CW00894879

OTHER BOOKS BY JANE RULE

FICTION
Desert of the Heart*
This Is Not for You
Against the Season
Theme for Diverse Instruments*
The Young in One Another's Arms
Contract with the World
Middle Children
Outlander
Inland Passage
Memory Board
After the Fire

NON-FICTION
Lesbian Images
A Hot-Eyed Moderate
Loving the Difficult

*Available from Talonbooks

Taking My Life

Portrait of Jane Rule taken on the occasion of her retirement from writing, 1991
Alex Waterhouse-Hayward

Taking My Life

JANE
RULE

TALONBOOKS

Copyright © 2011 by Estate of Jane Rule
Afterword copyright © 2011 by Linda M. Morra

Talonbooks
PO Box 2076
Vancouver, British Columbia, Canada V6B 3S3
www.talonbooks.com

Typeset in Sabon and printed and bound in Canada.
Printed on 50% post-consumer recycled acid-free paper.

First printing: 2011

The publisher gratefully acknowledges the financial support of the
Canada Council for the Arts; the Government of Canada through the
Canada Book Fund; and the Province of British Columbia through
the British Columbia Arts Council and the Book Publishing Tax Credit
for our publishing activities.

No part of this book, covered by the copyright hereon, may be re-
produced or used in any form or by any means—graphic, electronic or
mechanical—without prior permission of the publisher, except for
excerpts in a review. Any request for photocopying of any part of this
book shall be directed in writing to Access Copyright (The Canada
Copyright Licensing Agency), 1 Yonge Street, Suite 800, Toronto,
Ontario, Canada M5E 1E5; tel.: (416) 868-1620; fax: (416) 868-1621.

LIBRARY AND ARCHIVES CANADA CATALOGUING IN PUBLICATION

Rule, Jane, 1931–2007
    Taking my life / Jane Rule ; afterword by Linda Morra.

ISBN 978-0-88922-673-9

    1. Rule, Jane, 1931–2007. 2. Authors, Canadian (English)—
20th century—Biography. I. Title.

PS8535.U77Z476 2011   C813'.54   C2011-902479-9

CONTENTS

Taking My Life by Jane Rule
1

Afterword by Linda M. Morra
229

Commentary
251

Omitted Text
257

Acknowledgments
273

About the Authors
277

Taking My Life

WRITING AN AUTOBIOGRAPHY may be a positive way of taking my own life. Beginning in the dead of winter, mortal with abused lungs and liver, my arthritic bones as incentive for old age, I may be able to learn to value my life as something other than the hard and threateningly pointless journey it has often seemed. I have never been suicidal but often stalled, as I have been now for some months, not just directionless but unconvinced that there is one. No plan for a story or novel can rouse my imagination, which resolutely sleeps, feeding on the fat of summer. And so, I take my life, with moral and aesthetic misgivings, simply because there is nothing else to do.

I remember remembering when I was born. My practical young mother said nobody could. But I did remember dreaming and dreaming and that first waking to the hard light. By the time she read me *Mary Poppins*, I realized that I, like most people, had forgotten not just my birth but apparently the language of birds, the ability to fly, to walk into the landscape of pictures and to be at home among the stars. Just that one sensation remained—the painful brightness. It was not enough to make me into *Mary Poppins*, but memory became for me the earliest self-discipline I had. I couldn't, after I learned to write, keep a diary, just as I couldn't later take notes in lectures. Writing anything down seemed a way of forgetting it. I wanted to memorize my life so that whatever experience taught I would not forget. The difficulty, of course, is that what may seem to be static interference could be instead the very melody of life, the dismissed clutter, the real furniture of the soul. The fear of such loss, even our starkest nightmares, are consolation, for they store and restore to us things we have not chosen to recall.

I remember Josephine, our black servant, the more vividly for the nightmares she inspired. Perhaps because she was real, she spared me a random racial bigotry harder to sort out. I did not, at three, confuse her with "that black trash" on the playground with whom my brother and I were not allowed to play. They were simply children like us, victims of adult whim and anger, as were the kittens Josephine kicked out of the kitchen back down the basement stairs. Nor did I confuse her with Rose, black nurse for the children we were sent to play with on Josephine's day off, who was wonderfully, shockingly permissive. We could turn over all the furniture on the porch and play doctor on the youngest and most natural victim among us, a little boy we also regularly lost in the woods. On one Rose afternoon, a gang of us, ranging in age from three to six, broke into a vacant house on the rumour that there was candy in the garage. Our young fathers had to make up a party to restore bashed screen doors, broken windows.

Afternoon outings with Josephine were rigidly supervised, arm-wrenching walking, full of negative lessons in deportment. The only consolation is that sometimes our destination would be a building site our father was supervising. In those days, he was working for his father, helping to develop Wychwood into a residential section of Westfield, New Jersey, the acres of the old family farm.

We lived in the large gatehouse of the development, built to advertise it and given to my parents when my older brother, Arthur, was born. Mother came home from the hospital to the enormous relief of her own house. They had been living with my father's parents, among others of his worried sisters and twin brother, for the first year of their marriage, a hard requirement for my mother, a materially spoiled and emotionally deprived only child. Her mother-in-law's attempts to teach her house-keeping had not been markedly successful. The butler, swearing her to secrecy, did her kitchen duties since she was queasily pregnant. When she moved to her own house, she knew how to make mayonnaise and cheese soufflé. Her experience in ordering food for that large clan prompted her to spend a month's food budget in the first week. She didn't know how you could buy less than five pounds of butter at a time.

Perhaps because there had been servants before Josephine, dishonest or syphilitic, Mother loved Josephine. They were the same age. Josephine could wear Mother's cast-offs when she wasn't in uniform for a party. She knew how to cook and clean. She welcomed and took good care of guests. Since Mother assumed the care of us when she was home, she did not know Josephine's violent temper or the terrifying tales she told. I developed a phobia about food because Josephine spun stories about cooks who put poisonous snakes in the soup, whose leprous fingers fell off and were ground up in the hash.

I became such a problem to feed that my mother turned to the nursery school my brother and I attended for help. They suggested I stay at school for lunch for a time. We were not allowed milk or anything else to drink until we had finished the main course. Each day for a week, I resolutely cleared my plate, then stood up and vomited, and was sent to lie down. The school finally gave up. I knew, in a perverse way, my mother was proud of me. I would have shamed her as well as myself if I'd let the school do what she hadn't been able to. She simply didn't understand that Josephine and the school cook were trying to poison me. I loved my mother, but I couldn't trust her in such matters. She didn't even know how to cook.

The only person who did understand was my brother, but he had a reckless courage about eating and an ability to reason with authority. Sixteen months older than I was, he often tried to stand between me and the world. Our classrooms were separated only by a curtain. When, at nap time, I lifted my head off my rug to look around, a chair was put over me. Arthur must have heard my indignant protest because he came from the other side of the curtain to explain to the teacher that I was too young to understand such a punishment and must be treated kindly.

Arthur had an odd combination of talents. He was instinctively tactful, never made the blundering comments that were to become my trademark; yet he couldn't distinguish between what had happened and what he made up. His teachers thought of him as overly imaginative. I suspect it was I, a moral primitive, who first called him a liar. I had a passion for getting things straight. I have a more vivid memory of the closet where the hockey sticks were stored than I do of my classroom, the chapel or the dining room at school. I was sent to that closet after asking impertinent questions in the time set aside for that purpose at the end of chapel service. Once I asked why Santa Claus wasn't superior to God since he brought presents. Arthur never was inadvertently naughty. But he was dismissed from a car pool for saying "Grunty" in front of proper little girls and their mother. I don't think for the first five years of my life I had a very distinct sense of myself as a separate human being. I was half of what made up Arthur and Jane. We were named for our parents, who also seemed to me each half that made up Mother and Father. Oh, one fought, Arthur sensible enough to hit so that the wound didn't show, I leaving punishable teeth marks. He, the more tender of the two, asked me not to pull earthworms in half. I sometimes told on him. But we were central to each other. Occasionally, when he was taken off with older cousins for an event in New York and I was left behind with my cousin Frank to stand on the curb, shouting "It isn't fair!," I had warning that the world didn't think of us as I did, naturally inseparable. But he would come home, content to perform operations on my dolls (I remember only two, called Jesus and Barbara, who slept in bunks of a toy Pullman car I had been given). I could protect Arthur from the dogs that terrified him. And we could discuss all manner of things, from why brown cows gave white milk to what God tasted like when the grown-ups ate him.

When not under Josephine's thumb or in school, we were more permissively raised than our cousins. Mother had resented her mother's always siding with her teachers and was resolutely and often unreasonably loyal to us and our versions of the truth. Dad was eager to teach us to reason and to explain. All our grandparents had the conviction that we would be killed in the street while one of our parents stopped to explain the reason for getting across. Grandmother Rule, who had raised five children and didn't stand for any nonsense, gave Mother more advice about raising us than she wanted, and we were glad to be left less often than our cousins in Grandmother's care. Our grandparents at that time lived just across the street from us in the little Gatehouse. Grandfather had built a replica of Robbie Burns's cottage in a field next door and stocked it with children's books for all the grandchildren.

One afternoon, four or five of us were playing hide-and-seek in Farmer Brown's cornfield when someone decided we should pick some and cook it for ourselves. We gathered the corn and went to the cottage where there was a fireplace. Like our mothers, we didn't have much idea about cooking, but one of the boys said Indians roasted corn over an open fire. We had just got a good blaze going, a triumphant exercise for a band of children under six years old, and were dropping our corn onto it when someone spotted Granny Rule, coming out of her house and not hesitating in her stride as she snapped a branch off the apple tree. Arthur and I went out the back window, somehow managing to take four ears of corn with us. When we presented the corn to Mother, she asked if we had stolen it.

"Farmer Brown's got lots. He should share," I replied, not old enough yet to know the moral communism of childhood did not extend into adult territory.

We could hear the cries of our cousins being beaten with the apple branch. We had our first whole ears of corn for dinner that night, right under the veiled but disapproving eyes of Josephine.

Josephine moved with us when we left the Gatehouse just before my fourth birthday. My grandfather's various business ventures, too much mortgaged, were near collapse and selling that impractical, lovely storybook house was one of the ways my parents could help. Josephine, who had lived in one of its turrets, now had a room in the simple attic of a house we rented on Harrison Avenue. For the first time, I had a room of my own, away from my brother, and there was no balcony off it over which, in the Gatehouse, we had peeked at the grown-up world down below, whose sounds drifted up to shelter our sleep. What I remember of that house on Harrison Avenue are nightmares and sickness. All of us were sick: Dad with appendicitis, Mother and Arthur with mumps, and I had the only real earache of my life. Josephine was finally sent home to her own people to die of what was then called galloping consumption. "If she'd lived, she would have come to California with us, even without pay," my mother was fond of saying, but loyal Josephine, my nightmare bad mother, was gone for good.

With her went the world my mother had expected to live in. Grandfather was near bankruptcy, Grandmother ill with arthritis. There was no work for my father. The yearly journey we had made to California to visit Mother's mother and stepfather was, the year I was five, to be one way. With a legacy from her grandmother, Mother paid for the home in California. My father's mother didn't forgive him that decision for years.

We went first to Palo Alto, to our grandparents' house, which was so very unlike either the large, ramshackle family house of the Rules or the quaint little Gatehouse they'd moved to in leaner times. The new house at 1111 Hamilton was on a corner lined with magnolia trees. If one leaf fell, our step-grandfather, Colonel Packer, went out to pick it up. The inside of the house was immaculate, cared for by a string of maids and a faithful Mexican cleaning woman, whose husband was the gardener. It was a Spanish house with red tile floors, protected by handsome, dark, oriental rugs. The beehive fireplace in the corner of the living room had never been used, fire being both too messy and too dangerous to consider a pleasure. Both the living room and dining room opened onto an enclosed patio, at the far end of which was a covered area with a small waterfall and goldfish pond. Beyond that was the real garden, entered through a tall gate and under an arbour of grapevines and wisteria. Fruit trees were espaliered to the walls. Parts of the garden were separated from each other by hedges. In the rose garden, there was a lily pond full of mosquito fish. At the end of the picking garden, there was a raised platform with an elaborately tiled barbeque and picnic table. I remember eating there only once. The garden was not a social place, haven rather for the solitary pleasure both grandparents took in gardening, and for my brother and me when we had behaved too well for as long as we could. Arthur had learned to whistle, and his toneless accomplishment was hard on Mother Packer's nerves.

We stayed there long enough to be enrolled in school. The first day, to Arthur's acute embarrassment, I offered to stand on my hands in the cement schoolyard and promptly broke my nose. He was already suffering badly from being the only boy in short pants on the playground. Neither of us was sorry that our stay there was brief.

When Dad found a job as a salesman with the U.S. Gypsum Company, we rented a bungalow in a more dubious neighbourhood of the same town, a Filipino boarding house on one side, the large family of a postman on the other. Across the street lived an eccentric old maid who drove a large, ancient car after which loped her great mongrel dog, Gyp. Her Victorian house is all that's left of that neighbourhood now, a heritage house among new high-rise apartment blocks.

At 727 Cowper Street, we began our real life as a family. Though the Colonel and Mother Packer were as prone to interfere as our other grandparents had been, Dad didn't work for them, and they didn't live across the street. In fact, they seemed reluctant to come into the neighbourhood, as were many of Mother's girlhood friends in San Francisco, whose money was old and secure enough to withstand the Depression. At first we had no furniture because of a dock strike in New York. We lived for some months with cots, card tables and porch furniture borrowed from an aunt and uncle of Mother's, and from our grandparents. But even when the furniture bought for the Gate-house arrived, along with silver and china, Mother and Dad did not resume the social life they had in New Jersey, which had not been too far for even San Francisco friends to come in the days of plenty. My parents, in their prosperous old age, have forgiven or forgotten those slights, attend the weddings of grandchildren, the fiftieth anniversaries of old San Francisco friends.

In 1936, when they were beginning again, they did so with a sense of new freedom and adventure. Dad was proud of what seemed to him his first real job, for he could not be called away from it to make cocktails for his mother's luncheon guests, and he held it on his own merit. Mother finally learned to cook, and, if her timing was a bit uncertain, the charred hamburgers and baked potatoes were love offerings, not poison. Gradually, she became a very good cook and enjoyed it. Cleaning the house was never anything but a chore, for which she got help when she could afford it. But for a time, we were alone together. Dad spent weekends building himself a darkroom, building us swings and an exercise bar, a ladder up the almond tree, from which we could climb onto the garage roof.

I learned only much later that Mother Packer, whose inherited income had been little affected by the Depression, had offered to send me to private school to spare me the rough companions I would find in public school, a sheltering it did not occur to her to offer my brother. My father, in most ways simply grateful to his mother-in-law for her generosity, refused. He did not want me among children with much more than I had. Though he had been raised by Southern parents, he somehow escaped a sense of horror at exposing his own children to the multiracial population of our own neighbourhood school.

It seemed to me just one more evidence of freedom from Josephine that I could go to school with and make friends with black, Japanese, Chinese and Mexican children.

The shock for me was of a different order. The curtain Arthur had so easily parted in our first school became a wall. The big kids in the first grade had nothing to do with the little kids in kindergarten, and girls didn't play with boys at recess.

At first our newness to the place made us dependent on each other out of school hours. We fought almond and walnut wars against the mailman's kids next door. We made lead soldiers and turned the backyard into an ankle-threatening trench war zone. On Saturday mornings, we walked together three blocks to the movies, sometimes staying on for the adult movie in the afternoon, watching our father's head against the screen as he patrolled the dark aisles trying to find us, then reading the typed message that moved along the bottom of the screen, "Jane and Arthur Rule, your father is waiting for you in the lobby." On Sunday mornings, we walked to the Episcopal church. We both liked the church service and detested the Sunday school classes held afterward in the church hall, where fights could break out meaner than on the school playground. There was nothing to do but colour religious pictures with too few crayons. You waited for the blue crayon or turned Mary into a scarlet woman or switched.

One morning, crossing from church to Sunday school, we turned down the street instead and used our dimes for the

Carlotta Jane Hink Rule (Jane Rule's mother)
Jane Rule Fonds, University Archives, University of British Columbia

Arthur Rule Sr. (Jane Rule's father)
Jane Rule Fonds, University Archives, University of British Columbia

offering to buy Cokes at the drugstore. Since our father usually didn't get up on Sunday morning and our mother was busy with cooking, we decided it was a safe as well as pleasant solution to Sunday school. After it had become a habit, we sat in unguarded debate with the man behind the counter about whether there was more Coke in a bottle than in a glass, when Colonel Packer came in to buy a Sunday paper. Ushered into his Buick, we were delivered home for appropriate discipline.

"You don't go to church," I said to our only recently awake young father.

"I do sometimes. You don't have to go to church to be religious."

"Then why do we go?" Arthur asked.

Our father turned a matchbook on the arm of his low-slung chair, in the cracks of which we could usually retrieve enough change for a movie if our allowances had run out.

"Convince me," he said.

We did not go to church after that unless it was a family undertaking, Christmas and Easter Christians until years later, after Arthur and I had both left home, when our parents took up with the church again for some years, in a mood of community spirit, grateful to be together again after the long war, or as a new conservatism that age and some kinds of disappointments can bring.

Free of Sunday duty, I expected other kinds of adventures with my brother, but he was increasingly restless. Boys didn't play with girls, particularly kindergarteners. Only boys were supposed to play war and soccer. Why did he have to walk to school with me? Why did he have to take me to the movies? Kids did jeer at us. Arthur, the pacifist, walked more quickly, longing to run away, to escape the humiliation I was to him. I, the pugilist, jeered back, called our tormentor "a nigger, black trash," using the weapons Josephine had given me. One boy retaliated by tying Arthur up. Only when I bribed his sister with money to get her jump rope back did he let Arthur go. He didn't speak to me for a week.

I always had more money than Arthur did. He was both generous and careless. I hoarded. So, when he otherwise would have refused my company, I could sometimes buy my way in. I even bought my way into one of his clubs, its meeting place in the bar room in his friend's house. They needed light in there and first cut a small hole in the roof, good enough for a lookout but not for reading or playing cards. I bought candles to be allowed to join. One day I came home from school to find the whole store of candles laid out on my bed. Both Arthur and I were forbidden to play at the house again, pyromaniacs and carvers up of property that we were. Arthur, of course, blamed me. Secretly, I was relieved to be banned from that house where the brother's brutality to his sister made Arthur look a paragon of gentleness and forbearance.

When even being a patron of his projects didn't work, I spied on him and told on him, knowing I only confirmed his desire to be rid of my company.

The first Christmas at 727 Cowper, we were given a set of phones to be set up between our two rooms, mine next to my parents', his at the back of the house behind the kitchen. The instructions for setting them up were burned with the wrappings, and the phones were never connected. Mine stayed on my bedside table and for some time received the secrets and questions Arthur no longer wanted to hear.

The first-grade reader was as personally insulting. I would not read "Dick and Jane." I said "Arthur." Corrected again and again, I finally wouldn't read at all, for the story not only confirmed my separation from my brother, but revealed the source of his growing prejudice against girls, who only watched boys play or helped Mother. As for Spot, we didn't have a dog, and Arthur had taken to tormenting the cat even more cruelly than Josephine had done, dropping it from the garage roof, kicking it. When it died, Mother said she didn't really like pets. We could bring home any strays we wanted, as long as they were human.

I did begin to make some friends of my own. Wally, Chinese, and Chiaki, Japanese, were the two brightest boys in my class and they weren't as averse to playing with girls as the other boys were. They were even willing to captain opposing mixed teams at recess, called the Japs and the Chinks. We knew that, in the grown-up world, the Japs were bad and the Chinks were good, but those two boys, best friends, were equally liked. I sometimes invited them home after school. Mother Packer thought them odd companions, "like little rats," she said, silently scurrying by her when she was there one afternoon to take care of us. She didn't have much use for Eddie, the Jewish boy down the block, either, but there we sadly agreed with her. Eddie hung around me as dismally as I tried to hang around Arthur, and I was no kinder. Eddie was a mama's boy, fat, easily given to tears, the neighbourhood butt of most jokes. I was learning right along with my brother what a boy should be, and, though I sometimes detested the cruelty—I can still see a cat hanging from the top of the school flagpole—I detested a sissy with the rest.

Arthur was increasingly in trouble at school. Often when we changed classes, there he would be, sitting on the principal's detention bench, and everyone in the class would hiss, "There's your brother." If I tried to speak to him, he ignored me. He often had to stay after school. When he arrived home, famished, Mother said, "Gee, if your teacher is going to keep you this late, you ought at least to ask her to serve tea." The next day, even later, he said, "She didn't think it was funny."

Given tests, Arthur was labelled unusually gifted, one of the children to be studied by a Stanford research team. He was in trouble so often at school, our parents were told, because he was bored. The label didn't help. His teachers bullied him with it and he withdrew further. I think now he was probably as frightened as I often was, first by the newness and strangeness of the place, then by the often-bewildering requirements of the school. Told he was bright enough for the work to be easy made him more self-protective. He avoided. He lied. At least I was spared the brutality of being a boy. I, meanwhile, fell in love with my second-grade teacher. For her, I would even try sometimes to read aloud and, since she had no misgivings about my left-handedness, my printing improved.

Arthur never did his chores at home unless he was reminded, but then he usually did them cheerfully enough. If he was punished, he took that cheerfully, too. I didn't have to be reminded often, but, when I was, I sulked. Punishment of any sort sent me into a silent, revenge-vowing rage. I would stay in my room for

Arthur Rule Jr. (Jane Rule's brother)
Jane Rule Fonds, University Archives, University of British Columbia

hours, planning hunger strikes, go days refusing to speak. Only my father could break my will. He always did it with kindness, sitting down next to me on my bed, putting an arm around me and asking, "So what is the problem, Cookie?" All my resolve failed into furious tears, after which I had to agree to forgive and be forgiven. I adored my father, but even then his power offended my sense of myself. He would often say, "You know, if we could just shuffle the two of you together, we'd come up with a pretty fine person." Since I already felt the bereaved half of a strong identity, his view seemed to confirm that loss. I didn't know how to replace or find for myself all that had gone from me in the broken bond with my brother, who felt required to root out of himself the gentleness that had linked us.

I have little recollection at all of the indignities I suffered at my mother's hand. I suspect, therefore, most of them were invented, ways of taking out on her the bewildered sense of hurt and fear I felt. I grew increasingly frightened of the dark. Listening to the radio broadcasts of some of Edgar Allan Poe's stories made me sweat in such fear that my mother thought I had wet the bed. Those black gloves coming out of a secret panel in the wall over the bed in the film *The Cat and the Canary* gave me nightmares of Josephine come back from the dead to get me. The evening news Dad read in the paper while I sat on his lap made me dream of Japanese soldiers, the size of our lead soldiers, marching across my bedstead. I was as huge as Gulliver, waiting to be bound up. When I asked my father how big Japanese soldiers were, he answered absent-mindedly, "Small, very small." I didn't ever say I was frightened, but I called out every few minutes, sometimes for several hours, after I was in bed, listening to hear the weight of Mother's footsteps to see if her anger had become more frightening than the dark. To comfort myself, I got a fingernail file out of my bedside-table drawer and gradually filed off all the finish of the leg nearest me. If Mother noticed it, she never mentioned it.

Once we were taken to San Francisco to spend the night with my father's aunt while he and Mother went to a party. Auntie Sue went out after we were in bed, I out on an enclosed back porch, Arthur in a bed in the next room. Thinking we were all alone, which was terrifying enough, I suddenly saw the kitchen light go on. I rushed in to Arthur who decided to explore to find out who was there. We had not been told or hadn't taken in that Auntie Sue ran a boarding house. We crept along the dimly lit corridor upstairs, peeking through cracks and keyholes, finding several of the tenants in. Since they seemed comfortably at home, we decided the person in the kitchen meant us no harm, but I begged Arthur to let me get into bed with him. Grumpily he agreed, if I would sleep next to the wall. I lay awake and tense, listening to strangers move about the house, and then I began to peel paper off the wall, a task as comforting as the filing of my table leg. I was still awake when my parents came home and carried me into my own bed again. The next morning, up early to get back to Palo Alto in time for school, I walked into the bedroom door and fainted. Though I'm sure Mother and Dad heard about that wallpaper, they didn't discuss it with me, and we never stayed with Auntie Sue again.

SUMMERS, IN CONTRAST, WERE LIGHT-STRUCK months for me, perhaps for my brother, too. Each year around the first of July, we went to South Fork, 240 acres of redwood trees in Humboldt County, California, ten miles north of Garberville. It was officially Paradise Ranch, named by a fruit rancher who owned it until he was killed by Indians and my Great-Grandfather Vance bought it from his bank cheaply. Our only acknowledgment of that name was to call two dead redwood trees at the south end of our valley "God and the Missus." The Vances called it South Fork because it bordered on the south fork of Eel River and was their farthest summer outpost from Eureka, California, the town in which my great-grandfather was president of a bank, a railroad and owner of extensive property, a result of his rectitude rather than acumen. He'd inherited money from an uncle who had disowned all his children. The family's regular summer home was at Carlotta, a widening in the road with stone and a lumber mill named for my grandfather, which could be reached easily from Eureka by carriage or train in my mother's childhood. South Fork was an overnight journey from Carlotta by buckboard, past Indian encampments. The stay there never lasted longer than two weeks for trout fishing, berry and fruit picking. Mother Packer had inherited it, and she and the Colonel spent at least two months there every summer, where we joined them, Mother, Arthur and I for the summer, Dad for occasional weekends and his two-week vacation. In those days, before the Golden Gate Bridge was built, we had to cross from San Francisco to Marin County by ferry and drive nine hours to get there.

It was not a happy choice for my mother, who became resident cook and housekeeper. She and her mother never got along easily, Mother Packer sarcastically critical of Mother and us. Mother Packer and the Colonel didn't get along well either.

He was the sort of alcoholic who stays nervously sober for months and then goes on a suicidal binge, locked up in a hotel room with gallons of high-proof alcohol. Mother Packer would have divorced him, but she had divorced her first husband when Mother was four. To divorce again would have sealed the world's judgment against her. The Colonel might have left her had he not enjoyed the comfort of her money. So they bickered and flared. One night, separated from them by the thin redwood walls of the summer cabin, Mother was sure the Colonel was trying to kill Mother Packer. Twice there was a heavy thud and then a scream, before Mother banged on their door and called in to them.

"Gov is trying to kill a bat right over my head," Mother Packer explained in exasperated fear while I lay in bed and giggled nervously.

I was never afraid of the Colonel. While adults tiptoed around his tense silences, I was as apt to seek the shelter of his quiet lap. I did not know then he was not my real grandfather, and, though he had a temper, it was more often pathetic or funny than frightening. Once making ice cream out under the relative cool of the great fig trees, he cranked and cranked without results until finally, in a filthy mood, he opened up the freezer to find that the women had forgotten to put in the dasher. His parade ground vocabulary was wondrous to hear. Our laughter excited the Colonel's German shepherd to barking and the Colonel stamped off into the cabin, leaving us to get on with the job. He was a kind man, in his shy way. He did not lay claim to us as he might have had we been his, but he made a personal effort, always choosing Christmas and birthday presents for us himself, separate from those Mother Packer gave us. They were often books carefully selected for our interests. Once he gave me a real army canteen, something I had no idea I wanted until I had it. Though he often protested my father's willingness to take me along for a day's fishing trip, that canteen was his way of giving in. We had rituals with him, raising the flag each morning, saying the salute, lowering it each evening, folding it properly, never letting it touch the ground. The flag served a practical as well as patriotic purpose, for it could be seen from the highway across the river and signalled to friends and relatives that we were in residence.

We hadn't many visitors except on weekends when Mother Packer's sister Etta might come down from Carlotta, driven by Charlie Weedman, once blacksmith at Carlotta and suitor to Etta. He was sent away, but when my great-grandmother died, he returned to the blacksmith's cottage and did general chores around the place, companion to Etta until she died, living on there, tending her magnificent acre of garden for the rest of his life. Though they seemed to us far too old for such nonsense, we were encouraged to tease them, to call out on our way to bed, "Good night, Aunt Etta. Good night, Uncle Charlie." I suspect he was as much a natural solitary as Etta and that they had arrived at exactly the right proximity for their temperaments, Etta at the top of the hill in the family's large summer house, Charlie at the bottom in his two-room cabin, filled with neat stacks of old magazines and newspapers.

Arthur and I loved Charlie. It was he who taught us to fish and to hunt. Because my Great-Grandmother Vance had been a famous fisherwoman, wrapping her own rods, tying her own flies, women in the family were expected to fish. There is a picture of Mother Packer as a girl standing over a dead bear with a rifle in her hands, but generally the women didn't hunt. I recall landing numbers of small trout, but at dusk by the vegetable garden, when Charlie pointed out the ears of a jackrabbit, the rifle was always in Arthur's hands. He turned away from cleaning the kill, which I enjoyed, Charlie pointing out heart, liver, lungs, kidneys. I once counted twenty-six cherry pits in one pigeon.

Mother Packer's other sister, Ida, had died in childbirth years before. Because there had been a squabble over her estate, the family feared her widower would try to kidnap Mother and hold her for ransom, a romantic terror I almost envied her.

The only brother, Harry, lived in Eureka, blind from diabetes, rich from having inherited least of the real estate which had increased in value much more than the stocks and bonds held in conservative trusts for Aunt Etta and Mother Packer. Once a week, he lined up his family—wife, son and daughter, numerous grandchildren—and handed out their allowances. A mean man, fond of practical jokes, shrewd, his sisters would hear no word against him, not even that he was blind, a lesson I learned when I was about six. Etta and Mother Packer were quarrelling over choosing a silver pattern for a place setting for him, lighter and easier to manage than the family pattern. "What difference does it make if he's blind?" I asked and was sent to my room for twenty-four hours. "He was the only man I ever trusted," Mother Packer said when he died. My father, having looked into some of Harry's financial dealings with his sisters, shook his head and held his tongue.

Harry's family rarely came to South Fork, but once or twice a summer, a meeting place between South Fork and Eureka would be chosen, and all the family, as well as close family friends, would bring a picnic. I don't think I ever saw a sandwich at one of those picnics. There were fried chicken, ham, roast beef, meat loaf, quantities and varieties of potato salad, aspic salad, tossed salad, homemade bread and rolls, cakes, pies, cookies and whatever fruit and berries were in season. Though it got very hot, up to 110 degrees, the redwood groves we chose for picnics were always cool. And always a river ran nearby for keeping watermelon cool, for fishing, for swimming.

Our ordinary lives at South Fork were solitary. In the morning, before the day got too hot, I often set out with a coffee can strung round my neck to the wild meadow to pick blackberries or the more difficult, tiny huckleberries. It took me a couple of hours to get enough of these for pie. I loved that chore. Berries grew particularly thickly around the burned-out foundation of the house the original owner had built for the squaw he took to live with him. She had died in that fire, and some said there was buried treasure somewhere near that house. At least once in a summer, Arthur and I worked up enough enthusiasm to go digging for it. I loved the meadow full of sunny mysteries, but I had to be careful of poison oak because a bad case of that could keep me bandaged and house ridden for several weeks, not allowed to feel sorry for myself unless I was alone. Then I'd crank up the old Victrola (which still sits in my study today) and put on "Red River Valley" over and over again, weeping through my swollen eyes onto my blisters. Dad was best at doing bandages, his hands deft and gentle, his patience absolute.

Just before lunch and just before dinner, one of us would be sent to the garden or orchards to pick whatever Mother needed. The garden was put in for us and tended by an old resident caretaker, Mr. Wheeler, who lived in the original house with bullet holes in the porch where the owner had been gunned down in revenge for the death of his Indian or for his treasure. The orchards dated back to his time and went largely untended, to my mother's distress. She always pulled out deadwood while we picked prunes, plums, peaches, apples, figs and pears in their seasons.

The enforced rest after lunch would have been more tolerable for me if I had been, like Arthur, a reader. I fidgeted on my already-too-short cot in my parents' bedroom and called out every ten minutes or so until it was at last time to put on a bathing suit and go to the river.

Mother Packer was fearful of sunstroke. We all had to wear ancient, floor-length dusters and large straw hats for the walk, through the vineyard, vegetable garden and the first orchard—I, trying not to eat so much on the way or we'd not be allowed in the water—before we came to the path through a fringe of great trees out onto the riverbank.

Our stretch of the Eel was a gentle river in summer, rarely more than twenty feet wide or deep, large calm swimming holes alternating with riffles. The banks were rocky, difficult and satisfying to walk along around clumps of willow and boulders. I had a particular nest among the willows, altered in some way each year by the spring floods. There in hiding or sitting on a large boulder in view of the highway, I could spend hours, the sound of the summer traffic faint above the sound of the river, reminder rather than disturber of solitude.

We were not taught to swim. We had inner tubes. When Dad was with us, we'd hang on to the straps of his old-fashioned bathing suit and he'd take us to the bottom for a handful of rocks to prove we'd been all the way. He had been a champion swimmer at Annapolis, and playing with him and watching him were all the instruction we needed to become strong swimmers ourselves.

Sometimes we had a rowboat, sometimes a raft, but we preferred, as we grew older and more independent, to walk along the shore, wading or swimming across the river when we came to impenetrable forest or cliff. Arthur almost always carried a rod, as he carried a rifle if we went into the woods. Very young, I set aside these excuses for a hike and went empty-handed, sometimes with him, increasingly often alone.

There was no electricity in the early days. We played cards by kerosene lamps, listened to old records, ragtime and Harry Lauder, and Mother Packer told us stories, sometimes real ones about her own childhood visits to South Fork, sometimes ones she made up. Arthur always asked for frightening ghost stories, I for magical forests where candy grew on trees and rivers ran full of lemonade.

For me, the real landscape of summer could hardly have been more magical. Just sitting on the porch steps, I could watch lizards, toads, butterflies, dragonflies and chipmunks. In the early morning and at dusk, deer fed in the orchards. Wildcat and boar occasionally appeared at the edge of the deep forest. One summer, skunks lived uncomfortably near, under the house. I never felt the lack of human companionship, except in the estrangement from my brother, for the ghosts of my grandmother and mother as children happily haunted my days, the past and present losing their distinction.

At least once in the summer, I would go back with Aunt Etta and Charlie to Carlotta for a week by myself. Charlie drove particularly carefully along the twisting road because I was prone to carsickness. Aunt Etta distracted me by asking me to sing, which I was only too happy to do until I was hoarse, sitting between them watching patches of hot road flicker out into the deep shade of the trees. Too tired to sing, I'd name the familiar signposts, the straight several miles of road called "the crooked road to Pepperwood," the Scotia mill and hotel where Mother as a child had spit tomato juice on a white tablecloth. Mornings I gardened with Etta, allowed to cut deadheads off the roses in my great-grandmother's garden, then allowed to find my own way around Etta's garden, where formal paths radiated out from a circle in the centre. At the edge nearest the redwoods, she had planted a garden of miniatures. There minutely grew the smallest rose in the world against a backdrop of trees over a thousand years old. I could also explore the kitchen where the cook was baking donuts or cookies or pies or cakes, depending on the day of the week, great pans of milk on the back of the wood stove being made into cottage cheese. I could stand on the landing of the stairs and look out the different-coloured panes of the stained-glass window onto the world below. In the afternoon, Charlie would take me down the hill, past the fruit orchard, past his vegetable garden which was larger and much more various than our own since it was to supply needs all year round, to the great barns, around the pasture where the bull was kept, to pick hazelnuts or loganberries. At night, instead of choosing any one of five empty bedrooms, I slept in Aunt Etta's large bed with her, or tried to. She snored, and, when she stopped, I could hear the cook snoring in her bedroom down below, but that irritant was a small price for the delicious safety of summer nights, in my parents' room at South Fork, in Etta's bed at Carlotta. I remember weeping only once at Carlotta. I was kneeling beside Aunt Etta saying night prayers when I peeked out and saw her poor bare feet, distorted with bunions and corns. I could not confess to her the source of my tears. Mother Packer told me later, "Oh, it's just that Etta's always been so vain about her feet that she wears shoes that are too narrow and too short." They were close, but not kind, those sisters.

Usually the whole family would come to fetch me, and that was always an occasion for a grand picnic. Etta had a summer kitchen out under the trees, next to which was a huge picnic table. While the cook did the ordinary preparations, I helped Aunt Etta with fancy, to me inedible salads, but I was never forced to eat anything I didn't want, and there was always plenty to choose from. When Arthur arrived, we'd go together to the more dangerous places, the garbage dump, which was like a diving board built out over a ravine above which buzzards circled and crows scolded. Or we'd walk down the front-door lane to the locked gate, climb over it and buy penny candy at the country store, just the journey my mother was never allowed to take for fear of kidnapping.

Evenings with everyone there at Carlotta were often occasions for the neighbours to drop by. The women all had handwork, not mending for such social occasions, but embroidery or needlepoint or even a quilt on a frame for everyone to work on together. While they reminisced and gossiped, the men talked crops and swapped fishing and hunting stories, country conversation, and, if we were quiet enough, it might be quite late before anyone remembered it was long past time for us to be in bed.

I remember the family house in Eureka where Aunt Etta spent the winter much less well, but its third-floor ballroom, turned storage room, with a turret seat that looked out over the harbour became one of the settings in my novel *Against the Season*, though the characters who lived there are not even a ghostly echo of the real inhabitants of the house, a sheltered, narrow family, my grandmother the only one ever to escape loving and possessive parents.

She married the first man who offered to take her away from Eureka, Lester Hink, a young merchant from San Francisco who managed a branch of his father's department store, J.F. Hink and Son, in Berkeley, California.

It was on the porch at South Fork—though I was older then, perhaps in my early teens—that Mother Packer read out a bit from the paper, a habit of hers we ignored, preoccupied with our own reading: "Frigid women are the victims of violent fathers." She paused and then said, "Mine never laid a hand on me."

She was the youngest of the family, named Carlotta, but called Tot into her old age. Sheltered and spoiled, she was obviously not prepared to deal with her husband's sexual demands. Nor was she prepared for the submission he expected in all areas of their living. When he shouted that the gravy should be dark brown, the colour of his shoe, she put his shoe alongside the gravy the next time it was served. When he wanted her money to invest in the store to make him more independent of his dictatorial and hated father, she refused. Giving birth to my mother was an experience Mother Packer never quite recovered from, the physical horror of it perhaps underlined by her older

Carlotta Mae Vance, Lester William Hink, Ida Vance Hauk
Jane Rule Fonds, University Archives, University of British Columbia

sister's death in childbirth. When Lester took a mistress, she divorced him, deposited my four-year-old mother at Eureka and went on a long holiday. She met Gouvenier Packer, whose first wife had died in childbirth, and married him before Lester married his mistress.

In papers I found after Mother Packer's death, there is the opening of a letter she intended to write for her grandchildren, half apology, half justification, claiming that the three wives Lester Hink had taken after her proved he had never been able to find anyone to take her place. The letter goes on to recount a couple of amusing incidents in her childhood. Her first day in school, when she was told she was not allowed to talk, she sang whatever she had to say. Perhaps the impetus to go on with that letter failed because she had already shared her childhood and girlhood with us, in fact, there at South Fork and Carlotta. We played in the places of her childhood, picked from the same bushes and trees, listened to the same records, looked at issues of *Godey's Lady's Book* and dressed up in the clothes and hats packed away in the attic. It was my mother's childhood as well, for she'd spent every summer at Carlotta. But for her, it became a prison rather than an escape once her beloved grandmother was dead.

I was named for my great-grandmother, Jane Vance. I don't remember her, but I have looked at pictures of us together when I was about sixteen months old, of her standing alone in a rowboat, wearing long skirts and a hat, holding her beloved fishing rod. I could not miss her as my mother did, sensed her presence rather in the domestic routines of Carlotta, in the Indian baskets that hung on the walls of South Fork. I learned to fish with one of her rods.

Even as a child, I sensed that this way of life, like the way of life at the Gatehouse in Westfield, was receding into the past, would not be there for yet another generation of children to play their timeless games in the shadow and warmth of friendly ghosts. One winter, a heavy snow caved in the roof of the barn at South Fork, and it was not repaired, housing nothing but an old buckboard and carriage, used only for our imaginative games. Honeysuckle pulled down the vineyard fence, and that,

Mother Packer
Jane Rule Fonds, University Archives, University of British Columbia

too, lay where it was since the grapes were never seriously harvested. One summer, when we opened up the rat-proof store-room at the original house to get out extra mattresses, we found that grapevines had pried their way in, inviting not only rats but birds. The door was simply closed again, for old Mr. Wheeler had died, and the house stood empty of a caretaker.

Carlotta was not so derelict while Aunt Etta lived, but, even when we were all there, it had an empty feeling, Etta, more care-taker than mistress, with no children and grandchildren of her own to call those musty-smelling bedrooms back to the present. Even the clutter of the house was two generations old.

Summers were so long for us, I forgot the life of school and town. One fall, when we had to stay in the President Hotel in Palo Alto for a couple of nights before our summer tenants moved out, I followed the bellboy into the room and said, as he flipped the switch, "Oh look, electric lights and everything." I hadn't lost my habit of embarrassing as much as amusing my parents and brother.

At seven, I was trying to learn to be tactful. Sitting at the dining-room table busy at some project or other, I watched my mother walk through the room.

"Gosh, Mom, you're getting fat," I said and then braced myself, recognizing that I'd made too personal a remark.

"Am I?" she asked mildly.

I don't remember how long after that she told us she was pregnant. I remember how full of self-importance I was when I announced the fact to my second-grade teacher, how deflated when she replied that she already knew. I hated being caught out by adult superiority, a secret or a discovery turned to nothing in its light.

Mother was the only grown-up I knew who never wrecked a surprise or triumph in that way. Only years later, when I heard my much-younger sister telling her a joke I'd told in my time and Mother's gratifyingly surprised laughter did I have a sudden qualm. "You already knew that joke," I accused her later. "I'd forgotten it," Mother said, protecting the genuine wonder I needed to be to her every day, protecting my sister's right as well.

Carlotta Mae Vance Hink
Jane Rule Fonds, University Archives, University of British Columbia

Mother sheltered us the more with her loving attention because she could not protect us from the critical and civilizing influence of our grandparents, often harder on her than on us. Sunday midday dinner every week at 1111 Hamilton was a test of our table manners, at which I usually failed, but I could go out and play in the garden while Mother heard about it and Dad slept on the living-room floor. Once sure she'd made Mother miserable, Mother Packer was ready for a game of cards, a pastime her own mother wouldn't have allowed on Sunday, though she saw nothing wrong with playing mah-jong. At home for Sunday supper, we always had something delicious, waffles with maple syrup or cottage pudding with chocolate sauce and large glasses of cold milk, just the four of us, like children together.

My parents were young, Mother, nineteen, and Dad, twenty-three, when they married. Arthur was born thirteen months later. Living first in the house of Dad's parents, then in the same town, first beneficiaries and then victims of Grandfather Rule's financial circumstances, they achieved only a minimal independence when they moved west, for Dad's salary as a junior salesman was modest. Though they lived much more simply than they had, they still needed the financial help Mother Packer could provide, not only free summer holidays but all the luxuries for us, clothes, peddle cars, bicycles, music and dancing lessons. My parents were the more vulnerable, therefore, to any criticism about us or themselves. Neither of them much admired their parents as parents, nor did they think much of the relationships between their parents. But often their own judgment had to give way to the more formal and conventional requirements of their parents' worlds.

Arthur and I were, for all our fallings from grace, politer children than our friends, better spoken and better dressed. When we went downtown together, Arthur walked on the outside even when there was no grown-up to tell him to. We both said "please" and "thank you" without being reminded, and, though I felt like a spastic orphan at my grandmother's table, I was a model of good manners, for my friends' parents.

Let out of the requiring grandparental world, we all relaxed. Dad taught us risqué songs, gave us whole quarts of ice cream to eat out of cartons. Mother let us run barefoot (not allowed all summer at South Fork) and occasionally forgot to brush our teeth. Arthur was not stopped from telling us the same joke at the dinner table every night for weeks ("Do you have Prince Albert in the can?" …). We could turn over the furniture, put on plays, get dirty, even torn, if only we'd please behave as we should with our grandparents.

It was not always difficult. A couple of times a year I went to San Francisco on a shopping trip with Mother Packer. The mornings were a bit of a trial, trying on clothes that sometimes puckered under the arms or were scratchy or were too babyish. But patience meant lunch at the Palace Hotel. I always ordered waffles and asparagus, and the head waiter poured melted butter into each of the waffle squares, then onto the asparagus, which I was allowed to eat with my fingers, asking advice about how to keep the butter from running down my elbows. The Palace Hotel dining room had great chandeliers. Mother Packer told me about an uncle of hers who had ridden into that very dining room on a horse and swung from one of the chandeliers. It was a much more sedate place in my time, but I loved it just the same because at one side of the room a forest grew with a real little waterfall and stream. After lunch we went to Chinatown. I was given a dollar to spend, but Mother Packer paid for everything I picked out, tiny ivory monkeys ("hear, see and speak no evil"), a parrot in a birdcage two inches high. I loved miniatures and was creating a park with a zoo on a bookcase shelf in my room. I had begged all the pocket mirrors from Mother's and Mother Packer's handbags to make a lake for tiny ducks and swans to swim on. When I was exhausted, we'd go to Mother Packer's hat shop. While she tried on the hat being made for her, I'd be given a small hat box in which to pack all my treasures.

On the ride home on the train, I could ask any questions I wanted to, like why the head waiter was so particularly nice to us.

"I tip him," Mother Packer explained, "so that we can get good service and let you sit near the forest."

The cab driver who took us home to 1111 Hamilton saw how nearly asleep I was and carried me, as well as the packages, all the way to the front door.

"You must have tipped him an awful lot," I said before the front door had closed, my only faux pas of the day, and Mother Packer decided to be amused by it.

The dancing lessons she insisted I take are as bleak in my memory as those San Francisco trips are bright. I had taken ballet lessons without trauma in Westfield when I was three or four years old. Even the public performance during which I angrily shot my parasol at the laughing audience ended happily with ice-cream sodas and a drive home in the amazing darkness. Tap dancing—I only now realize it was probably all Shirley Temple's fault—simply embarrassed me. I was no good at it. At seven, I was a fair swimmer and a crudely accomplished soccer player. I had begun to ride. Aside from the noise I could make with my taps when I wasn't trying to dance, I hated it, facing for the first time the possibility that my height was not a natural superiority, but a fault. Wilful as I always was about my dignity, I would have refused that weekly humiliation if it hadn't been a trade-off for riding lessons. Mother Packer said no tap dancing, no horseback riding. A child obsessive about promptness—it was a matter of honour, never to be late to school—I was always late for dancing lessons, and I was late getting home because I had to sit on the curb for a bit and cry before I could face anyone.

An old Indian ran the pony ring out on El Camino Real. He had five or six ponies, one small horse and a goat and cart. On a Sunday morning, he'd lead me across the highway on the horse and turn me loose for a long hour's ride in the Stanford grant-land eucalyptus forests. She was a hard-mouthed, ill-used creature I loved nearly as well as my bicycle, which I called Silver. I often went to the ring early and helped curry the animals. The day I was offered free rides for helping to clean out the goat pen, I was liberated. Though Mother Packer protested that it was no job for a small girl, I was beyond bargaining with. The smell of a goat could hardly be compared to the punishment of dancing class.

I considered my relationship with the old Indian purely professional, but he must have been fond of me. Once he took me with him to call on a friend who raised and trained polo ponies. Mounted on one of those elegant, high-strung animals, I reined for a light turn and was taken round two full circles, while the two men stumbled with laughter. There was no humiliation in it for me. I was too amazed and then delighted at how light and quick a hand I needed. He said to me on the way home, "Yes, you could ride, little girl. You could ride."

Because the Colonel had kept horses in the army, Mother and he had always ridden. I loved to look at pictures of them on horseback in Golden Gate Park, while they were stationed at the Presidio, to learn the names of the horses, Whaland and Tzar. But that, too, was a world irretrievably gone.

Mother was also musical. She had a beautiful singing voice and had studied at the conservatory in San Francisco, though she'd never had professional ambitions. She belonged to a singing group in Palo Alto and sang in performances only days before my sister was born. My father, though he had no training, had not only a true voice but a knack for picking up and playing nearly any musical instrument. I could carry a tune, even with concentration sing a part, but I was bored with the piano lessons Miss Bone came to the house each week to give Arthur and me. For a brief few weeks I tried the violin instead. My arm got tired and, when Arthur asked if I'd ever get the squeaks out of the instrument, I knew I wasn't curious enough to find out. The birth of our sister relieved us both of the burden of our musical education. Mother simply didn't have the time or patience to keep us on a practising schedule.

Another great bonus of that pregnancy was Dad's decision to add a small room for the baby right off their bedroom. He did most of the work at night with floodlights which shone into my bedroom window. The light, the noise of the sawing and hammering, banished the terrors of the dark, and I slept, peacefully. Dad finished it before cutting the door through, a ceremony to which the long-suffering neighbours were invited. We all sat on my parents' bed and cheered as Dad bashed through to the new nursery.

Mother went to the hospital in the middle of the night on February 23, 1939, but Libby was not born until around eight o'clock the next evening when Arthur and I were already in bed in the big guest room at Mother Packer's. The maid, Bertha, came in to tell us the news. Arthur cursed. I cheered. Then he said, "Oh well, at least a girl won't be allowed to tag around after me." Had he been imagining a companion worthy of him? I hadn't really thought beyond the fact at all. Just before Mother came home from the hospital, Arthur and I came down with the measles and had to stay two weeks longer at 1111 Hamilton, an increasing trial to our grandparents and Bertha.

Libby was nearly a month old by the time we saw her. My interest in dolls had never been great and disappeared as soon as Arthur wasn't willing to play with me. My chief interest in the baby was showing her off, rather as I might a new bike or Brownie camera. Until the novelty wore off, I was cheerful about taking her round the block in her carriage. Her real value in my life was to end my role as the baby of the family, which had never seemed to me anything but a disadvantage.

WHEN DAD ANNOUNCED that he was taking us on a holiday to Yosemite, it was Libby who was left behind in a nurse's care. I was eight years old. I didn't like the cabin we stayed in because it was surrounded by other cabins, and everywhere we went in the park, there were other people. Used to the solitude of South Fork, I knew wonder as a private emotion in the silence of the great trees or enclosed in the wind on the river bar. I was embarrassed to be so moved by huge waterfalls surrounded by strangers.

At the observation point where a fire was built and nightly pushed off to drop a mile to the valley below, Arthur and Dad climbed over the barrier to stand on the fire site.

"Do you suppose you could dive from here and hit the motel swimming pool?" Arthur asked.

I had stayed behind the barrier. When they climbed back to safety and started back down the trail, I couldn't move. Dad had to pry my fingers loose from the fence rail and carry me away from the mesmerizing terror of that height. That night, while everyone else watched the fire fall, I closed my eyes and simply listened to the soprano sing "The Indian Love Call." I had never been afraid of heights before, had walked logs over creek beds, crossed the Eel River on a swinging footbridge high above the water, dived into deep pools from fifteen or twenty feet up a cliff. But those were all imaginable distances, not a mad death wish like my brother's, to leap off the edge of the world toward the postage stamp of a swimming pool a mile below.

Dad came home often in those days with news that he was to be transferred. We would go off to school with the important announcement that we were going to Chicago or St. Louis or Cleveland. Weeks would pass before we'd be told that, no, in fact, we weren't moving this time. We were labelled the kids who always told lies about moving away. When we finally did go to

Chicago, I had told nearly no one. Libby was eighteen months old, I nine, Arthur ten.

For years, Mother has said to us, "Never say 'never,' or you'll end up in Chicago." It was a place she had said she'd never live, and the year we spent in Hinsdale, a suburb of that city, did not change her mind. Dad travelled a great deal. Sometimes he had to take the car, leaving us without transportation for two weeks at a time. Sometimes he went by plane, which worried Mother. On the weekends, when he was at home, he was often too tired to be anything but physically present in the house, sleeping away most of the day. Mother hired Minnie to help around the house and give Mother some freedom from the baby but she really had nowhere to go. Newcomers were suspect in that conservative town. Mother was offended to be treated like a nobody, for the first time independent of family. Some of Dad's business connections were friendly, but it was a very lonely year for her.

School for me was a new rather than familiar terror. In California there were half terms, and I had begun first grade in February. In Illinois, I couldn't begin fourth grade in February. I had either to go back to third or join fourth grade halfway through the year. I sat in an empty third-grade classroom in a cramped, little desk, the third-grade teacher and the principal standing over me while I stumbled through the hated *Dick and Jane* reader.

"Well, just the same," the second-grade teacher said, "she's too big for the furniture."

So, though my reading was a failure, I was put into fourth grade anyway. The school was so large that I lost track of Arthur the moment he got off the school bus and didn't see him again until the end of the day. One morning, after we had been entertaining other passengers on the school bus by teaching them bawdy songs we had learned from our father, we were told we could no longer ride on the bus. It was in the middle of winter, twenty degrees below zero, and Mother had no car. We were a good three miles from the school. Furious with the school rather than with us, Mother hired a horse-drawn sleigh to take us to school and deliver us home, complete with blankets and Thermoses of rich hot cocoa, and we could sing any song we wanted to at the top of our lungs. We would have been glad never to have to ride that bus again, on which fights were always breaking out, but we were duly reinstated.

Mother did what she could for our social life.

Arthur and I were both enrolled in ballroom-dancing class. The girls all wore white gloves, black patent leather shoes, regular school dresses except for special parties given at Christmas and Valentine's Day. The boys wore jackets and ties. They sat on one side of the room, the girls on the other until the order was given. Then the boys had to cross the room. Each chose a dancing partner, by bowing and saying, "May I have this dance?" At the end of the hour we lined up to be paired off. There was always hurried counting and switching places to avoid being ludicrously coupled with the too tall or too short, too clumsy or disliked. For a reason I've never been able to discern, both the tall boys in my class liked me; therefore, what should have been another of an endless series of social ordeals, preparing me for a world nearly vanished in which I would never live, I actually enjoyed myself.

In the spring, Mother drove me out into the country to find a riding school. We got lost several times on the way.

"This damned place is so flat, everything looks the same," she complained.

I could not, as I had in California, simply mount a horse and ride off into a forest. There were a dozen other children to ride with, all with proper riding habits. The horses were large, the saddles English. Instead of sitting in the saddle, I was told I must learn to post. The first afternoon out, trying to do as I was told, I put my weight on the stirrups and one broke. I fell off the horse, the only fall I'd ever taken. Nothing but my dignity was hurt, but I would have suffered less from a broken bone in front of those strange, snobbish children. I went back occasionally, but, since the riding was far more a trial than a pleasure, I gradually gave up any interest in horses.

Dad took a vacation and decided we should all go to the New York World's Fair. We had been several times to the world's fair in San Francisco, about which I remember nothing but refusing to go down the slide in the funhouse after Bertha and Arthur had both hurt themselves on the way down. I remember little about the New York World's Fair except that Dad thought Playland a waste of time and took us to incomprehensible educational exhibits instead. The lineups to see the future dome were too long, so we didn't see that. As we dragged wearily along after him, he said, encouragingly, "Now how many kids can say they've been to both world's fairs?" just as he always tried to cut through our boredom on long trips with, "Now how many kids can say they've been in this many states?"

Libby was the only good traveller among us. She sat, perched on a boxed-in potty, on top of suitcases just behind the driver's seat where she had a good view. Every time she had to use the potty, she'd shout, "I have to be a good girl." Minnie, who travelled with us, would lift up the lid, and Dad would empty the potty without slowing down.

The trip east, I suspect, was really for a reconciliation with Dad's parents whom we hadn't seen since we'd moved west. We stayed at the little Gatehouse in a clutter of cousins, ones we'd known when we'd lived in Westfield and a new batch around Libby's age. There were finally fourteen of us, ten boys and four girls.

An unplanned and, for Mother, alarming family reconciliation took place soon after we got back to Hinsdale. Mother's father phoned her from Chicago, on a honeymoon with his third wife, who wanted to meet all his family and reunite him with them. Mother phoned Dad at the office, something she never did, and told him he had to come home at once. She had not only to prepare dinner for her mythically particular father, whom she hadn't seen since she was a child, but also explain to us we had a grandfather we didn't even know existed, evidence of Mother Packer's bitterness Mother had felt required to serve all these years. She cried a good part of that afternoon.

For Arthur and me it was a marvellous piece of information, for it suddenly solved a puzzle we weren't clearly aware of until we had the missing piece. We had great-grandparents in San Francisco, to whose apartment we had occasionally been summoned for a meal. We liked to go. Oma always telephoned ahead to ask what we would like to eat and catered happily to my suspicious whims. Once I had chicken livers when everyone else was eating rare roast beef. Oma had a box of toys for us. There was a beautifully painted miniature German village to set up. We took turns sitting on a child-sized musical chair. Opa always made special drinks for us when the adults had cocktails, and he personally scrubbed our hands before dinner and lay down with us for a brief nap after the meal. Opa spoke with such a strong German accent that we could only tell he'd made a joke when he laughed at it himself.

We also had a great-uncle O.K. (Oscar Karl) and his wife, Lucille, who lived in Palo Alto. Uncle O.K. owned a department store there, called J.F. Hink and Son. We went to their house for dinner, to the store to buy clothes. There was an uneasy friendship between them and the Colonel and Mother Packer. Lucille had also grown up in Eureka.

"So Uncle O.K.," Arthur said, "is this guy's brother."

"And Opa and Oma are his parents, and he's why we're related to them," I added.

We put on our dancing-school party clothes for dinner.

"What are we supposed to call this guy?" Arthur asked.

"Granddad, I suppose," Mother said, the sound of tears still in her voice.

"What about her?" I asked.

"Gretchen? Oh, I don't know. I don't even know what I am supposed to call her."

Granddad was not as big a man as we were used to for a relative, shorter than either the Colonel or Grandfather Rule. He was as bald as Grandfather Rule. Gretchen was a slight, dark woman, too young to be a grandmother. She had children, she said, not much older than we were. Neither of them was as strange as Mother. I had never seen her shy, even meeting strangers, nor had I ever seen her trying not to like someone. Gretchen seemed to us really nice, not just because she brought presents but because she talked to us as if we were people. Mother cried again when they left, but she seemed more relieved than unhappy. After that, Granddad sent her a cheque every Christmas, most of which she gave to us for our savings accounts. We were curious about him, but we didn't ask many questions until years later when he became a real fact in our lives.

Oma Vance

Jane Rule Fonds, University Archives, University of British Columbia

All the photographs of Arthur in Hinsdale are sullen. He was hanging around with boys who stole light bulbs from the hardware store and then smashed them in people's driveways. When Dad was home, Arthur would become suddenly talkative, bragging about fights he'd been in, about how fast he could run, how many races he'd won at track.

"I bet I can still beat you," Dad said.

"I bet you can't."

Right after dinner they raced each other round the block, and Dad won.

The next week Arthur started stealing the new nickels Dad was collecting. He wrapped them in bits of paper and threw them out my bedroom window. When Dad got home, Arthur showed him the nickels in the garden.

"Janie must have been stealing them from you."

I was furious with Arthur and, at the same time, sorry for him. So many of his lies were too elaborate to be credible. Sometimes it seemed as if he told them to get caught.

Granny Rule, perhaps aware that Arthur's behaviour and moods puzzled and worried my parents and, confident in her ability to handle children, offered to take Arthur and two other cousins on a trip to Washington, D.C. To forestall my protests, Dad promised to take me to Kentucky where I could visit for a week at the Rule family farm in Goshen.

I wanted so much to go on my first plane ride that I kept myself from thinking about staying alone for a week with people I didn't know. Only Mary Lily, a much younger cousin of Dad's, had visited us for a week. While she was with us, Dad's men friends joked about wanting to help her babysit. I had to judge her attractiveness from their behaviour, which seemed to me distinctly stupid. She was tall with long, strawberry blonde hair, I was interested in her breasts at a time when I was apprehensive about someday having to have them myself.

"All this talk about what a vamp she is!" Mother said to Dad. "She's just a nice, simple, country girl. Your sister's just jealous. She's used to being the youngest and best-looking woman in the family, that's all."

"What did she do?" I asked.

"When she was staying with Aunt Lib and Uncle D.B. at West Point, she was popular with cadets," Mother said. "She's an eighteen-year-old girl. What's the matter with that?"

Her looks interested me most because she looked more like Grandfather Rule than any of his own children.

It was a strange household Mary Lily had grown up in, made up of Grandfather Rule's three older brothers: Clarence, a widower; Wallace, a bachelor; and Lucian and his wife, Ida, who were Mary Lily's parents. Lucian was an ordained Presbyterian minister. Clarence and Wallace were both lay preachers. Grandfather Rule had built them a small church, much in the same spirit that he'd build the Robbie Burns cottage for us, but they never had much of a congregation, travelling Baptists forever stealing away their neighbours. Clarence kept himself busy with farm chores. Wallace hired himself out as a water-witcher. Lucian studied and wrote religious poetry which Grandfather Rule had privately published. After Lucian died, Granny Rule found erotic poems which she promptly burned.

Ida looked after all of them, no easy chore since they didn't keep the same hours or eat the same food. Lucian, who read most of the night, was going to bed, just as Clarence was getting up to do the milking. Wallace, who would not sleep in the house, had a tent platform out in the side yard and appeared for food any time he was hungry. The original farmhouse had burned down. A servant and her illegitimate baby had been killed in the fire, a hellishly Presbyterian fate, which might have frightened Wallace. His father, a Presbyterian minister, convinced of hell but not of heaven, was finally unfrocked. The grass was still dead in a patch by the front porch where he was said to have spent his last days, rocking and spitting tobacco, tended by his saintly wife.

For me the peculiarities of the household were a great comfort, for there was always someone awake to dispel night fears, and there was never a family meal to test either my table manners or my appetite. Like everyone else in the house, I simply told Aunt Ida what I wanted when I wanted it. There was always fried chicken in the refrigerator and large pitchers of fresh milk. Ida baked bread and cookies and fried potato chips every morning early "before the heat of the day." I could pick vegetables and eat

them raw in the garden, and there was a country store across the
road where I was sent on small errands in the company of
Goggles, the collie, with the direction to keep the change for my
penny candy, a Coke or a chance on the punch board. Ida was
surprised that I made my own bed. I think I was the only one in
the house who ever did.

Those were Mary Lily's last few months on the farm. That fall
she ran away to New York where Grandfather Rule got her a job
as a Powers model, making his own daughters and Granny Rule
the more jealous and critical of her. Mary Lily was for me a
revelation. Even at my stubborn worst, I had never stood at the
top of the stairs and screamed at anyone, Mary Lily's tactic when
she was crossed by any of them. The old men and her mother
were worried about her and frightened of her, the very image of
Eve, the temptress, for every man in the county. One day she took
me to the reservoir to swim and pushed me out on an inflated raft
where I dozed in the sun for hours while she flirted with half a
dozen young men. I came home badly sunburned and my bed
rocked gently all night. The next day, contrite, she read me parts
of her diary. I was too flattered by the attention to mind being
bored, puzzled and embarrassed by turns.

Aunt Ida took us to the races. She was the only one who
knew how to drive. A great talker at any time, she drove to the
mood of her continually shouted monologue, as slowly as five
miles an hour for sad parts of stories, up to fifty for the exciting
bits. I don't think any of the men were deaf. She shouted over the
phone, too, could often have simply opened a window to
converse with her neighbours without aid of the phone. Dark
stories were told about Ida. Dad's sister Mary claimed Ida once
chased her around the house with a fingernail file, and Granny
Rule said she went berserk at every full moon and sometimes
had to be put away. She said Uncle Lucian had been tricked into
marrying Ida, her family not telling him she was a lunatic.
During my first visit and every other time I went to the farm in
Kentucky with the family, Aunt Ida was the warm centre of the
world, tending all that odd crew and her guests without even a
complaint, making work to make people comfortable.

Clarence was the other gentle one in the household. As thin as Ida was fat, he had a high, lilting Southern voice. He was also the only other one who laughed, leaning up against a wall as if he might otherwise simply fall down. He took me to the barn and taught me to milk. He let me feed ears of corn into a machine that took off the kernels, saving the stripped cobs for the pigs. He only forbade me to watch when he had to kill chickens, an activity not fitting for a girl. Even when I explained to him that Charlie let me hunt pigeons and rabbits, Uncle Clarence just shook his head. So I took a fly swatter and killed the hundreds of flies always clustered on the screen door that led into the kitchen.

Later, when the whole family visited, Arthur and I explored the limestone caves Dad had discovered as a boy. We swam in the Ohio River out to the riverboats from which passengers would throw us small change. They were gambling boats, we were told, steering their way across state lines whenever a police launch came out to challenge them.

I don't suppose I stayed at the farm more than several times. Though South Fork and Carlotta remained my spirit home, Goshen, Kentucky, with its traces of my father's boyhood, the stories of his grandparents, his eccentric old uncles, was a masculine counterpart to the very feminine world my mother had grown up in. One of Dad's brothers-in-law, angry at Granny Rule's social pretensions, said, "They may talk high and mighty, the Rules, but they were just a bunch of poor Kentucky dirt farmers." I was grown before it occurred to me that those people were poor, living on Grandfather Rule's handouts, the only one to have escaped, like Mary Lily after him, to make his way in the world. He was unfailingly generous to them, perhaps sometimes, as Granny claimed, at the expense of his own family. He respected their lack of worldliness, admired their service to the church and did not set his own successes above theirs.

Grandfather Rule, always sentimental about family if often not very practical, wrote a monthly newsletter which was sent not only to his own children but to other members of his family. Scattered as we increasingly were, we always had news of our cousins. The family for me was my own private soap opera, often more interesting than those I listened to after school on the radio or in the morning if I was sick in bed. Mary Lily's face on an increasing number of the covers of national magazines under-lined the glamour of my relatives, but I was always more drawn to the old stories, fixed in people's memories and told over and over again, like ballads.

Arthur's trip to Washington, D.C., was not such a success if Granny's report of it can be credited. While young George comported himself with dignity, going into famous buildings, Frank and Arthur chased squirrels around the grounds until Granny locked them up in the car. She had particularly high expectations for Arthur because he was Arthur Richard Rule III, and he was not carrying that dynastic burden with grace.

Again there were rumours at Dad's office of promotion and transfer. Mother was inclined to think that nothing could be worse than Hinsdale. I, having been assigned the task of making a leaf notebook and terrified of any project that took longer than half an hour, put it off in the hope that we would be gone long before it was due. I did not know the names of trees in Hinsdale, nor was I interested. Real trees grew in forests and orchards. The only authentic wonder we found in Hinsdale was the ruin of one of the hideouts of the underground railway where we could play at being runaway slaves. There were no black children to play with, or Chinese or Japanese either. But again the move was postponed, and Mother finally had to go with me into the neighbourhood to collect the leaves and identify them. The first snow had fallen, the day I lined up to get on the bus with the note-book finally completed. The girl next to me knocked it out of my hand, the papers scattering in the slush. I tried to turn away, to run home, but the kindly driver—surely not the one who had reported us the winter before?—got out and collected my soggy leaves for me and coaxed me to school. Something of the dread and then grief of that project made me fear long assignments all through my school life, to hope for reprieve rather than to settle to work. I think it odd, nearly perverse, that I have spent my adult life, pursuing the difficult, therefore precious and vulnerable busi-ness of writing books.

DAD'S TRANSFER CAME THROUGH just about the time my Valentine's Day dress arrived from Mother Packer. We had to leave before I could wear it and enjoy the last episode of my brief social success. Dad had been appointed district sales manager of the St. Louis region. Mother found a house in Kirkwood, Missouri, a suburb of St. Louis, and once again the large Gatehouse furniture, including the grand piano, and all the wedding-present china, silver and glassware, was moved into a house crowded by its pretensions.

It seemed a happier place for Mother, mainly because Dad was much more often at home. Our neighbours on Circle Drive were friendly. They gathered at each other's houses and sang in harmony all evening. Though I couldn't understand why they sang so many different tunes at once or why they laughed at so sad a song as "Miss Otis Regrets," I liked to fall asleep to the sound of their singing. For the first time since Westfield, Mother and Dad had a circle of friends.

Arthur and I weren't as lucky. Out of necessity, we banded together walking to and from the local school, I having learned to be passive before the jeers, the occasional rocks thrown at us, thinking bitterly that sticks and stones would break our bones and names did hurt.

I sat, as always, in the back of the classroom, far behind in work and bewildered. I was expected to do long division when I had not been taught the multiplication tables, to pick up the meaning of a book halfway through it. The only familiar subject was geography. In the course of my first years of school, I studied South America three times and had never heard of Europe or Africa. I could draw a map of South America free hand. Other students volunteered to run errands to the principal's office to escape the boredom of the classroom. I couldn't because I didn't know where the principal's office was. I didn't even know where the girl's bathroom was. I hadn't in Hinsdale either, but long trips had disciplined my bladder.

The gang of girls I would have liked to play with was a closed clique, the leader of which had broken her arm in first grade and consolidated her position by letting only a select few write and draw pictures on her cast. I tried to figure out a way to break my own arm without having it hurt. Failing that, I made friends with a twin brother and sister, but their closeness and kindness to each other underlined my unhappiness with my brother. I played with other girls who hung around the edges of Margerie Fraser and gang. Their idea of adventure was to steal their older sisters' sanitary napkins and peel them open to discover the mystery, to tell dirty jokes I didn't understand. I would so much rather have been roaming the fields with my brother who had finally been given a BB gun, but he went alone or with a foul-mouthed boy my age who was the terror of the neighbourhood and with whom no one else was allowed to play. He told incomprehensible jokes, too, one of which I repeated at the dinner table.

"Do you know what that means?" my father asked.

"Not exactly."

That evening my father came to my room and explained to me how babies were conceived. That a man had to put his penis inside a woman was unbelievably disgusting.

"They do?"

"Yes, they do," he said brusquely and went off to my brother's room, which proved a less difficult assignment.

Though it was clear to me that under such circumstances I would never have a child, I drew some comfort in the knowledge that my father was not simply the man my mother had married but actually my father. There was a reason for my looking like him. At about the same time, he discovered that I needed to learn the multiplication tables and taught them to me, solving the mystery of long division.

I was now growing taller than even the tallest boy in my class. The taunts which had before been impersonal were now physically mocking. "Giant. Big nose. Big feet." For the first time, too, I was forced to notice how much lower the pitch of my voice was than any other child's. The music teacher asked me not to sing because I carried my part a full octave lower than any other child.

At the same time, my mother began to fret about my hair. I was sent to the torture of a permanent, which made my hair impossible to comb. "Suitable" clothes were increasingly difficult to find, and I had to go to a special shoe store for corrective shoes.

Finally, it was discovered that I needed glasses, a disappointment my parents could not hide. I had turned from a pretty child into a great, lumpish ten-year-old, negatively self-conscious and sullen.

For me, neither my parents' depression over my glasses nor the new taunt "Four Eyes" could lessen the wonder of being able to see leaves on trees, individual pebbles in the driveway, birds in flight, what the teacher wrote on the board, people's expressions in the movies.

Mother, who had grown progressively heavier after each of us was born, began to worry at me about the weight I was putting on, lining open-faced peanut butter sandwiches up the length of one arm every day after school and sitting by the radio listening to soap operas. Arthur could do the same thing and stay thin as a fast-growing young tree. The doctor decided I needed thyroid pills, which turned me from depressed wordlessness into shrieking fury. One day, Dad took both my mother's and my thyroid pills out of the medicine cabinet and threw them in the field. We were, for a while, able to be civil to each other.

My parents found a not-quite-completed house just a block away which they could buy for a reasonable amount and Dad could gradually finish. I suppose the down payment cancelled our summer trip west. I campaigned for at least two weeks at a summer camp in the Ozarks, away from my disappointed father, scolding mother, boring little sister and hostile brother.

I had no real friends to go with and chose a time when the friends I had wanted wouldn't be there. But, of course, I took my baffled and unhappy self along. Camp made Yosemite, in retrospect, magnificent. It was at least beautiful, and I hadn't had to eat and sleep and even share an outhouse with strangers. In my cabin were five other girls and my last winter's teacher, who looked very odd in shorts or jeans and appalled me by trying to be friendly. The river we swam in was a mudhole, and I was disqualified after winning a race because I didn't breathe at every stroke.

"Neither did my father, and he's a champion!"

I was terrified of the food, of the physical intimacy with people I didn't know and of the friend each of us drew to do nice things for in secret. I didn't so much mind leaving candy bars and wild flowers for the girl I had drawn, but I was threatened by the secret and extravagant affection I received.

"Yours must really love you," my cabin mates taunted, jealous I suppose, but I would gladly have traded that passionate attention for lacklustre duty or even failure to respond.

I forgot to spit out my gum one night and woke up with it in my hair. I ran out of clean underwear. I got a migraine headache and was refused pills for it. At the end of the first week, I demanded to go home. When I was refused that, too, I found some visiting parents and was so eloquent they offered to drive me home.

When we stopped for lunch, I insisted on paying for my own. Then I bought presents for each member of my family so that I wouldn't have to present them with the grotesque clay bowl and the wallet, so thick Dad couldn't get it into his back pocket, which I'd been forced to make in crafts.

The new lawn was up at our new house, measuring for me the century I'd been away. Mother did momentarily gloat at my being glad to be home.

Arthur that fall went on to junior high, which meant he had to ride the streetcar and I had to walk to school alone. But I was no longer new to the neighbourhood or to my class. The new girl now really was fat and nearly blind, and she made a mistake I never did: she looked frightened. One afternoon other kids in the class invited me to help chase her off the playground. I ran at her, snatched one of her galoshes and threw it down the steps after her. A few minutes later, on my way home alone, I threw up my lunch and breakfast. I could not bring myself to make friends with that outcast, but I never took part in tormenting her again.

The Colonel and Mother Packer came to visit, he staying only a few days before he was off on a trip of his own, perhaps to visit his spinster sister in the East. Mother Packer stayed on, sleeping in my room with me, which meant I could no longer read comic books by the radio light at night. We had a maid at the time. Though that meant less work for Mother, it also gave her no escape from her mother's company. Except for Libby, who was a generous, affectionate and cheerful child, Mother had much to answer for in the looks and behaviour of her children. Critical of and baffled by us herself, she nonetheless defended us fiercely.

In that defence, I heard more clearly my mother's dissatisfaction with the world we lived in. How could we learn good manners when Dad's office staff gave us a surprise housewarming and got drunk and sick all over the house, leaving water stains on the grand piano, when our neighbours had murals of naked women in their recreation room and raised vicious dogs, when there was no civilized entertainment for adults or children, bring-your-own-bottle parties and rowdy public Easter egg hunts? When schoolchildren were taken to the symphony in St. Louis, the conductor finally refused to go on with the concert they were so badly behaved. It was an awful place. The people were awful.

My mother was as unhappy as I was. My own loyalty was roused; I took her side against Mother Packer when I could. And I tried to remember how to be a child again, easily amused by card games, easily pleased by ice-cream cones, obedient. Mother had hay fever. I had migraine headaches and, finally, a kidney infection.

When Mother Packer left, the doctor said, "You're allergic to her, all of you, that's all."

Yet Mother wanted, above all things, to move back to California.

I don't think that I did, except for summers I missed at South Fork. I didn't like it where I was. I was afraid of the black children who went to separate schools and even separate movies, who stepped off the curb when I passed but spat at the same time. I was afraid of my own classmates, too, and yet the most persistent cruelty I suffered from was at home where Arthur rarely spoke a civil word and was frequently violent if we were left alone with the maid or a babysitter. He would have to go wherever I did, intimate evidence that the scenery changed but unhappiness was probably a constant. I began to wonder, even then, if the world my mother wanted to live in really existed.

"We were nice to each other when we were children. We had fun together."

"You didn't have a brother."

"My friends did. If you were nicer to him, he'd be nicer to you. Somebody has to begin."

During one of our uneasy truces, Arthur and I had gone to a Sunday afternoon movie together. When Dad picked us up, he was unusually solemn.

"Japan has just attacked Pearl Harbor. We're at war."

There had been talk of war ever since I could remember, and it had increased in the last two years. Two of Dad's brothers-in-law were graduates of West Point, professional soldiers, and another, a classmate of Dad's at Annapolis, had already re-enlisted in the navy.

"Will you fight, Dad?"

"I don't know," he said.

Walking to school the next day alone, I kicked through the last of the autumn leaves, thinking over and over again only "we're at war."

Very shortly the letters began to arrive for Dad. He had three children, and he was a year too old for the draft, but he was a trained officer. His country had paid for his education, and it needed him now.

His sisters were on the move now, following husbands as far as they could. Uncle Keg was going out to the Pacific. Aunt Pat stopped with twins, Patsy and Artie, who were eleven years old, on her way back east from seeing him off. Arthur and Artie spent hours playing elaborate war games with miniature grey fleets, knowing the real distances guns could fire, torpedoes strike, and they memorized the silhouettes of enemy and allied planes. Patsy, taller than I was, even taller than her brother, still wore bloomers to match her dresses and fancied herself a singer. She had a tiny record she had cut which she played over and over again.

"God, I thought you were bad," Arthur remarked.

It was a small, odd but real comfort to know I had a cousin even more detestable to my brother than I was. I couldn't stand her either, but was too much like her in her brother's eyes to be allowed to make common cause with him.

The war had given boys a new dignity and concentration on real violence, from which girls of any sort could be excluded.

My father went on working on the house on weekends, finishing the upstairs where Arthur already had his room and where I would eventually move, but he was restless and distracted.

At school I found a note from my teacher on my desk, "Arthur Rule's Pig Pen Taken Over by Jane Rule." I hated being compared to him, knowing every teacher began with negative expectations of me; yet I usually defended him because I had no more allegiance to school than he, only resisted in more passive forms.

I was sent one day to a room in the school basement to see a speech therapist. Used to being ridiculed for my low voice, always threatened by a stammer when I was nervous, I was tempted simply to hide somewhere until the hour was over, but I hadn't Arthur's courage for disobedience. There were only a few students there, lispers and stutterers all. When my turn came to read, I said, "I don't like to read."

"Why not?"

"I don't like to make mistakes."

"Do you know any poems or songs by heart?"

"Yes."

"Well, sing me one."

" 'The breaking waves dashed high / On a stern and rock-bound coast,' " I began and found it easy enough to go on with so small and daunted an audience.

When I had finished, she dismissed the other students but asked me to stay behind.

"I want to tell you something. You have a perfectly beautiful speaking voice. One day, when you've grown up to it, you'll be able to do anything with it you want. Don't believe anyone who tells you anything else."

The intensity of her attention embarrassed me, but into the huge vacuum of my inadequacy, there rushed a sudden hope that growing up could be an answer to my voice, to my body, even to my fear and anger. After that, when I mouthed the words I wasn't allowed to sing, I began to listen to my own voice in my head at least. When I was told to hand out programs instead of taking part in a school concert, my mother decided she'd take me to a movie instead.

My fear of junior high, of having to ride the streetcar, of having to find my way around from class to class, of great numbers of new and hostile people, of being in my brother's territory again, was diminished by the sudden banding together of the children I'd been in school with. We rode the streetcar together providing safety in numbers. We sat together in classes, helped each other with homework, and because Margerie Fraser decided to play the clarinet in the school band, several of us rented clarinets to keep her protective company. We practised together after school, even occasionally played popular tunes in the local ice-cream parlour. I wasn't asked to exclusive birthday or slumber parties, but I had a public place far more secure than before.

I even began to feel a bit cocky, brave enough to object when, week after week, I was always assigned to wash dishes in a home economics class.

"For that you'll stay after school," the teacher announced.

"Can't. I have band practice."

"You'll go to the principal right now."

The principal's office was in the adjacent high-school building. No one I knew had ever been sent there, except, of course, Arthur. I had to ask hall ushers the way. Waiting in the outer office, I was indignant rather than afraid.

He was a little man, shorter than I was by several inches, obviously not used to dealing with junior high-school girls.

"How old are you?" he asked mildly.

"Eleven."

"What's the trouble?"

I told him I didn't need to learn how to wash dishes. I did them every night at home, and I'd done nothing but dishes for a month in class.

He looked at his watch. "It's my lunch time. Why don't we have lunch together, and you can tell me about what you think of junior high."

There I sat in the cafeteria with the principal, having an amiable lunch while my friends looked on, amazed. I never did dishes again, but I didn't learn to cook either. I lived in stiff truce with that teacher all term.

When Margerie Fraser decided we should take some cooking classes offered by Westinghouse, we all signed up. We were supposed to cook and then eat a dinner each week, but Mother always saved my dinner for me at home. The only thing I learned how to make that I liked was candlestick salad, forcing half a banana into a pineapple round, putting a cherry on top for a flame and dribbling mayonnaise down the side for melting wax. When I tried it a home, the bananas were too large for the holes in the pineapple. The bananas were grey with my fingermarks by the time they arrived at the table.

"It's what I call 'handled food,' " my mother said.

There my interest in cooking ended for some years.

When our names were published in the local paper for having completed the course, we all got obscene phone calls for some weeks. Learning how to deal with those was more useful to me in later life than anything the classes themselves taught me. And, of course, living through such an experience with my friends strengthened the bonds between us, giving us all a sense of new self-importance. Even Arthur asked, "What did he say? What did he say?"

I didn't tell him they were just dumb things like, "Do you wet your panties?" which had no overtly sexual meaning for any of us. He might as well have chanted, with the stupid boys on the street-car, "I see London, I see France, I see someone's underpants."

The day after my father told us he decided to enlist, he left for Chapel Hill. When he came home months later, he was in a lieutenant commander's uniform.

Mother, left to sell the house and be ready to move either with him or back to California if he was ordered overseas, set the back field on fire the day after he left and nearly burned the whole neighbourhood down. She told such stories on herself with gusto: "Just my part of the war effort." Cheerfully, she sold the Ping-Pong table he'd just been given, most of our books, nearly all Dad's civilian clothes. I'm sure she sold things of her own, too, but I remember what we objected to. Mother adored sales, "My merchant blood coming out in me."

We left, as usual, before school was out. We went to the Colonel and Mother Packer at 1111 Hamilton, and Arthur and I were again walking to school together, this time from the right side of the tracks, passing potentially dangerous bands of children, some of whose faces were familiar.

The first morning, the principal over the PA system asked students from our homerooms to come for us at his office. He handed each of us a schedule of classes, and that was that. After homeroom announcements, we were all dismissed to find our first classes. The homeroom teacher asked another student to show me where my math class was. When that was over, I went out into the hall with no idea where in that maze of corridors I should go next. Finally I went back into the math room and stayed there all day, the teacher taking no notice of me. The next morning, in homeroom, my name was called over the PA system to report to the principal.

"Maybe you can get away with cutting classes in Missouri," he began.

"I didn't cut classes. I couldn't find them. Don't you even have a map of this place? Don't you have any idea how to treat new kids?"

"You should have asked for help," he said gruffly.

"There's a rule against talking in the halls."

A student was assigned to show me around for a week, and my homeroom teacher asked every morning how I was getting along.

Before the first week was over, Arthur had enough demerits so that he had to stay after school, either working in the victory garden or digging dandelions out of the school lawn. While I waited for him, I caught sight of Wally, my Chinese friend from years ago.

"Hi," I called to him. "Where's Chiaki?"

Wally laughed. "He got sent to concentration camp with all the other Japs."

It was as if Wally felt he'd won a long, personal argument.

"Chiaki didn't do anything wrong," I said at the dinner table that night.

"Neither did my maid," Mother Packer said irritably, "but they wouldn't let me keep her."

"They're our enemy now," Mother said. "Some of them might be spies."

"But aren't they American, just like us?" I asked.

"They're Japs," Arthur said and pulled his eyes into slits.

When the Colonel took us to San Francisco, he had a pass that could get us through the restricted zones of the city, but, when Mother Packer and I went to Chinatown, half the shops were shut.

"You tell the difference between Japs and Chinamen by their feet," Mother Packer explained.

I noticed on the way home that all the cutting gardens along the bay shore were gone, even what we'd called Mount Beauty, a hill vibrant with colour at every season of the year.

"They were Jap gardens," the Colonel said.

In Kirkwood, Missouri, there had been nothing at all to indicate that the country was at war. In California, it was impossible to forget it. There were training camps everywhere, and new hospitals were being set up to receive the wounded. We could practise recognizing service and rank even on the streets of Palo Alto, where young men loitered, waiting to be shipped out or recovering from wounds. Even at 1111 Hamilton, there were blackout curtains, vegetables growing where flowers had been, and Mother Packer, after the first submarine scare, had put her flat silver in the bank.

I joined the school band, was issued a uniform of my own. At my first practice, I discovered Eddie Hootstein, playing the cymbals. Once, after marching in a parade, playing patriotic songs, Eddie tried to walk me home, but his feet hurt and he gave up halfway there.

I didn't see any point in trying to connect with old friends or make new ones since we didn't know from day to day where we were going. School was a way of getting out of the house, of killing time.

Libby didn't have that distraction, and she was the one who took the brunt of nervous irritability our presence there created in everyone. Mother Packer corrected and scolded her at every opportunity until that amiable four-year-old turned on her and said, "You don't love anyone. You didn't love Granddad, and that's why he went away."

Granddad had never been mentioned in front of Mother Packer. She turned away from Libby in freezing silence.

"She's only a little child, Mother," my mother pleaded after days in which Mother Packer refused to speak to Libby.

School let out, but there were no preparations to go to South Fork. Gas was rationed. Summers there, like so much else, were postponed "for the duration."

We moved instead to Orinda, California, behind the Berkeley Hills because Dad had been ordered to St. Mary's College, now a pre-flight school where batches of young officers were turned out every six weeks. We rented a house on a small lake, a game preserve, near the college. Among Dad's duties, which were various and often nebulous, he was band officer. The band was made up, in part, of members of Count Basie's orchestra. Royal, a trumpet player, was the leader. His brother, Ernie, played the clarinet. Through that summer he gave me clarinet lessons, back of the stage in one of the dressing rooms. We nearly always surprised some of the other band members shooting craps. They would scramble to mock attention for me, and I would say, mocking back, "As you were, men." It never occurred to my father or to me that I was in anything but the most protective and solicitous hands.

The one person my father both mistrusted and detested was the captain of the station. At one of the marvellous USO shows put on to entertain the men, Royal announced that the band would play a special piece dedicated to the captain, who sat through it smiling broadly while the rest of the audience stifled laughter. It was an instrumental piece called "Big Fat Butterfly."

As band officer, Dad had to attend football games. We went with him in a station wagon filled with guns, with which the drill team would perform at the half. Thirteen busloads of cadets followed us, and, when we reached the Bay Bridge, we were picked up by a police escort. We drove across the bridge and through the city, sirens screaming, traffic lights ignored.

The beauty of the college, the glamour of all those men in uniform, formal graduation ceremonies every six weeks at which at least two or three men would faint from the heat and be carried off in ambulances waiting at the edge of the parade ground for that purpose made that summer, which might otherwise have been lonely, a wonderful time. I could finally imagine what it must have been like for my mother, growing up on army posts. For Dad, though I'm sure he enjoyed providing so much happy entertainment for us, the place was a mockery of everything he understood about the military, and his jobs were pointless, even sometimes humiliating. A man of his age, with three children, would not be sent to active duty unless he volunteered for it. He was facing yet another crisis of conscience.

ARTHUR AND LIBBY WERE ENROLLED in local schools, but I was finally to be sent to a private school, Anna Head's, in Berkeley, three-quarters of an hour's drive from where we lived. The father of another student would drive four of us in each morning, and mothers would take turns picking us up. I had to have a uniform, a grey skirt, white blouse and grey sweater. Drab as it was, I was delighted not to have to think about what to wear every morning. Mother decided it was also time for me to have stockings and high-heeled shoes.

I initiated them when Arthur and I took Libby to see her first movie. I walked into the lobby, feeling like a large puppet on strings. Libby stood amazed at the size of the room, the carpets, the murals on the walls. The place impressed her far more than the film, and all I remember was my physical uncertainty and my growing sympathy for a whole population of grown women for whom that sensation was constant.

"What does your tie feel like?" I asked my brother.

"Like a tie, stupid," he answered, a discomfort he'd been familiar with for years.

Arthur is the one who should have been sent to private school, far more alienated than I was, in much greater need of the attention he would have had in small classes. But Mother Packer was paying the bill which, even though I had a serviceman's scholarship, Mother and Dad couldn't have afforded on his navy pay. Nothing but a private school could take a six-foot-tall, twelve-year-old barbarian in hand and make a civilized young woman out of her. Mother Packer had no similar interest in Arthur, whose natural manners had always been better than mine, whose even greater height was a social asset rather than a disaster.

I was introduced to my travelling companions before school began, and, though I felt the usual dread at new beginnings, at least I would begin with a few girls that I knew, though none of them was to be in my class. There were only fourteen of us, and five of us were named Jane. I was already restless with the jokes people made over the phone about big Jane and little Jane, old Jane and young Jane. My mother's godmother had called her Jinx when she was growing up, a name that appealed to me. I accounted that I would be called Jinx, but it took me about a month to get used to it. Mother indulged me at home, but Dad would have nothing to do with my new name, resisting as he always did any change in his children.

The school physically was so different from any place I had ever been. The two- to three-storey buildings surrounded a court-yard large enough for basketball games but edged with trees under which were benches for shaded sitting. Paths led to small patches of garden, intimate and quiet. The school buildings, too, had nooks and crannies, having been built before people were concerned about waste of space, which has always made a place liveable. The main house, where the boarders lived, had a large imposing entrance hall, lounge and dining room with real rather than institutional furniture.

The eighth-grade classroom was on the second floor of the school building, wedged in under the eaves, windows opening onto a sunny, gently sloping roof, onto which we occasionally climbed without more cost than a gentle reprimand. We were encouraged to feel at home, taking all our studies but art and music in one place.

About half of us were new girls, and those who had come up from the lower school, rather than banding together to exclude us, the only social strategy I expected, went out of their way to make us feel welcome.

The absence of boys from that whole city block the school occupied gave me a sense of giddy freedom and then growing power. Being the tallest girl in the school was a mark of distinction rather than a bad joke. Because we did all our academic subjects until one o'clock, and chose from an offering of sports in the afternoon, I was allowed to join the high-school basketball, volleyball and swimming teams. I was welcomed by the older girls, and my classmates were pleased with my distinction because it reflected favourably on them. As the highest class in the lower school, it was important for each of us to be looked up to.

Academically I was much less successful, bringing with me such uncertain skills from the grab bag my education had up to that point been. The one highly developed talent I had, which was hiding my ignorance, was of no use to me. I had not been in school a week before I discovered that teachers at Anna Head's wanted to find out what we didn't know not to mock and judge us but to help us.

By unhappy accident, the eighth-grade teacher fell down the stairs and broke her arm soon after school began, and the principal, whose husband had gone off to war, had a nervous breakdown. The assistant principal, Mrs. Knapp, an old school friend of the principal, who had been brought in to fill gaps, took over our class for several weeks until the first of a series of unsuccessful substitute teachers could be found. In those few weeks I was taught with an attention and perception I had not known existed. Each of us had private appointments with Mrs. Knapp in her own bed-sitting room in the boarding house. There we discussed our problems and set up individual programs for solving them.

"When you don't understand, say so," she said finally. "That is the first mark of intelligence."

Why was a word I had not used outside my home for years. Slyly at first and then with something like abandoned greed, I asked and asked. Mrs. Knapp set up a tutorial hour for me once a week which continued even after she had left the class.

I worked so hard at home, for such long hours, that my father finally said I must set limits.

"But I have to," I said. "I don't know anything."

"Teach yourself to concentrate," he said. "When you're over-tired, you daydream."

It was true; so I set myself time limits for my assignments and found I could get through the work much more quickly, but I was edgy with excitement every night, often unable to sleep and, in that state, old fears of the dark returned to me.

My room opened onto a stone terrace, past which a small creek flowed down into the lake. On stormy nights, tree branches would scratch at the window, and the creek was a wild throat. Too old now to call out to my parents with fake requests for drinks of water and more blankets, ashamed of the childish fantasies that terrified me, one night I got up, put on my shoes and a coat over my pyjamas, and went out the French doors onto the patio. I followed the path by the creek down to the road and began to walk along it, sure every shadow was a madman and murderer or a vicious wild animal or an evil spirit. Light-headed with terror, I nevertheless forced myself to go on. Gradually, my stride grew less timid. I began to be able to turn my head and look around me. It was a wild night, wind pushing broken clouds across the face of a bright moon, setting the trees to dancing. I was not victim to it now but part of the spirit of the storm. I began to run, intoxicated with the energy in me and all around me. I ran the full circle of the lake, came home and slept. I was never afraid of the dark again. I had taken it into my nature.

That kind of energy can be a disruptive force. I was often that autumn too happy to know what to do with myself, energy spilling over into nearly hysterical high spirits. When we didn't have a teacher with as sure a hand as Mrs. Knapp who could use our energies, we became torturers.

"You're acting like silly children," one of them snapped, her patience nearing an end at our noisy joy.

I suggested we all bring our younger sisters' and brothers' musical animals, wind them up and put them in our desks. The room was full of the faint twinkling of a dozen different music boxes, and our teacher quit.

We grew proud of our ability to discourage substitutes. Rumour now had it that our original teacher hadn't fallen but had been pushed down the stairs, and it was the behaviour of the eighth grade that had inspired the principal's nervous break-down. One of our motivations was to force Mrs. Knapp to return to us, but our pranks were mainly inspirations of high spirits.

Expecting yet another substitute to turn up one morning after chapel, we got into boxes of yarn to be distributed to us to knit squares for afghans for soldiers. We strung the whole room with it, I climbing up to hook it to the ceiling lights, another girl binding the teacher's chair to her desk. Hearing footsteps on the stairs, we raced to our seats and sat waiting for a reaction to our decorative achievement.

It was Mrs. Knapp who opened the door. There was the faintest flicker at the edge of her mouth.

"Well, get us undone," she said. "It's clear who will have to get it off the ceiling."

In ten minutes we were sheepishly, happily at work, arguing fine points of grammar, a skill we had developed so well only Mrs. Knapp could beat us at it.

At home I was rebellious about the amount of time I was expected to spend with Libby. I started reading her my English text, not to waste the hour, and the poor child even put up with that if it was all the attention I would give her.

When Arthur looked at us and sighed, "And I wanted to be the football player in the family," instead of responding with some rudeness about his protruding Adam's apple, I burst into tears and left the table, a reaction as surprising to me as it was to him.

The next morning I had my first period, about which I felt as physically awkward as I did about wearing stockings, but, though it was still commonly called "the curse," I was glad to have it and to cross the line that divided those who didn't from those who did.

My father had a long talk with my brother which must have had to do with the mysterious emotions of women and how they must be treated. From then on, though there could be irony in his tone, his attitude toward me was faintly flavoured by the protective concern he had been so generous with when we were little children.

When elections were held about a month after school started, I became judge of the lower school court, a position of even greater prestige than president of the class. More often than not, I was one of the offenders and had to turn over my position to the president of the class while my own trial was going on. Mrs. Knapp pointed out that my example wasn't very good for the younger children, but I sensed underneath her rebuke a tolerance for my run of high spirits, stealing from an abundance of neighbourhood flowers to bring her a bouquet, climbing the tallest tree on the grounds and chucking hard candy down to my schoolmates. About matters of real moral importance, I was dependable. Cheating was despicable, lying about anything important unthinkable. I loved the solemn ritual of chapel that began each school day. In the alto section, my voice was perfectly acceptable, and Mrs. Knapp's morning comments about truth, beauty, self-discipline and kindness gave me a few moments of saintly aspiration each day, which had nothing to do with giving up pranks, rowdiness and laughter but rather to do with some unimaginably noble and self-sacrificing act that would save Mrs. Knapp's life in a more dramatic way than she was daily saving mine.

She had the virtues of cheerful respect and fairness, and, though she devoted herself to us, she stayed aloof. I never felt the five inches taller than she that I was. And I bitterly resented her sudden demotion when Mrs. Hyde, the principal, returned and took Mrs. Knapp's place on the podium.

With Mrs. Hyde was her husband, on mercy leave to help her in the first month of taking the school back under control. One of her first acts was to hire a teacher for us who would stay, a dull but stubborn woman who outlasted our rebellious stunts with the help of Mrs. Hyde's harsh disciplinary measures. We were punished as well for our devotion to Mrs. Knapp. Our tutorials were abruptly stopped.

Outraged and heartbroken, I protested my banishment.

"Don't cross her, Jinx," Mrs. Knapp said, tiredly. "She's not a person to be crossed. You have to grow up in these matters and accept what you have to."

The whole tone of the school changed. We attended formal teas at the principal's house at which academic subjects for conversation were frowned on. When I had an opportunity to speak with Mrs. Knapp, I discovered neither of us was very good at small talk. Mrs. Hyde made surprise inspections in the classrooms and was sarcastic about what displeased her, which more often had to do with housekeeping and personal appearance than with lessons.

Then she announced a series of surprise tests unrelated to our ordinary work. My academic confidence was so new and frail that I felt unfairly challenged and at the same time required to live up to the hours of individual instruction Mrs. Knapp had given me. In the middle of the math exam, I discovered the girl across the aisle copying answers from my paper. Nothing like it had happened since I'd been at Anna Head's, and my pride in the standards of the school was offended. I told her to report to the next student court.

The faculty adviser who should have attended that meeting was called away to another emergency, and I carried on the meeting without her. The cheater was charged, found guilty and given a week's suspension from school. I went home, maniacally self-righteous about having seen that justice was done, only to discover that I myself had been suspended from school indefinitely.

The next day, my father went to school for an appointment with the principal to be told not only of my unprecedented behaviour in suspending one of my classmates behind the adviser's back but also of my arrival at chapel every morning reeking of smoke. I was in matters of general deportment a very bad example to younger students.

"I don't smoke!" I said indignantly.

What I did do was ride every morning in a closed car with a man who smoked a cigar.

A meeting was arranged with Mrs. Hyde for me and my parents. When we arrived, Mrs. Knapp was also there.

"Because Mrs. Knapp has been in charge while I was away, she has asked to sit in on this meeting," Mrs. Hyde explained.

I could not look at her or at anyone, feeling at once betrayed and ashamed and in terror of being shut out of the only school I had ever liked.

Even when Mrs. Knapp spoke at length in my defence, I could not look up. I was sure that I would recognize the pattern of that carpet for the rest of my life. She said that, while I had certain immaturities and was too headstrong in judgment, I had a natural reverence of spirit, was an eager student and a good athlete and I was well liked by all of my classmates if not always a good example to them. I had made a serious error which, once I understood it, she was sure I would apologize for.

"As for the smoking ..." my mother began, never patient with even the mildest criticism of her children, however couched in praise.

"Do you understand why what you did was wrong?" Mrs. Knapp asked.

"She did cheat," I said defensively.

"You had no business sending a student home from school on your own authority," Mrs. Hyde snapped.

"I'm the judge of the court," I said. "I didn't do it behind anyone's back. The adviser had to leave."

Mrs. Hyde gave an exasperated sigh.

"Do you understand why it was wrong?" Mrs. Knapp asked again.

"Because it was unkind," I said.

"Are you ready to apologize?"

It was my turn to sigh, but I nodded my head.

I could return to school, but I was no longer judge of court. Someone with a clearer understanding of the limits of justice and authority was put in my place.

"You know that saying, 'I'd rather be right than president'?" my father asked. "Well, sometimes it's probably better to be president."

"Or anyway not pick out the richest girl in class who's only there because her father makes large donations to the school," Mother said indignantly.

Neither of their views had the clarity of the judgment Mrs. Knapp had drawn from me. I had been unkind to someone more frightened of that test than I was, someone needy and unsure and unhappy.

Dad, meanwhile, had obviously decided for himself that he'd rather be right. He had volunteered for overseas duty and had orders to join his ship in Seattle. We would last out the school year where we were and then move back to Palo Alto to a house of our own until the war was over.

Mother had made contact with her father, whose department store, J.F. Hink and Son, was in Berkeley and who lived not far from us. His first gesture was to give Mother a forty-percent discount at the store. Then he bought us a membership in the Orinda Country Club where he liked to play golf. His wife Gretchen invited us to dinner where we met her son and daughter. Zane was in uniform, a handsome, silent boy about to leave for the Pacific. When we younger ones were left alone after dinner, he said suddenly and viciously, "I hate his guts!" His older sister tried to calm and distract him.

"Anyway," he said finally, "I'm leaving and I won't come back."

He was killed in action three months later.

"He's tired of her already," Mother said on the way home. "He says three years is really his limit."

By then we had been to the store and met his three sons by his second wife who still lived in Berkeley.

I wrote on my basketball shoes, "Jinx thinks Hinks stinks," wanting no part of the reflected glory when my grandfather was made first citizen of Berkeley that year.

A mother of one of my classmates said, "Are you Lester Hink's granddaughter? I always thought he was a bachelor."

When I repeated the remark to Mother, she said, "I'm afraid that's what he thinks, too."

But into the hands of that self-centred, self-serving man, my father commended our lives, as he commended us to Arthur: "You're the man of the family now." He was not yet fourteen years old, six feet and three inches of awkward bone.

The epidemics had begun before Dad left, inevitable with the numbers of young men living in close quarters. Spinal meningitis and polio were the killers. Our next-door neighbours couldn't go to the funeral of one child, dead of meningitis, because they were quarantined with another with polio. Swimming pools were closed. We no longer went to USO shows or the movies.

Libby, always prone to ear infections, ran a temperature of 106 degrees and had to be taken by military ambulance to Oak Knoll Naval Hospital in Oakland, rows of quickly set up Quonset huts on a hill of golden grass behind the city, receiving mainly men who had lost limbs. Stanford Hospital was taking the blinded and those in need of plastic surgery. There were also isolation huts for the contagious diseases, and one hut for the children of navy personnel.

Libby was given sulpha and broke out in a rash. That allergy kept her longer in the hospital than the ear infection.

It was a forty-mile round trip for Mother each day, and she had to apply for emergency gas rations. I lost the coupons, and she had to go yet again and stand in line.

On weekends I went with Mother to visit Libby. We walked past eighteen- and nineteen-year-old boys, the basket cases without arms or legs, wheeled out into the sun. Then we sat with Libby, who seemed to grow thinner and longer each day, black circles under her still-feverish eyes, her arms blotched red, without even the energy to complain. We read to her, brought her colouring books, sat quietly while she dozed, and I didn't dare ask my mother how sick Libby really was.

Mother herself was running a fever. She'd come home from the hospital, put on supper and then go to bed. After a few days, Arthur was sick as well, and he went straight to bed and stayed there. I'd had the fever several days before I admitted it, not seeing how Mother could go on without what little help I could offer.

She called her father, desperate to find someone who might come briefly to look after us all. He came himself, bringing a box of candy and a stack of health magazines, and kept Mother up until midnight telling her his marital troubles.

Arthur recovered in about ten days. Lib came home from the hospital so that Mother didn't have to make the daily trip and could rest, but it was several weeks before she was well. I was in bed for a month, unable to shake the fever. When I finally went back to school again, I had lost so much weight people didn't recognize me. And Libby was back in the hospital with another ear infection and dangerously high fever.

She was in and out of the hospital all that spring. When she was home, we worked at making her eat to gain back what weight and strength she could. We dyed milk different colours and made custards, not knowing until several years later that one of her chief allergies was to milk.

Each time the ambulance came, I wondered how much more that child could take. Mother, too, was strained and often silent. Arthur avoided the house as much as he could, but it was he who finally went to the hospital with Mother to wait through Libby's mastoid operation.

A young orderly, homesick for his own younger brothers and sisters, made her a bracelet with adhesive tape and small coins while her head was shaved. Her two arms were dotted with needle marks from the newly discovered drug penicillin, not yet available to civilians. When she finally came out of surgery and had to be kept still and without anything to drink on that very hot day, the family of her roommate sat and drank Cokes while she begged for water.

Arthur came home murderous, Mother in tears of mixed anger and relief. The timing of the operation, crucial and so much a matter of guesswork, had been right. The infection was full blown enough to get it all, and it hadn't yet affected the bone protecting the brain. Libby was going to live.

Granddad, who had not appeared again in all those months, phoned to suggest that he take me out to dinner. I didn't want to go, having no idea what to say to such a man, alone with him. But Mother wanted to accept any gesture he might make.

Taller than he in my one pair of modest heels, bone thin under my button-down-the-front dress with a "Chubbettes" label, thirteen awkward years old, I went. I needn't have worried about what to say. He talked about himself without a moment's failure of interest. He told me what I was to hear over and over again each time I couldn't avoid seeing him over the years. He was an excellent golfer, had been a professional boxer, was a genius at business, Berkeley's first citizen and a poet.

We went to the St. Francis Hotel to the main dining room. There, waiting for our meal, he explained why he never sold his poetry, published it himself in a book called *Musings of a Merchant*, which he gave away to his friends.

"I could make a fortune with it if I wanted to," he said. "I could syndicate."

He took an elegant repeater pencil from his pocket and wrote the figures of his imagined fortune on the white tablecloth. I wondered if the waiter would throw us out. The orchestra had begun to play, and my grandfather asked me to dance. I said I didn't know how.

"Well, I have a surprise for you after dinner," he said. "I'm going to take you to see your great-grandparents."

Remembering the German village, the musical chair, the energetic old man who had scrubbed our hands and napped with us, the gentle sweet-faced old woman who had liked my mother to sing for her, I was wonderfully relieved.

It was to be a surprise for them, too.

My great-grandmother opened the door of their apartment, looked at Granddad, looked at me and burst into tears.

"Lester, she's too young!"

"Mama," he protested. "This is your great-granddaughter."

All through our short visit, while Granddad was out in the kitchen following his father's directions about putting chopped ham onto a butter saltine (press the cracker face down into the ham), Oma apologized to me, obviously hoping I hadn't understood the source of her distress.

"I'm an old woman. I cry easily. I was surprised."

"*Ja*, she cries all the time," Opa confirmed. "Last night I fell out of my bed, and I was laughing too hard to get up. She was crying too much to help me."

On Mother's Day, I recited my grandfather's poem to his mother:

> I am thinking of a Mother
> Who happily is mine,
> And I can best describe her
> By calling her divine.
>
> Divine because her nature
> Is free from selfishness,
> Divine because her life reflects
> Her fine ideals, I guess.
>
> If one could take self-sacrifice
> And understanding, too,
> If one could take a kindly heart,
> A spirit that rings true,

If one could take these heavenly traits
And merge one with the other,
The outcome would perfection be,
And there you have my mother.

He might have made a fortune. The stuff was bad enough.

I never saw those tiny, distressed old people again. Opa died in his nineties, and Oma lived on for ten more years in a rest house, recognizing no one. I was in my midtwenties when she died, and Granddad rode to her funeral, his hat on the seat between him and the woman who became his fourth wife, so that they could hold hands. She was older than me by maybe ten years. She'd been his housekeeper's daughter, whom he gave away in marriage and then took back. After she bore him his final son, the same age as his first great-grandson, she drank herself to death.

My brother was fair and blue eyed and full lipped, like the Hinks. His remoteness and indifference, symptoms of an unhappy adolescence, reminded Mother of her father. She hadn't been raised with brothers. Her stepfather was also a remote, unhappy man. Without the one man she knew and trusted and loved to help her with her bewildering son, she could sometimes assume he was as he was because he was mysteriously male and a Hink. In most crises, he vanished, but he could, like Granddad, suddenly take on a gallant role for himself. He took me to my graduation dance at Anna Head's, picked out a corsage himself, and did not desert me for my prettier friends, danced with me all the steps we'd learned together back in Hinsdale days, and we even showed off some of the boogie-woogie we learned ... where? Maybe at St. Mary's from the cadets. It was my first experience of Arthur as an attentive, courtly brother with whom my friends all wanted to fall in love.

At graduation itself, I puzzled over Mrs. Knapp in a dress, her fine, short-groomed head out of keeping in that feminine finery. She looked all of a piece in the tailored suits she normally wore.

Dad came home from the Aleutians on mercy leave in time to get Libby out of the hospital. She had talked so much about him that the whole staff lined up to meet him. Libby refused the wheelchair, ready to take her to the car. She set off down the corridor herself and had walked about twenty feet when her long, bony legs gave way under her, and Dad caught her before she fell, lifting his tall, frail five-year-old with her shaved head into his arms.

He stayed long enough to move us back to Palo Alto to the square house on Waverly Street where we would live until the war was over.

Arthur, all the time Dad was home, nagged him about being allowed to drive the car.

"I already know how. Why can't I?"

"You're not old enough to have a licence."

But, the last day of Dad's leave, when we pulled up in front of the house and Mother and Libby got out, Dad tossed the keys to Arthur and said, "Okay, son, put it in the garage."

I didn't have time to get out before Arthur was behind the wheel. He gunned the car around the corner and smashed it into a telephone pole.

"Well," my father said to my mother later, "it's an expensive lesson, but I don't think he'll nag you about the car for a while."

Angry as I was to be left to be a victim of that accident, I was angry for Arthur as well. So many of Dad's tests for him seemed designed to humiliate.

"The clutch stuck," Arthur said, determined to maintain the bluff that he knew how to drive.

Dad laughed.

The Rule family

Jane Rule Fonds, University Archives, University of British Columbia

THE LONELY SUMMER BEGAN. Libby, playing on her tricycle out in front of the house, stopped a high-school boy walking along the street and asked if he knew any little girls her age with whom she could play. Arthur wandered farther afield and found the local pool hall and bowling alley. Mother and I had an appointment at Castilleja School for girls, only a block away, where I was registered to begin high school in the fall, Libby to begin kindergarten. When I wasn't settling into my new room or arranging a sunroom I shared with Arthur where our player and record collection were kept, I was reading poetry and writing letters to Mrs. Knapp, who answered them for the few months before she died of cancer. And I walked, round and round the school property, trying to imagine what it would be like to be a student there. I often walked at night and saw the light on in the principal's office. Once I dropped in to see her, and she welcomed me easily enough, but she was younger and cooler and less sure of herself than Mrs. Knapp. Miss Espinosa had been a student at the school, then a Spanish teacher there, now principal in her early thirties. There was fear rather than laughter underneath her guard.

"Not enough experience in the world," was my mother's judgment of her.

I could hardly remember now what Mother and I had found to quarrel about when I was younger. Dad's leaving, Libby's long sickness, Arthur's increasing withdrawal from us had all contributed to a growing closeness between my mother and me. I had not looked up to her as I had to my father until I watched her coping without him and began to understand the power of her steadfastness, courage and love. Her fierce loyalty to us was in such contrast to her father's total indifference, her mother's sharp criticism. Though Mother complained about her parents and was often hurt by them, she did what she could for each of them as long as they lived. To other people, she was always inclined to make funny stories of her troubles, a clown rather than a martyr to hard events.

"Don't you take anything seriously?" her mother would complain.

"Not if I can help it," Mother replied.

She never came home from even a quick trip to the store without a silly story or two.

"I stuck out my hand to turn, and the man in the next car shook it!" or "A woman at the butcher asked for the left leg of the lamb. When I asked her why, she said it was the leg with the tail on it. You learn something new every day."

Her advice was nearly always irreverent. "Don't learn to do anything you don't like, or you'll end up having to do it the rest of your life."

When I was bored with something I had to read, she'd read it aloud to me in changing accents.

Laughter was the antidote to pain, boredom, fear, hurt pride.

"Never mind, darling. It will make a good story later on."

Mother did what the British call "dining out on" her life, a survival technique I owe her, for I was not a natural comic.

In fact, at thirteen, I was chiefly aware of a great capacity to suffer without the experience to spend it on. I had, of course, decided to be a doctor, an ambition I cherished for three years until I took chemistry and could get nothing but original results in all my experiments, had no hand for lighting Bunsen burners and couldn't clean out a test tube without getting a sponge stuck in the bottom of it.

A more tentative interest in being a poet prompted me to write metrically correct, rhyming verses on topics like "My Blindness," an avocation brought to a premature end by my mother's laughter. Stung as I was, I did have to admit the comic potential of my morbidities.

I have been able to use quite a lot of the material of my child-hood in fiction, but I have never been able to use the years of my adolescence. In the great range of characters in novels and short stories, it is as if people between the ages of thirteen and fifteen didn't exist. And I not only lived through those years but taught students that age for two years with comprehension and delight.

What has put me off, I think, is the odd blurry line between emotional ignorance and dishonesty which characterized those years for me and misshaped my understanding for much longer.

The troubled and troubling bond I had with my brother made me mistrustful of the few boys I knew, grateful for the protection of a girl's school which could put off the question of how I could ever be a woman loved by a man. But I was frightened enough by that eventual failure to invent "David," off fighting in the Pacific, my only fantasy life with trying to decide how he would die, how I would mourn him. I loved all poems about the death of lovers, particularly Amy Lowell's "Patterns," ending with that fine, "Christ! What are patterns for?" which she may have written with motives similar to mine.

Mother laughed about a lie she'd told her French teacher about a baby brother who had been drowned at sea.

"I was an awful liar—anything to get out of my homework."

That sort of a lie I would never have told. Even after my humiliation as judge of the lower school court, I was a fanatic about "the truth." So my "David" fantasy, which I occasionally committed to paper on a free theme day for English, was of a more desperate order of lying, a defence against future humiliations and pathetically unoriginal, since every old maid school teacher, however unattractive, was rumoured to be faithful to someone's memory.

I must have voiced something, my fear, to my mother who said, "Who you want to be is what's important. If someone comes along to share life with, fine. It's not something to worry about."

But Dad was her whole life. And I didn't question his masculine idealism which separated him from her and from us for years. He was off making the world safe for democracy.

I couldn't have known that first year in high school how much I presented myself to my teachers as a potential lover. I was arrogant and hopeful, willing to earn their attention with hard work, passionately loyal to those who taught me well, disdainful and rude to those who didn't. Though I made friends among the students, could win elections, be class captain of a team, it was the adults who mattered to me. I didn't have "crushes" on any of them. I wasn't a teacher's pet. I wanted to be known to them. I wanted to be, in the literal sense of the word, remarkable. An A without comment was less pleasing to me than a B with an explanation. I was intoxicated with the potential of my own mind and wanted the power that learning promised.

Miss Grant, the math teacher, a dry, ageless stick of a woman, with a jaw rewired as the result of an accident, was puzzled by any report of my misbehaviour because in her class my attention was fixed on the pure beauty of mathematics, the balancing equations of algebra, the unfolding logic of geometry. Among students who memorized or despaired and failed, I made Miss Grant's day, and she made mine. But poor little Miss Dively, the Latin teacher, who wasted the first ten minutes of each class counting the homework papers and kept discipline by not excusing students to go to the toilet, was tormented by my pranks and bewildered that I didn't respond meekly to threats of lowering my otherwise good grades. I was both interested enough and unsure enough in English—I couldn't spell and had a horror of reading aloud—to keep my mind on the lesson. I slept through German so often, Miss Espinosa complained to my mother that I wasn't getting enough sleep.

"She's bored," my mother replied.

I was in the office frequently to be reprimanded. Miss Espinosa said with some irritation, "We could do a good deal more with you if it weren't for your mother."

"Thank God for my mother," I replied.

I wasn't sleeping enough. I worked long after Mother went to bed, then often walked around the neighbourhood, and more than once I stood watching the late light in Miss Espinosa's office, knowing she didn't sleep enough either, irritated by her cold, humourless propriety, drawn by some half-sensed wish to break through it.

I was, in part, the same sort of challenge for her, I suppose, an undeniably bright student—and she had ambitions to improve the school scholastically—which was too wild, too lacking in respect, a threat to her control.

She added extra courses to my schedule to keep me from disrupting study hall. She suggested that the young Spanish teacher become my informal tutor to encourage me to read more widely and to be guided more firmly in matters of behaviour. Miss Read was only twenty-three, lived at home with her parents, waiting for the war to be over, for the young men to come home so that her real life could begin. I called her Sugarfoot for reasons I don't remember, walked her home in the afternoon, listened to her records and her complaints about her job, about Miss Espinosa.

"She wants me to spy on you, you know," Sugarfoot said. "She wants me to spy on the gym teacher and the history teacher, too."

"Why?"

"She wants to spy on everyone."

I would not have said I wanted to spy on Miss Espinosa, but I was as intently interested in her as she was in me. There were students and teachers in the school she wanted to wear her colours. Because I would not, she came to basketball games to cheer the opponents' team; to swimming meets to comment that I won too easily, being so tall. We wooed each other as stupidly and negatively as children pulling each other's braids.

Because I lived so close to the school, I made friends among the boarders and made a nuisance of myself after school hours as well, delivering contraband food and even cigarettes to the older girls. Also, I invited them home for weekends.

Among that group was a girl named Hina Gump, the half-Tahitian ward of Mr. Gump of the famous San Francisco store. She was no relation to him, a stray, unwanted child of one of his daughter's husbands on whom he had taken pity. A blind, ailing, old man, he couldn't care for her himself, but he could afford to educate her. Hina loved to come home with me. She would play with Libby and her friends, flirt with Arthur, talk with Mother.

"You're so lucky to have a home. Do you know how lucky you are?"

Mr. Gump, to express his gratitude that Hina could spend weekends in a family atmosphere, invited me to San Francisco for the weekend. His female driver came in a huge black car to collect us as well as another boarder, signed out to Mr. Gump for the weekend but dropped off before we arrived to meet her lover for the weekend. Hina and I taunted the throngs of sailors on the streets of San Francisco from the safety of that large car until the driver threatened to put us out. I suppose we were trying to seem as sophisticated as our friend. Perhaps Hina was.

Grandpa Gump's house on the Marina was filled with paintings and beautiful furniture. Hina had her own bedroom and sitting room, next to his study where he sat in the dark, smoking cigars. He had a nickel slot machine, into which he put five nickels each night, keeping any winnings he made. And there was a bar, arranged so that he could make his own drinks.

My first sight of him, sitting in the dark so that only the coal of his cigar lighted his wide-open blind eyes as he took a drag, frightened me a little. But he called me "Captain Jinx" affectionately and took my arm to go down the stairs for dinner. I was used to helping grandparents, felt comfortable with the weight of his arm on mine. Every few steps he paused, nodded to a painting and told me about it.

At dinner, his housekeeper presented Hina and me with full plates of deliciously cooked meat and vegetables in rich sauces. He had rice and a bit of white fish.

"You're having meat. I can smell it," he said crossly. "Aren't you, Captain Jinx?"

The housekeeper glanced a warning and shook her head. "They're eating just what you are."

"I should hope not. They'd starve. I am a prisoner in my own house, that's what I am, everyone lying to me."

I minded for him, but he settled to his meal resignedly. Both Hina and the housekeeper had such obvious, protective affection for him that their transparent deceptions became less painful to me, but I found it hard to lie to him myself.

How much more comfortable I would have been if I'd spent the weekend in his company at the store or in the house, learning about the great Oriental collection, listening to his grievances about his ungrateful and unhappy children, but he didn't suspect that a fourteen-year-old would find him interesting company.

Hina was allowed to go to a parking garage he owned across from the store and borrow a rental car though she had no licence. We careened around the steep streets of San Francisco until the car somehow caught fire and we had to be rescued by the fire department. Then we rented horses and cantered along the beach until we got tangled up in surf fishermen's lines. We went somewhere to a bar where prep school boys made oddly hostile advances to Hina, racially beneath them but rich. Then we went home and Hina got two pints of rum from Grandpa's bar, a large bottle of Coke for me, ginger ale for herself. I had never drunk anything but a beer or a Tom Collins, and, before that night was through, I had drunk the pint of rum and quart of Coke and was crawling to the bathroom to be sick.

I could not face Sunday, some kind of brunch at a hotel with the boys we'd seen the night before. I took a train back to Palo Alto the next morning, still ill, but what my mother saw was the sunny overlay of my ride on the beach. I had at last had a taste of her own glamorous girlhood in San Francisco, among the cultured and the rich. I hadn't the heart or courage to contradict her, confirmed instead the details of her fantasy. I was not able to eat so much as a rum-flavoured Life Saver for years afterward.

I ENTERTAINED MY MOTHER EVERY DAY when I came home to lunch with what went on at school. My own misbehaviour, whatever I organized—piling desks on top of each other, or wise-cracking, or leaving comic messages on the blackboard—was always in response to some authoritarian silliness to which I didn't think any student should be victim. I did not trouble her with anything that really troubled me. Libby was still often sick. Arthur not only routinely stole Mother's car but had been picked up by the police for truancy and vandalizing property and was threatened with reform school. Mother Packer and the Colonel, who might earlier have been some help, were having difficulty taking care of themselves without the domestic help they were accustomed to. Mother Packer, suffering a range of physical ailments and nervous disorders, was irritably demanding. I bicycled over to their house to do what errands I could, but Mother was the centre of their need as well as ours.

Tired and discouraged about how little her nagging or threatening Arthur reached him, Mother tried for a time to give him positive, generous attention. She asked him what he'd particularly like to do on his birthday. He asked for tickets to a concert in San Francisco and suggested the menu for his birthday dinner. But he left the day before and didn't come home for the concert or the meal.

Mother went to a therapist and tried to get Arthur to go, but he wouldn't. Mother continued with her sessions, and, though her relationship with Arthur continued to deteriorate, she at least had somewhere to go to find adult help.

"He says Arthur's not my problem, Mother is," Mother responded. "I wish the police agreed with him."

My relationship with Arthur was an on-again, off-again thing. Because he made no real friends of his own of the sort he could bring home, he increasingly depended on mine. At fifteen, he'd reached his full height of six feet and five inches and looked older than he was. His good looks, old-fashioned manners and taste for extravagant gestures made him much in demand, not only with girls our own age, but with young women.

"I'm a war substitute," he commented wryly.

Though he sometimes dated my friends, he preferred the less-formal arrangement of gang parties. A good many of the day students at Castilleja came from wealthy, indulgent, bewildered parents who offered up their houses to Saturday night parties for their teenagers, leaving them to do pretty much what they wanted to. There was always as much beer to drink as anyone wanted, and hard liquor wasn't difficult to come by. They were not the orgies some people suspected. We played cards, danced and some few got drunk and sick and probably pregnant. What was frightening was the dangerous ride home over the narrow winding roads of Woodside, boys driving as fast as they could bumper to bumper, when they shouldn't have been driving at all.

Arthur wasn't yet a heavy drinker, and he didn't want me to drink at all. Though we only occasionally danced together, he was always around at the end of the evening to see that our ride back to Palo Alto was among the safer choices. Nearly an ideal public brother, he was indifferent or hostile at home, unwilling to accept any kind of responsibility.

We gave a few parties ourselves, but, since it wouldn't have occurred to Mother either to serve beer or disappear, we worried about the rowdier elements of our loosely related group as well as crashers since we lived at a busy intersection and all teenaged parties were considered open houses. We could enjoy ourselves more easily away from home.

We also took up bowling together. We could set pins for the earlier part of the evening and earn enough to bowl ourselves when the alley was less crowded. Some of the newly blinded servicemen were sent to the alley, for bowling was excellent therapy for restoring a sense of balance. Arthur and I both graduated from pin setting to teaching. Arthur was particularly good with those who didn't want to participate. He never bullied them, but he had a way of sitting quietly with them until they trusted him enough to try.

One of the most sullenly reluctant who finally took his turn and pitched angry gutter ball after gutter ball would not believe us when he finally made a strike. He started to walk down the alley, his hands defensively before him, his balance increasingly uncertain until to keep going he had to crouch and then crawl to the place of toppled and scattered pins.

But such experiences made no sure bond between my brother and me. They could not even be referred to later. Arthur would-n't be lured into any kind of real conversation. He could tell jokes and pay compliments. Beyond those limits he refused to go. He would not give himself away. His favourite Steig cartoon was captioned, "Whenever I'm a good guy, people walk all over me."

Miss Espinosa offered me a job in the summer to assist the swimming teacher of the Castilleja day camp for younger children. How much more comfortable I was, at fourteen, being a member of the staff. The only other person near my age was a tall, conventionally pretty girl of sixteen called Mac who taught music and played the piano. She was a student from Palo Alto High School in whom Arthur took some real interest. I was much better friends with the swimming teacher with whom I worked very happily, pulling overconfident six-year-olds out of deep water, encouraging the timid to put their faces in water. Being good with those children made me sharply guilty at how impatiently and badly I taught my own sister. It was my first insight into ego investment, which made me doubt that I'd ever be a good mother.

I very much liked Ann Smith, the art teacher who supple-mented her teaching salary by doing charcoal portraits. She lived in one room behind a garage across the street from the school, saving money for the time her young husband would come from the war and want to go back to school. Ann also sang and paid Mac to accompany her for a couple of hours a week by doing her portrait. In the late afternoon, when the school day was over, I liked to go to the gym to listen to Ann sing or to her studio to watch her work on Mac's portrait, where Arthur occasionally also dropped by.

My pleasant leisure time lasted only a few weeks. The Colonel had a stroke, and Mother Packer had an attack of phlebitis. They were for a time in two different hospitals, Mother travelling between them. She tried to find a nurse or housekeeper to take care of them when they came home, but all such people were already employed in hospitals or at other war work. Finally, it was decided that I should move in with them. Mother Packer was well enough to do a little cooking. The Colonel was bedridden, one side partially paralyzed. He could no more than slowly get himself to the bathroom and back.

In the morning, Mother Packer needed help going down the stairs. She fixed breakfast while I made beds and helped the Colonel get settled for his day. I took his breakfast up to him, fetched the tray back down again, set up lunch and did whatever other domestic chores Mother Packer needed before I rode my bike the couple of miles to Castilleja to teach. I had to leave as soon as classes were over in order to help with dinner, clean up and get Mother Packer upstairs for the night. Then I went home to eat a late dinner with Mother, Libby usually already in bed, Arthur often not at home. Mother and I would plan the errands that needed to be done for each household. I rode my bike back to my grandparents by about ten o'clock at night and slept there.

No arduous duties, any of them, and the Colonel was pathetically grateful. He insisted on paying me a dollar a day, clumsily counting out the one-dollar bills I got him from the bank at the end of each week. I was acutely aware of how little he felt he deserved my help, how little kinship he had any right to claim. Yet, perhaps because of that, we made shy friends with each other during those weeks, I telling him about the friends I had made among the other teachers, about my students, he sometimes telling me about his early life, his disappointment at not being allowed to go to West Point. His father had forced him to take a law degree before he could join the army. The Colonel was ashamed of his helplessness, asked me not to tell Mother Packer when he could no longer feed himself. He began to have hallucinations about dozens of flies in the room, clothespins on his fingers, snakes in his bed. Mother, who visited as often as she

could, played along with his complaints, shaking out the bedclothes, rubbing his hands. I knew it was kind to humour him,
but I had difficulty lying to him. His dependence created a trust
I was reluctant to break.

Sometimes at night I woke afraid that, if anything happened,
I wouldn't know what to do.

When I raised a tentative question with the rushed and overworked doctor, he answered irritably, "There's no emergency
about death."

One night I woke vomiting and had to wash out my sheets
and blankets without letting Mother Packer know. To my great
surprise, my brother offered to take my place for a night. He
then told Mother a great deal about the care of Colonel, which
I hadn't. Half betrayed, half relieved, I admitted that he was
often incontinent, couldn't feed himself and was increasingly
irrational. Mother confronted the doctor who did finally get him
a place in an army hospital.

I don't know whether Mother had been hoarding gas
coupons or bought some on the black market, but the moment
the Colonel was in the hospital and my summer job was over at
the school, we left for South Fork, Mother, Arthur, Libby and I.

The day after we arrived, Arthur took off with the car and
we were stranded ten miles from the nearest town, two miles
from a telephone. For me, it was like a fulfilling of a childhood
fantasy to be left behind there to live in isolation and peace.
Libby, not knowing the place, was timid, excuse enough for me
not to encourage her company. I went alone to the hot berry-
scented meadows, through the deep woods to the creek, down
through the orchard to the river, to my old nest among the
willows. I had not known how tired I was until I stretched out
on a great rock in the sun and felt the heat as a snake must beat
out the deathly cold.

That night, when we turned on the radio, we heard about the
bombs, which seemed no more than a technical detail to prepare
us for the Japanese surrender. Mother wept, then made hot
chocolate to celebrate and talked for the first time about Dad's
coming home. "It's over. It's over."

After Lib went to bed, Mother said with tired energy, "Where is that damned brother of yours?"

It was another twenty-four hours before he turned up, a timeless sweetness for me, filled with the fragrances and tastes of my childhood. He had been delayed by celebrating, we had planned to stay only a few days and now Mother was anxious to be at home where there might be news of Dad. We needn't have hurried. His ship, having attended the Japanese surrender, was ordered through the Panama Canal to the East Coast. It was three months before Dad rode a train across the continent to get home.

Arthur had been missing for three days and turned up just in time to drive with us to Oakland to meet Dad's train, which was hours late. Arthur slept in the back of the car while we paced the platform. Mother watched a young woman with a fussy baby and nearly offered to hold it for a while. "But what if the train came in?" she asked and laughed.

Once Dad arrived, kissed us all, woke his son to say hello and got into the driver's seat, Mother asked him what he would have done if she'd been holding an infant.

"I'd have gotten right back on the train," he said, with confident amusement in his voice.

I sat studying the familiar back of his neck.

It was so obvious when we got home that our parents wanted time alone that Libby drifted off to play with a friend, Arthur to wherever he went and I back to school.

"I thought you had the day off," Sugarfoot said. "Didn't your dad get home?"

"Yeah," I said, puzzled by the awful sense of anticlimax after years of waiting.

What could he fix after all?

I had not seen the Colonel since he was taken to the hospital. Mother said he recognized no one. His older sister, Aunt Gussie, had come west and was staying with Mother Packer, where she complained that he had no right to die and leave her with no one to bury her. She and Mother Packer discussed what they would wear to the eventual funeral, and Aunt Gussie reminded Mother Packer that the Colonel wanted to be buried by his first wife.

"It's all right with me as long as she's dead," Mother Packer replied.

She had her own shelf in the family mausoleum in Eureka, designed by a father who didn't imagine husbands or children for any of his daughters.

When Dad went to the hospital the day after he got home, the Colonel gave him a weak salute, and whispered, "Welcome home, sailor."

However ineptly, he was the one male of the family who had felt a duty to Dad's absence and honoured it, refusing to die until he came home.

Our first family event was his open-casket funeral. I did not recognize the corpse and was as dry eyed as my grandmother, for very different reasons. I had no blood-right to mourn him with the noisy possessiveness of his sister. But in that grotesque public occasion I did know I had loved him and done what I could to let him know. The flag draped over the coffin lid reminded me not of his service to his country or the victorious country itself but of the ritual he had taught us each summer morning and evening, the care he took to teach us care. I didn't find that flag among Mother Packer's possessions when she died. Perhaps Aunt Gussie took it for the repeat funeral she had back in New Jersey, a day of such a blizzard that nearly no one could attend.

My FATHER HAD NO MILITARY FANTASIES about running his family when he got home. The war had not changed his genteel and reasoning nature. He did think he could take charge of his son. The man-to-man talks he had imagined left out the fact that Arthur didn't talk. He listened only when he had to and evaded rather than defied authority. Dad was left to discover that the understandings about school attendance and use of the car he thought they had come to were his own wishful thinking. Reasoning with Arthur, shouting at Arthur, depriving him of privileges had no more effect practised by Dad than they had by Mother. Though Mother would have been glad of a reformed son, I suppose in some part of her she was relieved that it hadn't been simply her ineptitude as a parent that had invited his delinquency.

I had always known Arthur was the more important though no more loved child for my father. It stung me when my father said to my brother, impatiently comparing our report cards, "With half the effort you could do twice as well."

At sixteen his son was a fair beauty, vain about his clothes, entirely bored with school, secretive about where he went, what he thought or felt, if he did either. If I had presented such an adolescent to my father, he would have been amused and indulgent. At fourteen, shaped like a telephone pole, I was stiff and awkward socially, still inclined to stand up when adults came into the room. (School friends of mine thoroughly embarrassed my father by standing up for him. "You are young women," he said. "Men should stand up for you.") I had no notion of what to do about my pimpled face or my long, limp hair. Since very few clothes fit me, I was indifferent to them. The one mirror I couldn't avoid was my father's face. It was a cold surprise to recognize how much I disappointed him.

Mother had not only welcomed but come to depend on my willingness to discuss family problems. Now she quite naturally confided in Dad, and he didn't take kindly to my observations.

After one failure or another with Art, Dad would say, "Well what should I have done, if you're so smart?"

I didn't know, but I could have told him that his beating us both roundly at bowling the first time he took him might have been tolerable if he hadn't added, "What's to this game anyway?" And I had a notion that Arthur had done so little work for so long that he couldn't simply "turn over a new leaf" with so many blanks behind him, no matter how impressive his IQ. I was in no mood to side with my brother against my father, but I often felt caught between them as I never did between Mother and Arthur.

My mother felt caught between my father and me, wanting to shield me from his disappointment, wanting me to be less disappointing. Since she had no more notion than I did what to do about how I looked except to trust I'd outgrow the embarrassment of it, she tried to show me how to soften my independence. "Ask your father instead of telling him where you're going. Get him to help you sometimes." She also explained his moodiness, first when he was looking for a job, then when he had taken one he disliked.

Dad was encountering all the men his age who had stayed home and made their fortunes from the war. Now he was asked to force people to buy leftover surplus goods in order to have their share of materials still scarce. The fair business practices he had been accustomed to were a thing of the past. If he'd had any illusions about the usefulness of his own service, it might have been less painful for him. He spoke very little of the war, but he did say, more than once, "If I ever get an idea like that again, lock me in a closet until I get over it."

For Mother there was no ambivalence about having Dad home. Her adult life was restored to her. Their love for and delight in each other had deepened through their long waiting. Only I was surprised that, rather than solving family problems, he added to their complexity.

All the veterans did, returning not only to families and the workforce, but to colleges and even high schools. The young ones with a couple of years' instruction in how to solve problems by violence were a glamorous menace. School for Arthur was now not only dull but terrifying, and our social world was invaded by a competitive sexuality we didn't know how to handle.

We were being asked, on the one hand, to become children again. On the other, we were being pressed into an adulthood we weren't ready for.

Ann Smith, who had finished portraits of both Arthur and Libby before Dad came home, postponed one of me now that her husband, Henry, had come home and started at Stanford. Her room across from school, which had been a haven, was now a private, intensely sexual place. She and Henry came to the house for dinner, as much our parents' friends as ours. Sugarfoot came, too, to be introduced to one of Dad's young officers, Walter Lord, who was now working with Dad. Walter took me to the movies once or twice which impressed my friends, but for me he was simply another of my childish duties.

At our own parties, fights broke out between the high-school boys and the veterans, unlike the drunken, half-athletic scuffles we were used to, mean and damaging. Arthur, never a fighter, was a target because of his height and looks. "Why would I fight over a girl?" he asked, sounding unpleasantly superior but probably simply bewildered.

Royal, the trumpet player from St. Mary's pre-flight days, was playing with a small combo at one of the roadhouses, and we sometimes went there to listen and dance to avoid larger parties, but the mood of any crowd was volatile. Also we were underage and could have been arrested in one of the frequent police raids. What we simply hadn't told Mother became lying to Dad. I didn't like any part of it, whether I was being one of the kids at home or one of the threatened crowd.

These were not problems to discuss with Mother, and Sugarfoot was so preoccupied with her sex life that I became dumb audience for her. Only Ann Smith and I occasionally talked while Henry was off at classes, first because I went to sit for my portrait, then out of the habit that formed. She was willing to discuss all the sense I had of my family and tell me about her own, her unconventional childhood, trailing around the world

ANN HIBBARD BURNHAM SMITH
NOVEMBER 1947

with an artist mother and alcoholic father, problematic older brother and sisters. Only when she talked about sexuality was I uncertain, guarded, not because I had anything to say but because I didn't. She'd been sexually involved with her older brother and asked me what my relationship with Arthur really was. The idea was not so much shocking as alien to me. My brother and I were so physically shy of each other we never touched except when we danced together. Though he'd long since stopped taunting me about how I looked, was always courtly to me in public, his private aversion to everyone in the family, against whom he locked his door as well as his heart, was the fact I lived with. I did find him attractive but in no conscious, sexual way. He was light on his feet, graceful. His fair head was beautifully shaped and, when he was neither sullen nor tense, he had a natural gentleness of expression, which Ann had caught in her portrait of him. Bewildered by him, angered by him, deeply hurt by his nearly inhuman indifference, I did love him, not exactly against my will. I wanted to love him, but I wanted him to be a different person, someone I could talk to, someone I could trust, the fantasy brother he played so well at a party.

Were there any boys I particularly liked? There were boys I admired, and they were all tall and fair like my brother and as remote from girls the likes of me.

"You have to show them you like them," Ann said.

But her specific suggestions embarrassed and repulsed me. I believed what my shy mother had told me, that if you loved someone very much, then you wanted to make love. When Ann told me she and Henry made love at least twice a day, I was reassured in the rightness of my mother's view.

"Sex has to do with love," I said. "I don't love anyone that way."

The first time I said it, I didn't add that I probably never would. Later I didn't add, "except you." It was in my head, but I had no idea what it meant.

My parents, my grandmother, even Arthur liked Ann. She and Mother were taking singing lessons from the same teacher,

opposite
Rendering of Jane Rule by Ann Smith
Jane Rule Fonds, University Archives, University of British Columbia

to whom Mother Packer had given the Colonel's old den, out by the garage, for a studio. Mother praised Ann's voice. Dad admired the likenesses she caught in her portraits, though he didn't like mine all that well, probably because it was stiffly, fiercely like me. Mother Packer liked Ann's serenity. She did look serene; yet the more she told me of her childhood, the more her face seemed to me a protective mask. She envied me my parents, the stability of my life.

The tension between Dad and Arthur mounted.

"The therapist told me just to shut his door when he didn't clean up," Mother explained. "He said not to nag him about little things."

For Dad the little things were emblematic of Arthur's total lack of discipline and his lack of consideration for other people. He was old enough to mow the lawn and wash the car without being told, to attend school and do his homework. Arthur listened to Dad's orders and lectures with a blandly courteous expression, but he would not answer when he was challenged. To all questions, from why he'd not come home for dinner to why he'd taken forty dollars from Mother's purse, he was either silent or said, "I don't know."

If I'd been challenged about anything I was doing, my mischief-making at school or my growing involvement with Ann, I suppose I would have offered excuses and explanations which might have convinced. But certainly I didn't know either why I really did a great many things.

Miss Espinosa's explanation, that I was simply an attention seeker and trouble maker, was descriptive enough, but not insightful.

I took my first IQ test. After the results were returned, Miss Espinosa called me into the office and charged me with doing badly on purpose in order to dishonour the school. Since I'd done as well as I could, I was horrified to discover that my score put me in the category of high moron. She wanted me to take the test again and do it properly. I refused, saying I didn't approve of IQ tests. I didn't admit to her charge, but I didn't deny it either. I couldn't bear being exposed as a moron. Could I really have done as well in school if I had been? Arthur did brilliantly in such tests and was accused, therefore, of failing his own great intelligence. What were tests for but to label and punish us one way or the other?

"I rated low moron," my mother said cheerfully. "And I get along just fine."

But I was still planning to be a doctor, not yet having taken chemistry.

Dad, like Mother before him, tried positive approaches with Arthur. Dad had learned to exercise on a trampoline while he was still at St. Mary's, and he'd ordered one for his ship so that he and other officers could combat the pounds their otherwise sedentary life encouraged. He bought one in army surplus and brought it home for our backyard. All three of us tried it. Libby and her little friends liked simply to bounce up and down on it until they fell into a giggling pile. It gave me such severe headaches, I soon very reluctantly gave it up. Arthur, surprisingly, enjoyed it. Though he wasn't interested in developing much skill at flips, he liked getting great height on it. It amused him to be able to peer in at me in our second-floor porch listening to records. He even made silly faces at me of the sort I remembered when we were little children.

One day, when Mother had to be with Mother Packer, I came from school early, in order to supervise Libby. I found her already home, sailing boats in an overflowing bathtub. As I turned off the taps, I caught sight of Arthur on the window ledge of our porch, about to try a jump from there onto the trampoline.

"You'll break your leg!" I shouted.

He didn't jump, but soon after that he did pull a ligament. He walked the metal peg off the cast he had to wear for some weeks.

Then quite suddenly Arthur was gone, and the trampoline went with him to a private school in southern California.

"They understand boys," Dad explained when he came home from delivering Arthur and his equipment, "even difficult boys."

Those first days the house was filled with a mood of silly, guilty relief. The long war of nerves was over. We could approach dinner now without wondering whether or not Arthur would come home. We could go to sleep without waiting for his footsteps on the stairs. We could answer the phone without fearing it was one authority or another to report his misdeeds. Mother didn't have to anticipate the car's being tampered with or taken just when she needed it most. Libby and I began to have glimpses of a father whom we'd nearly forgotten, who had time for jokes, surprises, treats.

He even took me on a business trip with him up through northern central California and over the mountains to the coast. We fished some of the way and arrived at Carlotta muddy and hungry at dinnertime. Aunt Etta was dead by then, the big house shut up; but Charlie greeted us warmly. He had nothing to offer us but whiskey and pink marshmallow and coconut cookies. We soon drove on into Eureka, and the next day stopped at South Fork on our way south again. I'd never seen it in May before, the meadow full of wild iris, the river high and smelling of dead eels.

I was shy with my father as I suppose he was with me. I was determined to be no nuisance to him, to entertain myself happily while he was doing business, to eat without complaint at greasy spoons. I had outgrown carsickness and could last longer than he could between comfort stops.

He made only one complaint. "Your mother talks to me when I drive."

I had no ambition to compete with my mother's ability to entertain my father. He and I were companionable because we were more alike in temperament, less interested in comfort and amusement than in meeting deadlines, able to accommodate long sidetracks for things we really wanted to do. Dad had his own love for South Fork. That our hours there meant we'd have to drive late into the night to get home troubled neither of us. And it was wonderful to drive toward home without the familiar half dread of what Arthur had been up to.

That taste of family ease made me much more resentful of Arthur when the school reported him missing about six weeks later. Dad drove down to talk with the authorities and came home bringing not only the trampoline but all Arthur's other belongings. He'd left, as he so often did, with nothing but the clothes on his back.

"His adviser said it was understandable that a boy with his experience would find it hard to adjust to school. Arthur told them he'd been in the merchant marine. His ship was sunk and he'd spent over a week in a life raft before he was rescued. And they believed him!"

The story didn't surprise us. I'd been with Arthur often when he took delight in lying about his own experience and getting away with it. He particularly liked claiming to have been somewhere another person had just visited. Always a voracious reader, Arthur held not only cathedrals and museums in mind but street and restaurant names. It never bothered him to have me there. In fact, he enjoyed having one person in the audience who knew how well he played his one-sided game.

Arthur turned up not long after Dad and the trampoline.

"Mostly what I did was work on a road gang," he said. "Can't see much point in that."

Summer was so nearly arrived that new plans for Arthur's rehabilitation could be postponed. I would teach swimming again in July. We'd go to South Fork for the month of August, taking Mother Packer with us.

She had fallen and broken her arm. That accident made her the more reluctant to walk alone. She had an elevator installed on the staircase and again had live-in help. She would have been more reclusive if it hadn't been for visits not only from the voice teacher but from some of her pupils. Mother Packer kept chocolates and salted nuts to offer drop-in guests, but it was her own wit and attentiveness that called to those younger women. She didn't have to be critical of them as she did of her own daughter.

I sometimes met Ann there after her voice lesson and biked or walked home with her.

Nancy Lockwood, the woman who rented Ann and Henry their garage room, was Mother's age with three daughters younger than me but older than Lib, and a husband who worked for the telephone company. Nancy taught piano, and they had a studio with two pianos that they also used for family parties, to which my family were often invited. Nancy and Ann were confidantes, and I liked Nancy, too, sometimes stopping to chat if I found Ann not at home.

"Nancy says you have a crush on me," Ann said one day.

"That's stupid," I answered hotly.

"What's stupid about it?"

"Crushes are stupid. I love you, but I don't have a crush on you."

"What's the difference?"

"I'm not a stupid kid. I'm your friend."

"You come to see me nearly every day."

"Would you rather I didn't?"

"I didn't say that."

Until summer school started, I was careful to see Ann no more than a couple of times a week. Nancy's friendly greeting which I'd taken at face value now irritated me. She'd become a spy rather than a friend.

"Don't be irritated with Nancy," Ann said. "She's very fond of you. She just doesn't want to see you hurt."

"How could I be hurt?"

"Nancy once fell in love with a woman herself."

"How silly!" I said.

"It isn't silly," Ann said sharply. "Women do sometimes fall very deeply in love with each other. It's very important for you to have your first experience with a man. After that, well ..."

"I don't care what other people do. I'll have my first experience with a man when I've married him ... If I get married."

"Oh, you'll get married," Ann said. "You'll want children."

I wasn't at all sure I did want children. I'd had enough first-hand experience with Libby to know how much time mothering took, and I was not patient with her as I could be with other children. Marrying I simply couldn't imagine.

I was beginning to meet young men with whom I could make friends, chief among them Bill Hennessy who had come back from being in the occupying army in Germany. He was a slight, dark, curly-headed Irishman, three inches shorter than I was, with a rollicking humour when he was sober, black anger and depression when he'd had anything to drink. He joked about his drinking, too.

"My widowed mother doesn't dare buy anything but black. She's never sure I'll live out the week."

Bill was taking education courses at San José State University, one of the very few men in those days interested in teaching in the primary grades.

He was having a hard time in an English class. When he asked me to help him with his term paper, I agreed if he'd choose a topic I was interested in. I chose American women poets, a subject which so startled and pleased his teacher that she gave him an A. By the time he heard the results, we had left for South Fork where there was no phone. He drove 250 miles to give me the news and stayed the weekend, delighting even Mother Packer who was usually suspiciously critical of young men.

Arthur shared in that friendship, more often dealing with the negative side of Bill than I had to. Drunk, Bill would seek Arthur out as the biggest man around and challenge him to a fight. Arthur kept him off, his large hand against Bill's forehead, his long arm keeping Bill at a flailing distance, saying gently, "Billy, Billy, come on now," and tried to keep him from driving, for he always seemed to pass out parked on a train crossing or in the middle of a highway.

Once Bill said to me, "The Germans weren't any more monstrous than we were. Men are evil."

He was among a number of our friends who survived the war, bringing unacceptable nightmares into the new peace, and did not live long. Bill ran himself into a tree four or five years later, after he'd become a very good teacher. He had said to me, not long before, "We're such good friends, we ought to have the sense some day to marry, but we never will."

That was as much romantic involvement as I could report to Ann, and neither of us was impressed with it.

I HAD GROWN INCREASINGLY RESTLESS and critical about school. Mother suggested I might like to go away to school for my last year. I was serious enough about it to apply to a girl's school north of San Francisco, to visit the campus and to feel a mixture of excitement and dread at the possibility of spending a year there. I was accepted, but a combination of their higher scholastic requirements and my low IQ scores would have made it necessary for me to stay for two years. I was far too impatient to contemplate that, and I'd invested a certain pride in doing four years' work in three. So I went back to Castilleja in the fall.

Aside from my impossible chemistry course, I settled well enough to my work. I was taking two English courses in order to complete graduation requirements, and I was also printing a column for the school paper.

Because I tended to comic insolence, most of the students as serious about their work as I was were cautious in their friendliness, except for Joy Ahrens, gifted and acerbic, who edited the paper. We wrote endless notes to each other, exchanging them between classes. She was a five-day boarder who went home each weekend. Very occasionally we exchanged weekend visits, but it was essentially a friendship of words on paper, as so many of mine have been over the years.

The other friends I had were the scallywags of the school, whose mothers hoped in vain that I would be a good influence. My friends overlooked or excused my academic seriousness for the fracases I could also inspire. But I was less involved in rebellious pranks and more seriously protesting that fall.

Along with required uniforms, we were not allowed to wear any sort of makeup, on or off campus while we were in uniform. Still, Miss Espinosa saw fit to hire a woman from a charm school in San Francisco, paid for out of the student treasury, to give us

lessons in makeup, wardrobe and deportment. First, she demonstrated makeup, using the girl who had been chosen to play the
Virgin Mary in the Christmas pageant. There in chapel the Virgin
was transformed into a whore. Then in the gym we were
instructed to imitate our instructor as she walked to music—in
stocking feet I was as tall despite her four-inch platforms. I threw
myself into that exercise with such abandon that Miss Espinosa,
ever watchful, hissed me off the floor.

"But she said to imitate her," I protested.

"There is a difference between imitating and making fun."

"Ah," I exclaimed in admiration of that fine distinction.

I went home to write an angry criticism about wasting our
own funds on such blatant nonsense when we should be being
taught to walk to the nearest college.

Our faculty adviser, the timid Miss Dively, saw the article,
but, when she was confronted by Miss Espinosa's wrath, she
claimed she hadn't, that we'd sneaked it into the paper.

I suspect Miss Espinosa, who had been irritated by my
attempt to find a better school and goaded by my increasingly
serious criticisms, had been waiting for a moment when she
could severely chastise me for something inside my own moral
framework. I was a sneak. Perhaps Miss Dively, too, lied not
only out of fright but with scores of her own to settle at my
merciless mockery of her own ineptitude.

I was, not for the first time, "sent home to think." After a
week, I was granted an appointment with Miss Espinosa. Her
terms for my reinstatement were that I give up all extracurricular activities, the paper, clubs, sports, that I leave the school
promptly when my classes were over, that I voice no criticisms of
the school myself and report to her anyone who had done so. I
walked out of her office to Palo Alto High School, where I was
immediately enrolled.

"It's your decision," my father said.

"Oh, how I'd like to get that woman!" my mother said.

Miss Grant, who never involved herself in school politics,
came to call on my mother and said she had pleaded with Miss
Espinosa. Students protested by stealing the school sign and
setting it up in our front yard, but the revolution I longed for did

not, of course, take place. Instead, my friends among the boarders accepted the order that my house was out of bounds. When Joy Ahrens's mother phoned Miss Espinosa to ask what I had done, her reply was, "For Jinx's sake and the sake of the school, I'm afraid I can't say, but she's a very bad influence." Joy was forbidden to see me.

Again, I found myself in the large hostile walls of public school. And once again my brother had been there before me, underlining the scandal I had created for myself. When my English teacher sarcastically chided me for not handing in a paper before I arrived in class, I stood automatically (something public school students never did) and defended myself. She apologized at the end of class.

"My name is Jinx, not Arthur Rule," I answered.

I was so far ahead of most of the public school students that teachers either dismissed me to go to study hall or set me independent projects. Except, of course, in chemistry. There, extraordinarily, in the last row of the class sat Wally and Chiaki, top students and apparently devoted friends.

There were other familiar faces from kindergarten, from junior high, but I was now not one but two grades ahead of most of them.

I joined the swimming team and made friends with a girl named Gerda Eisenberg. She invited me to dinner and to spend the night at her house in Woodside. I was reluctant to go, having been so recently excluded from that rich neighbourhood where I'd never been very comfortable. But she lived in an old farmhouse with large vegetable gardens, farm animals. She and her brothers and sisters had chores about the place. We ate homemade bread and jam for breakfast. It was like South Fork or Carlotta, if they had been real places, lived in by large families, rather than ghostly places of the past. At the first meet, when Gerda and I were swimming in the same race, I looked over and wondered what the point was. I didn't want to be better than she was. I wanted to be her friend. Yet I was shy of her and her large, wholesome family, where there was no place for the dark, complicating angers I felt.

After I'd been at Palo Alto High School for about a month, one of a group of girls came up to me and said, "We wouldn't mind if you ate lunch with us."

"Thank you," I said. "I go home for lunch."

After school I'd call on Ann or Sugarfoot.

"Why don't you have a cigarette?" Sugarfoot suggested. "She's not telling anyone why you were kicked out, you know."

"I wasn't kicked out. I left," I said. "What is she trying to make people think?"

I asked Ann the same question.

"Maybe she wants people to think you're a lesbian."

"But why?" I asked, astounded.

I was fifteen years old. My sexual experience went no further than a single struggle in the back seat of a car with a tall, blond veteran who was really more interested in finding a wife than in deflowering a virgin. He got no farther than my buds of breasts, laughed and gave up. I'd involved myself with that only because Ann thought I should.

Sugarfoot invited me to her engagement party. I have no recollection of the man. They didn't finally marry. I stayed afterward to help clean up. Sugarfoot was drunkenly triumphant. In her bedroom, she put her arms around me, her head on my shoulder while I stood in stiff surprise.

"Well, goodbye to all that," she said.

The high-school swimming coach sometimes gave me a lift home or to Ann's after practice. Occasionally, I went home with her and played with her two-year-old boy. She'd been dismissed from a school, and the students had staged a protest strike but she hadn't got her job back either. Once, also when she'd had too much to drink, she kissed me on the mouth and said she didn't want to interfere with my more important friendship with Ann.

"You don't," I answered, not meaning it as the rejection it must have sounded.

There was no one moment when I confronted my own sexuality. Consciously, I didn't desire any of these young women. If they desired me, they were too frightened to be anything but circumspect. Each obviously assumed I was lesbian, and all but Ann, of course, assumed I was having an affair with Ann. Had

Miss Espinosa, too? Ann lived right across the street from the school, and I had never made a secret of going to see her. At the time I was blind with outraged innocence, but I suppose I must have seemed for each of them a sexual time bomb that could go off at any moment.

Sugarfoot offered me cigarettes. Ann loaned me *Lady Chatterley's Lover* and *The Well of Loneliness*. The coach took me to a fortune teller, who told me I might not marry but would be involved with many children, and she remarked with surprise at how feminine my hands were. My hands were very much my father's, long and slender and accurate at small detail. No one ever mentioned that loving me would be a criminal offence.

In the spring, I discovered that I couldn't graduate because I hadn't had four years of gym. I had to return in the fall and take two periods of gym and whatever else might pass the time, finish in February and then have some time off to look around. I was really too young to start college anyway.

Dad, who had been looking for another job for some time, had accepted work in Reno, Nevada, as a manager of a building company. He suggested I fly up there and see if I could graduate from a Reno high school on schedule. Ushered into the principal's office with deferential ceremony, I discovered I'd been mistaken for the new gym teacher. As a student, I was of no interest at all.

The anger I felt at all authority was constant for me now. I wanted nothing more to do with any of them. Mother raged with me, but she was as helpless as I was.

She had the house on the market, waiting for its sale to join Dad in Reno, a town she looked forward to no more than she had Chicago. More seasoned a wife by then, having learned to count the blessings she had, she simply set her mind to going.

I didn't. My own plan was to spend the summer taking whatever I had to complete high school and be on my way to Stanford in the fall. I'd always planned to go to Stanford, and even now that my interest had shifted from medicine to English, no other university occurred to me. I hadn't reckoned on the fact that Miss Espinosa had a brother on the faculty there, or that the competition for the relatively few places reserved for girls was fierce, since not only men but women were returning from the war to complete their educations. None of us coming straight from school was a match for them.

Why my tutoring in third-year German became an acceptable substitute for another year of gym I don't remember. I agreed to it because I could get through it in a summer.

Mother and Dad wanted to make a trip east. Mother asked my swimming coach if she and her child would move in to supervise the household. We had a housekeeper and Arthur was away. The only real chores involved were errands and driving me to and from my German lessons with the head of the Stanford German department. It would be a sort of holiday for her. She agreed.

From the moment she moved in, I sensed something was very wrong. She had no patience with her own child, slapped him the first night at the dinner table and that alarmed my eight-year-old sister. Feeling responsible for the sense of a person I suddenly did not know, I tried to do what I could to make her stay easy, but she was edgy and sarcastic with me. If any of my friends came over, she pleaded a migraine headache and retreated to her room, complaining of the noise we made. One night she didn't hear Libby call, though their rooms were next to each other. I took Libby into my room and let her sleep in the other bed. When she woke and threw up, I changed her bedclothes and her pyjamas, then sat wiping her face with a cool, damp cloth.

"You're being so nice to me," she said in surprise. "I thought you'd be mad."

Because Mother had always been there to care for Libby, I had never needed to protect or reassure her about anything, or I had never thought to, and I had turned times of looking after her into a chore rather than a pleasure. She had no reason to expect help from me or protection from the hostile stranger in the house. I was both chagrined by and surprised at the fierceness of my need to shield her from what seemed to me somehow my own lack of judgment. Before a week was up, both mother and child were gone, and Libby and I moved to Mother Packer's until our parents came home.

The coach explained herself by saying she was in therapy, and her nerves were simply shot. She was very sorry.

When I puzzled the tale out with Ann, she had no comment to make. I sensed, as I often did with Ann, that some answers I'd have only when I figured them out for myself. I did not like being incompetently, ignorantly young.

The high-school German teacher set and marked my exam, which I failed, for, though my tutor and I had followed the outlined curriculum, questions having nothing to do with what I'd studied were on the exam. My tutor, from the authority of his university position, made a formal protest, and my mark was changed to a pass.

We went to South Fork at the end of the summer, taking Mother Packer with us. Ann came for a week, Henry joining us at the weekend to drive her home. She did watercolours for everyone in the family: the view from the porch of the dead trees at the end of the valley for Mother Packer, the corn crib for Mother, the view of the river from my rock and willow nest for me. She did an oil of the redwoods which she gave to Libby.

I loved being near her while she painted, reading poetry out loud or chatting or drowsing in the sun. I loved the pleasure everyone took in her presence. During that week, she told me she and Henry, who had finished his work at Stanford, would almost certainly be moving east early in September. She was expecting her first child in February.

"But then I won't see the baby," I protested.

She gave me an old, fond look. "You really do care about the baby, don't you?"

"Of course."

"You won't be jealous of it?"

"Why should I be?" I asked.

Missing the birth of the child had been the first thing that crossed my mind, but the fact of Ann's leaving gradually darkened the days for me. She was both more affectionate and more wary of me, and I began to memorize her face, the tones of her voice, her laugh, her hands. They were large, strong hands for a woman her size.

Ann and Henry did not move east, and I did not get into Stanford, but I didn't move to Reno with the family either. I stayed with Mother Packer and got myself a job as a typist in the purchasing department at Stanford. I had convinced myself that I'd been refused only because I hadn't finished high school until the end of summer. I reapplied for the winter quarter. Two of my Castilleja classmates had been accepted at Stanford, and I had lunch with them a couple of times, but I felt the gap between our circumstances bitterly and knew they were being nervously kind rather than friendly. I couldn't bear to think that anyone believed I deserved to be where I was.

The young tough boss of the purchasing department arrived every morning to stand by the water cooler, drinking glass after glass in order to put out her hangover. When I called her attention to lack of delivery date information on an order for a carload of live monkeys, she answered her standard answer, "You're paid to type." The monkeys arrived on a Sunday when no one was around, and they were all dead by the time they were discovered. Routinely, we were told to throw away any orders we hadn't got round to typing up at the end of each day. Departments, knowing not all orders were put through, often put in duplicates. If I spotted a duplicate, I was told to type it up anyway. When there was a staff cut, I was the one to go. My next job was in the general-secretary's department. I typed addresses on envelopes all the first day. The next day, they were all torn in half in a pile on my desk. I was supposed to have looked up new zip codes for each of them. About to protest the waste of a whole day's work, I remembered, "You're paid to type." Why should it make any difference to me what waste there was when I was paid by the hour?

I was terribly unhappy, bored and angry and increasingly frightened by my circumstance. I half knew I was in love with Ann, had no idea what that meant or what I might be expected to do about it. I had begun to lie to her about my sexual involvement with boys I occasionally saw.

I made an appointment to see the therapist my mother had gone to.

"Do you have your parents' permission to see me?" he asked.

"I have my own money," I said. "I don't want them to know, I don't want them to worry about me."

Reluctantly, he agreed and halved his fee when I looked shocked at the first amount he'd mentioned. What I needed to tell him was that I'd somehow lost a grip on my life, felt both pressured and stalled. The people around me who wanted to help, like my parents, didn't seem to know what I should do. And I was beginning to behave oddly, to lie to my best friend, for instance.

"What do you talk about with your therapist?" Ann asked.

"All sorts of things. That I've begun to lie to you, for instance, because I don't want to do what you expect me to do."

"Did you tell him you're in love with me?" she asked.

It wasn't the first time she'd kissed me on the mouth, but it was the first time I felt the ache in my gut turn to fire.

"You have to understand," she said, holding my face in her hands. "We can't make love. You have to make love first with a man, adjust to that, or you'll be a lesbian. You have to marry and have children. I want that for you just the way you want it for me."

"I want for you what you want," I answered.

"If it gets too bad, masturbate."

"What's that?" I asked.

"Don't you ever touch yourself?" she asked disbelieving. "You don't have to be ashamed of it. You don't have to lie to me about it. It's a perfectly healthy, independent thing to do."

"I'm not lying," I said.

Nightly after that I taught myself how to bring myself to orgasm, not even knowing the name for it.

Sometimes when I was with Ann, she didn't want me nearer than across the room. When I resigned myself to no gesture of affection, much less desire, she wanted me to lay down, holding her in my arms. There between us the baby kicked. I held them both.

I had given up the therapist. I did not want to tell anyone about my feelings for her, not out of shame which she so feared, but in protective wonder.

Ann's guilt and fear troubled me more for her than for myself. That she could acknowledge my love at all and teach me what it meant gave me so much new insight and so much more delight than pain that I accepted its restraints and understood her commitment to Henry, whom I also loved, for he was always a good friend to me. Ann didn't understand my lack of jealousy either of Henry or the baby. I didn't understand what there was to be jealous about.

"A child will mean more to me."

"So it should," I said, shocked that anyone would want to be more to a woman than her child, testimony to the mothering I had had.

The general-secretary's office had finished with a fund drive, during which I'd forged the president's, vice-president's and dean's signatures on acknowledgments, depending on the amount of the donation. Now we were set to send out the acceptances and rejections for the winter quarter. I typed my own rejection and signed the registrar's name. It didn't cross my mind to send an acceptance instead. What I did do was quit the stupid job. The woman at the desk next to mine had a BA from Stanford in creative writing; so what did an education matter anyway?

But it did matter. I hadn't direction enough in myself to get on with my own education. I wrote in a random way what usually turned into love letters to Ann. I didn't find books to read which really interested me. The routine at my grandmother's house suited a reclusive old woman better than a restless sixteen-year-old, though we got along very happily.

I went alone to a mother-and-daughter tea at the house of a friend, whose mother rather championed my cause. She introduced me to a woman who was a trustee at Mills College.

"I want you to tell her your story, Jinx."

I hadn't had enough opportunity to talk about what had happened, and I was still rawly indignant. Fortunately for me, my listener was indulgent. When she'd heard me out, she asked, "Would you be interested in going to Mills?"

"Don't know anything much about it. I'm interested in going anywhere I can get an education."

I made my application. I had to send for transcripts from Castilleja as well as Palo Alto High School. I had what I knew were good references from teachers, from my German tutor who was angry that I'd been refused at Stanford.

Without the sponsorship of the trustees, I doubt if I would have been called for an interview, for at that meeting I discovered that Miss Espinosa had also written to say that my academic standing should be disregarded since my moral character was such that I wouldn't be acceptable at the college.

Asked to explain her comments, I was furious.

"How can I defend myself against a general lie? My moral character, as far as I'm concerned, is a good deal better than hers."

"Why were you expelled?"

"I wasn't expelled. I walked out because the restrictions she insisted were intolerable and unjust."

Could one woman, I wanted to know, really have the power to prevent me from going to college? Didn't my grades, didn't the other letters mean anything?

"We've had some odd communications from this woman before," the registrar said to the dean.

"Tell me what you want to study," Dean Hawkes said.

The almost abrupt directness of her manner reminded me of my grandmother Rule, to whom I'd always felt required to stand up, to give an account of myself. Dean Hawkes was younger and handsomer, white haired, dark eyed, with a face I could read, probably because she wanted me to be able to. I told her essentially I wanted to learn to understand and then tell the truth. I wanted to be a writer.

"There's a difficulty about your test scores," she said, when I'd finished. "They can't be accurate."

"They are," I said. "I don't take tests like that well."

"You're particularly weak in language and reading skills. I find that hard to believe."

"I'm weak at the test's language and reading skills."

She smiled at me.

"I don't think I'm a moron," I said.

"No," Dean Hawkes agreed. "Yours is not only an irregular application but we don't usually let students in for the February term. We aren't really set up for it. You wouldn't be able to take all the courses you should."

"I don't think I can wait much longer to get back to work," I said.

In February, a month before my seventeenth birthday, I enrolled as a student at Mills. Mother came down from Reno to take me to Hink's to buy the furnishings for my room. I had been at home with her for the week before, buying more clothes than I'd ever imagined owning. Never having gone to college herself, Mother enjoyed all the preparations even more than I did, and laughed when she later read the instructions to parents that she shouldn't have come with me and influenced my choices. Mother has always been a follower of the dictum, "When all else fails, read the directions."

I did not settle easily into my first term of college. I was not as grateful as I should have been for my "provisional" status, proud of my academic record and still righteously indignant at what had happened to me. But I was not as confident of myself as I tried to appear. I had read nothing but required texts, some poetry and books about the lives of doctors. I had to bluff a background assumed for those students professing an interest in literature until I could, with years of all-night reading, make up for my earlier indifference. At that time, I was a slow reader though I had a good memory for what I had read. I couldn't spell.

I not only didn't know what was expected of me in assignments, I didn't know that anything in particular was expected. Asked to write a character sketch, I wrote three pages on Ann's hands. The paper was returned with every line crossed out and a question mark at the end. In a humanities course which was supposed to challenge our cliché-ridden young minds to some originality, I was simply suspicious of questions like, "Does a drowning man really drown?" I didn't want to be made a fool of by a bunch of condescending, smart-aleck male professors. In a course on religions of the Far East, the other students were all seniors in religion and philosophy with a vocabulary I didn't understand at all. At the final exam, the kindly professor said,

"Miss Rule, if you don't understand the question, just write what you know about the main words in the sentences," advice I followed for an hour of the three allotted. I had no more to say.

The remedial reading course I was required to take because of my low test scores was taught by a woman with a bad stammer which at times reactivated my own. Her advice, to read the first and last sentences of a paragraph and guess what was in between, was beyond my skill at reading poetry and religion texts, political argument and history.

I did not, of course, accept my failures humbly. I blamed the courses, the teachers, the texts, venting my anger and frustration on anyone who would listen, from impatient teachers, to my adviser, to the dean.

My complaints were not limited to my academic experience. I was amazed and appalled at the restrictions under which I was expected to live, signing in and out of the dorm, having to get signatures if I was to be away for the night. Because the only room available was a single on senior corridor, I was daily reminded of my lowly status and lack of privileges compared to the students I lived among. They were a friendly group, willing to sympathize with me and occasionally smuggle me out with them for a beer-drinking evening. They'd grown restless, too, with the hall meetings at which we had to vote on such things as whether we'd wear cotton dresses and sandals; skirts, sneakers and loafers; or formal dresses, stockings and high heels at our next open house.

Though I was an independent spirit, I was a domestic infant. I not only didn't know how to do my laundry (I sent my clothes out all through my years at college), but Mother had always washed my hair. I came from so private a household that the casual nudity in the washrooms was actually embarrassing to me. I contrived to find times when everyone else was out to use the facilities.

The suspicion, apparently so often entertained by so many people, that I was a sexual adventurer, seemed the more ludicrous for someone as young and physically shy as I was.

I did make friends of sorts. Alette, a Dutch girl who had spent three and a half years in a Japanese concentration camp in the Dutch East Indies, lived next door to me. When I was at my most

impatient with the restrictions and requirements of my new life,
she would counter my complaints by comparing the college to
the camp. She would point out the abundance of quite good
food, of hot water, the freedom to walk about the beautiful campus, to play tennis, ride, swim. The restrictions were, after all,
only silly, not cruel. She wasn't pious about it, simply detached
and realistic. She was herself marking time until June when her
fiancé would arrive from Australia and they would be married.
She spent a lot of time writing letters to him.

Occasionally, she'd talk about her experience in the camp,
being in charge for a time of rationing rice, a grain at a time, to
the other women and children. She said she'd never again be as
close to people as she had been then; it was a closeness with a
price too high to pay voluntarily.

Sometimes I made her laugh. Perhaps that was why we could
be friends. She could temper my bewildered anger, and I could
distract her from a deep, private mourning. Thirty-five percent of
the women had not survived. Fifty-five percent of the men in the
adjacent camp died. Alette's father had been beheaded.

Just behind the Mills campus was Oak Knoll Naval Hospital
where Libby had been. Now it was filled with men in the final
stages of rehabilitation, learning to use artificial limbs. Mills
students were asked there as volunteers. I went once or twice,
but I had no idea how to deal with their bitterness, the pressure
of their need to be reassured sexually. I was afraid of them and
ashamed to be. I could not as easily dismiss them as the sexually
confident, socially ambitious Mills students did, as "creeps" and
"weirdos."

Our own self-obsessed and sheltered life in that oasis of
beauty and luxury seemed to me peculiar and unreal. I took as
many weekends as I was allowed to visit my grandmother and,
therefore, Ann. The baby was born shortly after I arrived at
college and named Carol after Ann's favourite sister. When I was
with them, I shared Ann's preoccupation with her. In a way I
didn't much think about, Carol seemed somehow mine as well.
At her christening, however, I listened with some dismay at my
duties as her godmother concerning her spiritual life.

Henry had found a job in New York. Ann was preparing to join him. I would have been more distressed by her leaving if my father hadn't suggested I go east with him to visit his parents that summer. I'd be separated from Ann for only a couple of months.

Among the seniors, there were others like Alette announcing engagements, planning weddings. Most of them were also working hard to prepare for comprehensive exams and, if they were music majors, proficiency concerts. My corner room faced the music building. Perhaps some of the confusion of my own preparations had to do with nightly listening to the sounds from practice rooms: harpsichord, flute, piano, harp, voice. The seniors had time, too, for parties: receptions after concerts, major dinners with each faculty, engagement parties, balls. Sometimes I was included, but often I felt like a wardrobe mistress backstage, preparing all those attractive young women for their parts in a public show which had nothing to do with me. I did not usually mind.

As I had in high school, I invented a male figure for myself, this time called Sandy rather than David, far away not in the war but in New York. I received enough letters from Ann, addressed in her bold, androgynous hand, to make my story credible and excuse me my weekends without dates. The few details I offered about him, that he lived in a basement apartment two blocks from the Empire State Building and was an artist, were facts about Ann. Perhaps I should have invented him near at hand for Ann who still pressed me toward a required initiation into heterosexual life. I resisted on moral grounds, but, in fact, I had no gift or taste for men, except as friends.

Never having technically made love with Ann, thinking of her always as Henry's wife and now Carol's mother, I had no concept of being faithful to her, but I was both too preoccupied with her and too uncertain that anyone else would understand those feelings to wish any sort of intimacy.

I missed children. One day I saw several playing at the edge of a pond by the music building. They were trying unsuccessfully to catch pollywogs. I kicked off my sandals and waded in with their jar. As I was coming out with the jar full, a middle-aged man, elegantly dressed, hailed me. I was embarrassed to be found at so childish an occupation, but his amusement was clearly tinged with approval. He joined me and the children to examine my catch, raising his accented voice over the jumble of sounds coming from the practice rooms, and then he walked with me when I left the children with their pollywogs.

Nodding at the sound of a particularly commanding harpsichord, he said, "I hate it, like two skeletons fucking on a tin roof."

I discovered some days later that he was Egon Petri, the concert pianist, who instructed some of the best senior students. I envied them for their access to such distinguished teachers, their life slightly apart from the rest of the college, the distinction many of them had already achieved. Even their building, a gift to the college in the prosperous 1920s, called attention to them as the elite. Professional music critics came to most of the proficiency concerts. Darius Milhaud taught composition every other year at Mills, the alternate years in Paris at the Paris Conservatoire, and some students commuted with him.

I had no gift for music, no courage for any performing art. It was the high seriousness and cowardice that attracted me. My young, unpractised English teacher would never have walked along the path casually with a student, making any kind of conversation. The only authority she had was her podium, over which she peered on frightened guard duty against the barbarous freshmen.

Dean Hawkes was the only adult with whom I had any rapport, and I saw very little of her. By the time college was over in June, the few friends I had were graduating. What work I had done was so fragmented and uneven that I couldn't see much point in it. My attempts at writing were so sporadic and disappointing that it seemed more a daydream than an ambition. Perhaps it was really a lie.

I think I was a great deal more frightened of myself in those days than I could admit. I increasingly had migraine headaches, occasional blackouts and insomnia. I had traded my interest in athletics for a pack of cigarettes a day and a reputation for holding my liquor, punishing a body I had always been modest about but proud of in the pool, on the basketball and badminton courts. I could not look at the possibility that I was a woman, a sex pervert, a moral fraud who had been seen more clearly by Miss Espinosa than I could see myself.

Dean Hawkes was not distressed by the charitable C that I received in my religion course.

"You shouldn't have been in that course in the first place. It's for senior majors."

My other marks were not quite as humiliating, but I knew I hadn't taken firm hold anywhere, not out of lack of effort but out of lack of understanding.

"You'll begin well next year," the dean predicted.

Mother, too, was unconcerned, perhaps even relieved. She took my lacklustre performance as a sign that I'd learned to be less tensely serious about my work and was having some fun. I had dutifully reported the few frat parties I'd gone to, exaggerating my social success as I did to Ann, whose investment in my heterosexuality was no less than my mother's, if differently personal.

Though Dad was confident and happy with his new job, had picked out a lot at the edge of town to build a house, his relationship with Arthur was as bad as ever. I hated being back in that tension again. Unable to do anything about my brother's obvious unhappiness, I didn't want to be around it. After too brief a visit to San Francisco and a nightmare drive with my brother back across the mountain, knowing no one in Reno, I hid with the stacks of books I'd brought home and read with a will until it was time to go east with Dad.

Ann preoccupied my imagination, but I was also looking forward to seeing my grandfather Rule, with whom I'd started an independent correspondence once I left home. A dreamer himself, who honoured artists above all others, he had encouraged me and I'd confided in him all my young ambitions. He was the one adult who advised me against marrying early or perhaps marrying at all since I had so much to accomplish in myself and few men had either the vision or generosity to allow that. He assumed, with the sweet transposing vanity of a doting relative, that I was pursued by all men and must guard myself against shallow temptation. However inaccurate I knew that flattery to be, it was some comfort to me. And even as an old maid, I wouldn't disappoint him.

My father, too, had begun to find me more presentable now that I was well dressed and knew how to comb my hair. He was a courtly travelling companion, and he looked so much younger than his years, I enough older, that we were often mistaken for a couple. Even at college, I was teased about the glamorous older man I tried to pass off as my father.

We stopped first in Chicago to visit my father's oldest sister and her family. My cousin Patsy had, like me, improved with age. A year older than I was, three inches taller, she was still in high school and had no plans for college. Her twin brother had just gone off to West Point, following in his father's and older brother's footsteps. Granny Rule had promised to take me to West Point to see him, a duty she had taken on for her own daughters with the result that two married army officers, one a teammate of Dad's at Annapolis. Dad, listening to me talk about the things I was planning to do, suddenly suggested that Patsy come with us.

"Certainly not," her father said at once. "We can't afford it."

Later, when Dad was alone with his sister and brother-in-law, he offered to pay Patsy's fare. They agreed only on condition that she not know anything about it until the last minute, a tease so mindlessly cruel I felt entirely alienated from my aunt and uncle when the surprise was sprung only twenty minutes before we were to leave, Patsy's suitcase already secretly packed by her mother. Her father jeered the news at her so that she left feeling more the butt of a joke than the recipient of a holiday.

As soon as we had left, my father did what he could to make up for it, asking Patsy what kinds of things she'd like to do, giving her a sense that she had some choice in the matter.

My grandparents were living in the little Gatehouse the last time I'd visited them. Now they'd moved back to what was affectionately called "the shingle chateau," the original family house that Wychwood had developed around, and where Mother and Dad had started their married life with the whole Rule family. It was far too large and impractical a place for an old couple to be living in, but it had ample room for welcoming various members of the family for a visit or in transit, as so many in the family always were.

I couldn't now draw a floor plan from memory or recount the number of rooms. The large old kitchen on the ground floor and a suite of rooms on the second floor which could be reached by the back stairs were rented to a sister-in-law of Dad's twin brother, her husband and her daughter, Debbie, who was Patsy's age. What had been the butler's pantry had been turned into a small kitchen for my grandparents, but the arrangement was flexible enough to allow the Rule family to spill over into the large kitchen where crowds had to be cooked for.

My grandparents had a bedroom and bath on the ground floor since Granny couldn't manage the stairs. The only authority she had over the two floors above her was her voice, commanding up the stairwell for our presence at dinner, for our late-night guests to leave, for the younger cousins to be put to bed.

Dad's sister Mary and her family lived in Westfield. She came over rarely and always seemed to be just getting over or just coming down with a migraine. Her youngest son was away at camp for the whole summer, but both Frank and young George were at home. Frank, six weeks older than I was, was just finishing high school, but George had been away to college. I had expected to make common cause with him, partly because our grandfather had linked us as the brains of the family. George

was, however, very superior and dull, and he told Granny he
didn't think I was old enough to go out on dates.

Frank, on the other hand, all but moved in. Granny made no
complaint about feeding him, but she treated him more like a
lazy servant than a guest. He made great sport of outwitting her
and rather relished his role as the bad brother. Affectionate and
funny, always willing to be included in any outing, offering his
war-surplus Jeep for transportation, Frank obviously was making
up for the sisters he didn't have. He didn't have my brother's
polished manners, height or good looks. In fact, I thought all my
eastern cousins socially retarded. They didn't go to the theatre or
concerts in New York, only an hour away. They didn't give or go
to parties. But Frank was, at least, willing to learn.

We didn't have to organize parties because there was one
going on at the house perpetually. While Dad was there (he
stayed only ten days, and Patsy went back with him while I
stayed on for another month), great numbers of friends and
relatives turned up. Granny did most of the cooking of dinner.
Breakfast and often lunch were prepared for ourselves, and we
took turns cleaning up and taking Granny's long shopping lists
to the store. Addie Waddie, the coloured maid, and her daughter
Beatrice (with the accent on the "a") cleaned. The laundry was
sent out.

Granny was well organized and tolerated very little of the
long sitting on the back of one's neck that teenagers do. We went
upstairs to our rooms to relax. Once we entered the public
rooms, we were targets for conscription. There was always someone to be met at the airport, train or bus station. There were
chairs and tables to be put or taken down. There were children
to be entertained, old people to be helped out of chairs, up and
down stairs.

My grandfather still went into New York nearly every day to
his office to look after his various real estate investments. He had
recovered most of what had been lost during the Depression. A
quiet man in the midst of that large, very vocal family, he didn't
really try to listen and was apt, therefore, to introduce suggestions in conflict with plans already made. I was surprised at the
energy of my father's impatience with him.

"We can't go to the theatre tomorrow night. Mother's invited guests for dinner."

Granny, firmly in control with everyone else, was apt to give in and change everything around to suit her husband, not with the best grace in the world, but he didn't take any notice of her bad temper. Like my father, I sided with Granny, but I didn't feel the irritation he did.

In order to have time alone with my grandfather, I got up and had breakfast with him. He had ladyfingers instead of toast every morning, a habit I happily imitated. Though he occasionally asked a question, he liked better to tell me how gifted a poet his brother Lucian was or to show me the books of his that Grandfather had had privately printed. He told me about his friend Tony Sarg, a painter he'd commissioned to do a mural in the lobby of an apartment house on Jane Street in the Village. He confided that he'd like to found Rule University, devoted to teaching people to think.

Granny had no use for most of his schemes though she obviously let him indulge in those that were not too extravagant, and, when he came up with proposals which had a potential for profit, she encouraged and supported him. My father saw the conflicts between them more than their important co-operation. Though Dad admired his father's business accomplishments, he resented his father's neglect of his mother, and was embarrassed by how often his father sounded like a naïve crackpot, saved from folly after folly only by his wife's strong character. I loved my grandfather, but I felt closer to Granny, more able to talk with her. She didn't encourage me. She resented what she thought of as my grandfather's favouritism.

"I have to remind your grandfather that he has more than one grandchild. He can't do for one what he can't do for the fourteen of you."

She had favourites herself, of course, but that was different. Our fortunes rose and fell on our merits, not on a romanticized and idealized image. I did know my grandfather didn't love me. He didn't know me, but I was glad to be under his protection.

It was not for idle pleasure that Granny took Patsy and me for Sunday lunch at West Point. She was more disappointed than we were of the friends Patsy's brother brought along with him. Platoons were organized by height, and so the other two young men were as unusually tall, looking as my cousin Artie did in those unflattering uniforms like pencils with heads on them. Neither of them had military backgrounds or any backgrounds at all that Granny could discern. Neither their table manners nor their conversation impressed her. Of these my cousin was the only one who interested me. He seemed genuinely glad to see his sister, his grandmother and me. The affectionate friendliness of both Artie and Frank hurt me for my own isolated and hostile brother.

George, priggish and disapproving, was easily fathomable and therefore no threat. We formed an I-Hate-George-Coale Club dedicated to minor tormenting. When the rest of us went swimming, we played in the water. George swam laps. He, like his father and mine, was interested in competitive swimming. If he'd been at all amiable about it, we would have been an eager cheering section, but instead he bragged about competing at an exclusive country club in Atlantic City where we wouldn't be allowed in.

Frank and I drove over in his Jeep the day of the meet and passed ourselves off as competitors. We changed into our suits and joined some of the swimmers warming up in the pool. Frank suggested that I do ten lengths as fast as I could. When I climbed out of the pool, exhausted, Frank responded with great satisfaction that at least three coaches had begun to time me with worried expressions on their faces. George had, of course, spotted us, and would have turned us in as impostors if it hadn't meant embarrassment to himself. So we sat through the meet in the competitors' bleachers. George lost.

By the time we got home, he had already reported us to Granny, who suggested we might have better entertainment than plaguing George. We doubted it.

One evening we all did go into New York to one theatre, ten or twelve of us. The Coale boys were there, and Artie had a pass from West Point. Aunt Lib, Dad's youngest, tallest and handsomest sister, was with us. I don't remember what we saw. I do remember our standing together at intermission, people looking to see what kind of a platform we were standing on. I was the shortest one. My father's eyes were amused and proud in that forest of family.

I was less comfortable with Aunt Lib as we walked along Fifth Avenue together. A man coming toward us, candidly but quietly admiring her, was greeted with, "I don't stare at you because you're short!" Aunt Lib, Patsy and later my own sister, Libby, were more defensive about their size than I was.

I visited Ann twice that summer in an apartment they'd moved to near the George Washington Bridge. The second time, Henry was away. Ann made love to me gently, reluctantly, the last night I was there. I was afraid to make love to her in shyness and ignorance. I felt guilty, too, because she was afraid of what she had done.

A DAY OR TWO BEFORE I LEFT THE EAST, my grandfather announced that he'd arranged a little party at his Jane Street apartment house. The liquor had been provided, but he thought perhaps we should take some food along.

"We have to leave in an hour," Granny Rule said.

"Nothing fancy," he suggested.

It was a hot, humid August day. Granny pulled herself out of her chair, hobbled into the dining room and then lifted her dress off and slung it over a chair. I was ordered to bring bottles of chicken, celery and mayonnaise from the pantry, to fill a box with salted nuts, olives, cheese spreads and crackers. An hour later, I sat in the back seat of the car, a large bowl of chicken salad on my lap. Granny waited behind the wheel while her elegant husband still dawdled in the bathroom waxing his moustache, tooth brushing a bit of red into his fringe of hair, arranging the peaks of his pocket handkerchief.

Simply the mention of the Jane Street apartment block could put Granny in a bad temper because Grandfather had rented most of the apartments to people in the arts who often couldn't or didn't pay their rent. Grandfather, instead of giving them notice, indulged them rather as he did his brothers. If he could not be an artist, at least he could be a friend to artists.

Though I was curious, I was also apprehensive. I trusted Granny's judgment too much not to feel in many of my grandfather's plans the potential for disaster.

Until Great-Grandfather Rule had died of breakdown in the Depression, Grandfather had never taken a drink. On doctor's orders now, he had a glass of sherry before dinner, but he was not even what could be called a social drinker. Granny didn't drink at all.

The thirty or so people assembled in one of the larger apartments had not waited for their host and hostess (we were, of course, late). The enthusiasm of their greetings was more drunken than genuine. As Grandfather introduced me to one tenant after another, it was embarrassingly obvious to me that they saw him as something of a fool to be humoured for their advantage. Granny settled herself into a couch with a Coke and became rather as if she were waiting for a bus, rather than giving a party.

I detached myself from my grandfather as quickly as I could. The party was noisy and crowded enough so that no real conversation needed to be sustained.

A very good-looking, very drunk young woman sat on the floor, her back against the wall, saying to no one in particular, "If men were really more superior to women, there would be no problem."

"Look at my poodle," a man called out, "he's smart enough to eat the chicken and spit out the celery."

A man touched my elbow and said, "Your grandfather wants you to sing for us."

"I don't sing," I said. "He's mixed me up with my mother."

"She's just being modest," Grandfather insisted.

I looked toward Granny for help. She would not on my behalf. I was the inspiration for this farce. Whatever embarrassment I had to suffer for it was no concern of hers.

I protested again. By now half a dozen people urged. The music critic for the *New York Times* offered to play the piano.

"I really don't sing," I said frantically.

I sang, a song that eludes my memory.

I couldn't be angry with my grandfather, nor could I really despise that gang of cheerful freeloaders. That party was simply an early confirmation for me of my mistrust of groups of people with artistic pretensions or not. All parties were essentially frat parties. I gradually learned to be better at avoiding them.

I had confided to my grandfather that I was really uncertain about the value of going back to college. He urged me to stay in the East. I could be a Powers model like Mary Lily. Or he could get me a job as a book reviewer if that was my bent. Since he hadn't gone to college himself, he thought the world one's best teacher. Though I was touched by those daydreams, I wasn't deluded by them. I did have the sense to know I had to learn how to read books before I could review them.

I went back to college in the fall simply because I didn't know what else to do.

Because of my odd status, I had not been assigned a room on freshman corridor, and I couldn't be offered a room on sophomore corridor because the class was already too large for the space. One suite was vacant on junior corridor, consisting of two studies and a sleeping porch which doubled for a living room during the day. A sophomore who had not found a comfortable social place in her class volunteered to share it with me. Since it offered both privacy and space, I was delighted. Marty and I never became real friends. She was a bridge-playing, party-going non-student, as the majority were. I sometimes had to go on working with a bridge game at my feet, but weekends I had the place to myself, which suited me very well, for I had determined to make as much effort as I could to become a real student.

Since most of the courses I enrolled in were designed for incoming freshman, I had the advantage of already knowing my way around the campus and the library, and I had at least learned some of the things not expected of me as a young scholar. The first essays I turned in were thoroughly researched and conservatively presented, if still misspelled.

My English professor, Elizabeth Pope, had been on leave the year before. It took very little time for me to know that I was in the presence of a rare teacher for whom I wanted to be a rare student.

Badly crippled by polio as a child, Dr. Pope was not over five feet, standing on her good leg. To get the height she needed, she often sat on top of her desk, her lecture notes and the text forgotten on the lectern. It was a joke among us that she didn't know how to read because she needed neither notes nor text to deliver entirely organized and handsomely phrased lectures, enriched by long passages of quotations. Without the necessity to consult the printed page, she could watch her audience and play to it, not so much for dramatic effect as for requiring of riveted attention. She anticipated questions, bewilderments simply by reading the faces of her students and calling on them to ask at the moment they needed to. She was always glad to clarify, argue a point, encourage a new interpretation.

I had not before been in the presence of someone who had lived entirely for her work. Her long years in the hospital, where books were her only friends, made her dedication to her work intense and personal, an attitude more to be expected of eager undergraduates than of seasoned scholars. She was, therefore, able to reach students more easily than most other teachers, share their first wonder at learning because it was still her own.

In 1948, Dr. Pope was in her early thirties. Her PhD thesis on *Paradise Regained* had been published, and she had been at Mills long enough to have established herself as a central power in the department, cherished and admired by Donald Weeks, the sensitive, cynical head of the department.

The first year I studied with her, she lived first at graduate house and then in my own dormitory. When she finally moved to her own apartment off campus, it was open to her students at any hour of the day or night. She never made a real distinction between working and sociability. Conversations could be as intensely academic over dinner as they were in the office, and, in the office, she was as welcoming and warm as she was in her own living room.

From the beginning, we fought fiercely. I had grown so to mistrust authority that I needed to test all the way.

"All right!" she shouted at me one day, her large green eyes flecked with a spatting of yellow. "Don't see the point of understanding the great chain of being! Be a barbarian!"

"Quitter!" I shouted back.

She looked surprised.

"You have to fight long enough to let me lose," I said and knew I trusted her enough to give her that information.

I challenged the texts chosen for study, the methods of teaching, the questions on quizzes and exams.

"How can I possibly compare sixteenth- and seventeenth-century prose styles in one paragraph?" I scribbled instead of answering the question. "I give up!"

"Which one of us is to have the child?" was written in her neat hand across the bottom of the quiz, along with an F.

Critical as I was of all the details of my instruction, I didn't spare myself. I never refused to answer a question unless I knew I could have been adequate to it. Every argument I lost out of ignorance was an invitation to longer hours of reading. By the time I had finished my first full year at the college, the head librarian had given me faculty privileges.

Because Dr. Pope went to chapel, I began to attend. Any member of the congregation could propose topics for sermons. George Hedley lectured rather than preached, often on hard points of doctrine, and a group of us usually stayed after the service for coffee provided by Helen Hedley in their book- and record-lined living room. The debates were often literary and historical with some of the brightest and best-informed members of the faculty participating. Discussions of morality tended toward various kinds of responsibility rather than definitions of sin.

Only when I went back to the dorm for lunch did I feel in odd company among other students well dressed from their attendance at other churches in the neighbourhood, mostly Catholics and Mormons. My own friends were only recently awake, dressed for tennis or hiking or horseback riding, and I shared their pagan spirits.

Yet chapel hadn't required faith. Interdenominational, the service was more Episcopalian than anything, but it borrowed texts and ceremonies liberally from not only other denominations but other religions. When George Hedley dealt with faith, he did not assume he was preaching to the converted.

Still, often when I bowed my head in prayer, it troubled my conscience that I recognized no audience for that gesture by my fellow petitioners. And I envied what seemed to me the innocence of Dr. Pope's belief. It was among the few important things we didn't discuss.

I didn't ever speak about the nature of my relationship with Ann. I knew Dr. Pope would not have understood or accepted it. The relationship that was growing between us had to be defined by our work without any erotic overtones.

A graduate student, recently out of the service, was obviously in love with Dr. Pope, loitered in places where they might meet, offered to run errands, brought small presents, and I saw Dr. Pope's physical disgust and growing irritation.

"I can't stand people who fawn!"

I was used enough to the physical needs of my grandmothers to be able to know when Dr. Pope needed help and how to offer it without offending her fierce independence.

When the lovesick graduate student asked me outright how I managed to win such favour, I was frightened as well as embarrassed, for I knew she recognized the nature of my own devotion as clearly as I recognized hers. I felt sorry for her, but I wanted nothing to do with her or her self-despising, painful devotion.

I was suspicious of other more attractive offers of friendship. The natural reserve there was between Dr. Pope and me couldn't be assumed with people more or less my own age who expected exchanges of confidence. I joked in the dorm corridors, joined the group-singing at dinner, went out to a movie or to a bar if there was an empty seat in one of the cars, but I didn't join many late-night bull sessions after I discovered that what could begin as an interesting discussion about religion soon deteriorated into personal gossip about who was and who was not sleeping with her boyfriend, who did and who did not have crushes on the more attractive of our male teachers. Marty told me that sometimes there were sessions of "constructive criticism" of one or another of the group's members.

I hated the cruelty that flavoured the intimacy of dorm life. I would have nothing to do with hazing the freshmen, a stand that reminded the sophomores I hadn't been hazed myself. My radiator was smeared with cheese, my ashtrays dumped in my bureau drawers and onto my papers on my desk, my bed pied. Marty told me who had done it, a group of nearly identical girls who wore cashmere twin-sets and rolled their socks down over their ankles. I confronted them and threatened them with unspecified retaliation if it ever happened again.

"Well, you warned the freshmen about the room raid."

"And I will again," I said.

"They want to cut you down to size, don't they?" Dr. Pope observed.

"Nobody will, ever," I answered.

She cocked an eyebrow at me, for, of course, she cut me down to size all the time, writing comments like, "There is less in this than first meets the eye," on a particularly florid essay.

I looked out for rather than made friends with a freshman assigned to me for that purpose. Barbara Carson was a year older than I was. She arrived at college that fall so drunk that she had to sleep it off before I could take her the rounds to get her a mail-box, pick up her trunk and introduce her to the dean. Later I discovered she, like me, was another of the dean's gambles.

Barbara was far more contemptuous of dormitory life than I was. I even enjoyed a lot of the concocted nonsense. On the evening of our house mother's birthday, it was decided that we all should dress up as our favourite billboards. Just as I was about to go down to dinner, a large shell hung round my neck and "Clean Rest Rooms" tacked to the back of my bright-yellow sweatshirt, the dean phoned and said, "Is Barbara in her room? If she is, will you stay with her until I get there?"

Barbara was in her room, obviously not about to go to dinner. She had just dyed everything in the room black, curtains, bedspread, rug, all her clothes and even her hair. Her fingernails were painted silver. We stared at each other, and then Barbara gave a nervous laugh, at me, at herself, and offered me a cigarette. She was always very formal, her speech elaborately careful, whether she was drunk or sober. It was said she got As because her vocabulary was so esoteric that nobody could understand what she was talking about.

What the dean thought of the Charles Addams's cartoon she walked into I couldn't tell. She nodded a curt dismissal to me and said, "Thank you."

I never did find out what that episode was all about, and I wasn't curious. By that time the dean and I were a working team to keep Barbara from being expelled. Sometimes it required my going out with the dorm assistant at midnight or after to locate Barbara, nearly dead drunk in one of her favourite bars. Once it involved my persuading Barbara to pour a fifth of whiskey down her sink. Students who had drink in their rooms were routinely expelled.

Barbara would stay up for days at a time, chain-smoking, drinking coffee and writing her brilliantly incomprehensible papers. Then she'd sleep for days in her tomblike room.

I neither understood nor liked her. She tolerated my interferences with a show of patience laced with disdain. I think what I enjoyed about the task was my conspiracy with the dean, sharing her perverse determination to keep Barbara, if not out of trouble, out of enough visible trouble to get her through the year.

Barbara's rebellion gave my own a normalcy which probably reassured me. I didn't recognize her literary sources in such figures as Renée Vivien until some years later. At the time, she seemed to me an original.

Not until spring, after one of the assemblies at which we all wore our academic gowns, did Ellen Kay come up and introduce herself to me. She was a freshman at Mills Hall.

"I want to be your friend," she said with a candour that caught me off guard.

Ellen wanted to be a poet. She was not afraid of her ambition as I was of mine, partly because she had been writing poems for some years while I was just now struggling unsuccessfully with my first real short stories. Also Ellen saw nothing to be ashamed of in ambition. I was probably more superstitious than ashamed. I didn't want to make claims I couldn't fulfill. So I seemed the more modest of the two. In fact, one of our greatest bonds was the delusion of future grandeur so healthy and so derided in adolescents.

Perhaps because we met wearing our academic gowns, I tend to remember us dramatically clothed in black, caught up in the romance of being young scholars. Much of the time we spent together was devoted to work, either our academic pursuits or our own writing. We took many of the same courses, chose research projects that overlapped. We didn't share acquaintances, living in different dormitories. Nor did we share passionate loyalties, for Ellen was devoted to Donald Weeks, head of the department and a poet. She was never really comfortable in Dr. Pope's presence. I liked Dr. Weeks well enough, and I came to respect him as a teacher, but there was something snide and at the same time vulnerable in his manner that made me keep my distance.

Ellen, who dabbled in all the arts, sculpted quite a good head of Donald Weeks and kept it on the windowsill of her fourth-floor room, visible to him from his office window. If custom had allowed such blatancy on my part, I doubt that I would have displayed it. Even then I mistrusted the conventions for loving.

I left college reluctantly that summer to spend only part of it at South Fork. Mother Packer, who did not walk alone at all now, uncertain of her balance and fearful of falling, did when we were at South Fork practise walking with my steadying arm and her cane. One day we'd walk from the house up to the fig trees, the next down along the honeysuckled fence to our gate. One day we disagreed about which way to turn, and she struck out on her own. We were both proud of those few minutes of her independence.

Libby, who didn't really like the place, made friends with some elderly neighbours who tamed squirrels, chipmunks and birds. But she was often bored, missing her friends in Reno. Since she wasn't interested in fishing or hiking, disliked the moss in the river, the deer droppings in the orchard, she was a reluctant and complaining companion I was glad to leave behind. She and Mother Packer bickered.

My father, who had taken over a family-owned building supply company in Reno, had so improved it that the family were having second thoughts about the percentage of profit they had offered him originally. He began to mistrust the company lawyer; so he didn't come to South Fork for the holiday.

Arthur had joined the army.

Mother, caught between Libby and Mother Packer, missing Dad, must have been very glad to get back to Reno. There she had to put up with my restlessness and boredom. I made a pledge to myself that I would never spend another summer at home, one I kept the more easily since it was to be the last summer anyone went to South Fork.

How very different it felt to return to college that fall. I was again sharing a sleeping porch with Marty on junior corridor, and our own classmates had joined us, though I was half a year behind them. More confident of myself academically with a successful year behind me, I was less reluctant to make friends. Sally Millett and Edy Mori, two psychology majors, were amiable, bright companions. Ellen and I saw more of each other in classes we took together, and we made friends with other English majors. At the college shop for a morning or afternoon break, I had a comfortable choice of tables to join, though if Dr. Pope was there, I always joined hers. She made friends with my new friends, and sometimes Sally and Edy and I would invite ourselves to dinner, bringing steaks, making green goddess salad and garlic bread.

I more often went by myself for long evenings of literary debate. We shared now not only the curriculum but other books. We read C.S. Lewis, Charles Williams and Dorothy Sayers. I didn't share Dr. Pope's taste for Sayers's mysteries, but I loved her plays and her work on the *Divine Comedy*. We discovered Christopher Fry and read his plays aloud with other friends.

I would have said I had never been happier. Sometimes, working in the library, I would be so overcome by a sense of wonder at an image in a poem, at the rhythm of a line of prose, that I'd have to stop reading for a moment. I worked in my study at night long after other people went to bed, on essays, on short stories. I could always, even at four o'clock in the morning, telephone Mother Packer for company. She was usually awake listening to the radio and playing solitaire, but she didn't mind being roused from a light sleep. We'd exchange fond, rude messages, and then I'd sleep for three or four hours.

Edy, walking over to Mills Hall where we all had breakfast together, would tell me to put my hands in my pockets. She couldn't stand the greyish purple of my skin at that hour. One morning I fainted in the breakfast line.

I had the year before fainted even more spectacularly in class as I finished reciting, "I'll lay me down and bleed awhile, / And then I'll rise and fight again." Evaline Wright, the instructor, always after that opened a window when it was my turn to perform, and she harboured a notion that I was too high-strung to deal with college.

I was living in a restrained intensity I couldn't endure. I was too much in love, working too hard and far too frightened. Not being able to confront that fear and deal with it, I was living in a state of increasing anxiety. Some days I simply couldn't face breakfast. And several times I had to skip dinner, unable to climb the long flights of stairs into the dining room. I began to lose weight. Often I couldn't sleep when I tried to, lay listening to the campanile strike every fifteen minutes until it was time to get up and face another yet-more daunting day.

When I tried to distract myself, I listened to Sally's roommate planning to marry in June, not because she really wanted to quit college but because she was sure this was the only proposal she'd ever get and she couldn't bear not ever being married. Edy, who was being courted by a serious young doctor, saw no reason for such lack of confidence, and Sally went out with five different men, juggling weekend privileges to accommodate them all.

One midweek evening, they persuaded me to give up my books and go out for a friendly beer. In the ladies' room of a local bar, a very drunk and handsome woman tried to pick me up. Back at the table, Sally and Edy were amiably fending off young men.

I tried staying in bed for a couple of days. I went to see the doctor at the infirmary. She gave me pills for low blood pressure, which sent my head pounding every time I lay down. I went back again.

"Jinx, you've got to give up," she said to me.

"Give up what?"

She shrugged. Then she said, "I'm going to send you home. You need complete rest."

At home, I was far sicker than I had been at college. The altitude had always troubled me. Now I fainted if I went upstairs too quickly, I couldn't go anywhere by myself, not even into a store. I didn't know from moment to moment what negative trick my body would play on me, against which will seemed helpless.

Mother was attentive, patient, reassuring. She was willing to have me home for the year to let my overtaxed nerves mend. The thought of not going back to college horrified me. After several weeks, I begged to go back. Once I agreed to drop at least one course, Mother agreed to let me try it.

Dr. Pope, worried and inclined to blame herself for the academic pressure I'd been under, offered to feed me herself if the dormitory dining room was too much for me. She would waive the requirement for a second paper in her course and ask others of my professors to do the same. When I protested, she said, "Jinx, one of your papers is worth two from most other students." Never one to hand out compliments casually, she was telling me the only way she knew how that my love was returned. I knew it was. I also knew its limits and accepted them. Only a few months ago, Libby Pope wrote to me from a rest house on Mother's Day, saying that when everyone else bragged about their children, she reminded herself that she'd had about five hundred daughters, "Among whom, you are the most beloved."

It did help to drop a course.

Then Ann, pregnant with a second child, came down with polio and was temporarily, partially paralyzed. It was weeks before she could use her hands to write. Then she gave only the sketchiest of details. Her mother was taking care of Carol. Susan was born prematurely and had to be left in the hospital for some weeks.

So much in need of getting to her, I had no way of explaining that urgency to anyone. On the bulletin board in the English department, I saw an ad for summer schools in England. Immediately I phoned Mother to say it was exactly what I needed to do the following summer. I could make up the lost credits of the year and see something of England. At first she was reluctant, thinking I shouldn't work through the summer, but I persuaded her that a change of scene, an adventure, would be the right tonic for me. I wasn't at all convinced of it myself, still phobic on some days, but I had to get to Ann and was willing to risk anything. Mother persuaded Mother Packer to foot the bill. So I applied to the University of Birmingham to attend the summer school on Shakespeare at Stratford, and I was accepted.

Dr. Pope was far more excited at the prospect than I was. She had never been to England and took enormous vicarious pleasure in my going. She was also pleased that I had been accepted for what was billed essentially as a graduate school.

Most people left campus for the midwinter break in February, but some of us stayed on to work on papers, concerts, play productions, dance recitals. I liked the college best when it was nearly deserted. And early spring there was beautiful, the creek high, the scent of eucalyptus pungent, the daffodils in bloom. I always thought what a marvellous place it would be to take a real holiday, hiking up by the lake, swimming, lying in the sun by the high protecting wall at the pool. Yet once everyone came back, I was sorry I hadn't taken a break, gone to Carmel or down to visit Mother Packer. March was always a hard month, the pressure of work there, the term long from ending.

One night Sally Millett came into my room and said, "I'm simply fed up with this place. If I don't get out of here, I'll go mad."

"Then let's go," I said.

"Where?"

"Let's go to South Fork," I suggested.

There was no provision in the rules for students to declare short holidays of their own and simply take off. If we had asked permission, we would have been refused. So I signed us out, giving the address of the lodge across the river from our summer cabin, without going to the house mother to sign her permission. Then we took off.

It was an eight-hour bus trip from San Francisco in those days. We rode all night. Sally was small enough to curl up in the seat and sleep. Every time I stuck my long legs out in the aisle, the man in the seat in front of me reached down and took hold of my ankle. But we were going to South Fork, and I doubt that I could have slept under any circumstances.

The house, closed up for the winter with wooden battens on the screened porches, would be anyway too cold and damp to stay in at that time of year; so we checked into the lodge, and then set off on foot to cross the river, walk the bar to the stand of redwood trees through which we passed to the gate. I suppose the place must have looked dilapidated and unwelcoming to a stranger to it. For me it was alive with childhood, its lonely safety

Sally Millett and Jane Rule
Jane Rule Fonds, University Archives, University of British Columbia

and wonder. I knew why Mother Packer could walk here over this rough ground. We spent the day walking, into the orchards, the meadows, the woods, back down onto the river bar, across the swinging bridge high above the spring-running river. I slept that night as I hadn't slept in months, woke hungry and ready for another day out of doors.

The steelhead trout were running. At the lodge, we met a man who ran a radio program called *The Fish Finder*. Each week he fished in a different place and reported the conditions of the place for other fishermen. He complained good-naturedly that he had a trunk full of steelhead, and his wife and all his friends were sick of fish. He opened the trunk to prove his claim.

"Would you like one?" he asked.

Sally and I looked at each other.

"It just might help," Sally said.

"Help yourself," he said.

I reached into the trunk and shoved a fist up inside the head of a ten-pound steelhead.

"How are we going to get it back, though?" Sally asked.

"We'll get them to freeze it for us."

That evening I was called to the phone.

"Dean Hawkes here," the familiar voice announced. "Are you enjoying your vacation?"

"Very much," I said.

"When do you intend to come back?"

"Tomorrow?"

"We'll expect you then, tomorrow," she said and hung up.

In the morning, we stowed our frozen fish on the luggage rack overhead, and then Sally went back to sleep. I was content to watch for all the familiar landmarks of the road, one every two or three miles for the first fifty, whether the peach orchard where we stopped to buy particularly good peaches or the suicide bend where large trucks had gone over into the river. I knew the very place where Dad had had a head-on collision coming up to see us one summer when I was young enough still to be sleeping in my parent's room. He had hitchhiked the rest of the way and walked in cut and bruised but otherwise all right. I knew the legends of the road as well: Black Bart's Rock, behind which he had hidden to rob stagecoaches; the cliff off which the proverbial Indian maiden had leapt to her death in unrequited love. There was a favourite picnic site; there the turnoff to buy salami.

I looked up from my musing into the landscape to see our frozen fish drooping its tail over the luggage rack. The heating system was located in the rack. I took it down and, because Sally slept on, wrapped it in her coat as a way of insulating it. It had become more of a peace offering than a joke, though we still hadn't decided with whom we'd make the peace.

Into wine country, the weather getting warmer, I began to feel not apprehensive but eager to be back. Though I assumed we would be in some sort of trouble at the dormitory, I didn't imagine our punishment would exceed the pleasure of the trip. After so many months of illness and struggle, to feel younger again, reckless, and more or less sure of loving reproof, restored for me a kind of courage, a simple pleasure at being alive and in comic trouble.

When we arrived at the college gates around four in the afternoon, we decided against presenting ourselves without checking on the climate.

"Let's give the fish to Doc," Sally suggested, a name we'd by then given to Dr. Pope. "She'll know what's up."

She greeted us with warm relief, but she refused the fish, admittedly large for her needs. She had no idea what was planned for our return, but she suggested that we might better call on the dean and present the fish to her as a peace offering.

A lot of students were afraid of Dean Hawkes, whose eyes matched her name, whose temper was fierce. But Sally and I both trusted her sense of humour, and I knew her forbearance with Barbara was nearly limitless. She did, indeed, welcome us warmly, accepted the fish graciously and asked me recipes for cooking it. I had not ever eaten one and had no idea what she could do with it.

"Treat it like a salmon," I suggested, with no idea of the culinary manners for salmon either.

We didn't actually say we'd caught it, but we didn't correct her assumption.

"I can't invite you for dinner," Dean Hawkes said, maintaining her tone of sociability. "I'm going out. I suggest you'd be wise to check in at your hall in time for dinner."

Leaving us with no further clue as to our reception, she showed us to the door.

When we arrived, we went to the register to sign in, and there we found Dean Hawkes's own signature of permission which extended to nine o'clock that night. Nobody could touch us, not the house mother, not the student council. With the stroke of a pen, Dean Hawkes had made our holiday legal.

"But everybody else is mad at you," Edy told us, and she was irritated herself, for it's not easy to see even good friends so easily avoid justice.

Marty was not speaking to me. Along the whole corridor, no one was speaking to us. We'd been sent to Coventry, an expression I didn't learn until I'd spent a summer in England.

If the authorities wouldn't punish us and went so far as to protect us from student court, there were other ways of seeing that we were contrite.

"They're simply jealous," Sally said with a shrug.

"They think you're both very arrogant, that nobody should get such special treatment after breaking such an important rule, and, if you think they are going to start talking to you tomorrow, you're wrong."

The next night my Latin professor was a guest of the hall for dinner. Since no one was speaking to me, I sat next to him and regaled him with the story of our fishing trip, slightly exaggerating the size of our quite respectable fish. I did not know until some time later that the fish I was describing was in fact in his own refrigerator. Dean Hawkes had chosen him, for the size of his large family, to cope with our peace offering.

It was a week before, in the privacy of our own quarters, Marty finally broke her silence, not out of any friendliness to me but from pent-up frustration at not giving me a piece of her mind. I thought I could do anything, didn't I? Go home for several weeks in the fall, take a fishing holiday in the spring, write what papers I felt like, hobnob with the faculty. She was ashamed to be my roommate, and I'd better start looking for someone else for next year.

"Well, Sally's roommate is getting married," I said.

"You won't be allowed to room with Sally," she said.

"Why ever not?"

"Because you're bad influences for each other."

"Who's to stop us?"

"You'll see," she said.

I was surprised at Marty's venom. It seemed to me it must be nourished by months of unspoken grievances. Were my friendships with Dr. Pope and other members of the faculty really enviable to students who devoted their weekends to frat parties and balls, who studied as little as they could and talked of nothing but being free of the prison of college? I certainly didn't envy them the facts of their entertainments and interests, but I would have given a good deal to have had a male friend to shield me from social failure. My arrogance, the only protection at my own command, had been more effective than I thought. Since I had nothing else, I went on fostering it. For whenever I did try to accept a date, the gross attempts at the conquest of my body so disgusted me that I was less and less often tempted.

Edy soon relaxed her tone of disapproval, and both Sally and I had enough friends outside the hall not to be overly troubled by the righteous hostility around us on the corridor.

Only a few weeks after our escapade, we were returning some equipment to the hall from a party held elsewhere on campus. It was one of our amiable gestures toward doing our share of work even though no one was speaking to us. In order most easily to return stacks of chairs to their cupboard, we unlocked a side door to bring them in, then locked it behind us. That very night a member of the student council presented us with a charge of having disobeyed an absolute rule for leaving side doors locked after six o'clock.

"We were right there. We locked it behind us."

Our trial was comic. For our great sin, we were campused on alternate weekends for the rest of term. Since Sally and I rarely shared weekend plans anyway, it was no hardship for either of us.

The punishment was enough in the eyes of our fellow students to allow them to speak to us again, but nobody was unduly friendly.

"They finally got you, did they?" Dean Hawkes asked.

"That they did," I said.

"One of these days they're going to get Barbara."

I HAVE NEVER KNOWN THE DETAILS of Arthur's discharge from the army. Once he was AWOL, and I expected to be questioned by the military police. Then he was simply out of the army.

"My feet were too big," he said. "They didn't have boots big enough."

Because he had been in the army, a requirement for high-school graduation was waived for him, and he enrolled in college in San Francisco. When I asked him what he was taking, he simply shrugged. He told me instead about the people he was meeting in North Beach, poets and philosophers. Once or twice, I went with him to his favourite bar, but everyone there was too drunk to talk sense, and I was embarrassed for my brother that he was impressed with such pretensions and incoherent shouting. He sensed a genuine energy which I did not. Perhaps he also recognized his own pain in all that directionless passion. Out of it came Kerouac with *On the Road* and Ginsberg with *Howl*.

I remember the shock of recognition when I read *On the Road*, so different from the distanced aesthetic pleasure I had reading other books. It was the first time someone was speaking directly about experience which most people tried to pretend didn't exist. There were the crazed young men I knew, suicidal and violent, the human rubble of the war. I accepted the literary judgment of the book as undisciplined, negative romance, but I couldn't dismiss it.

I meanwhile wrote obscure, symbolic stories for my writing class. Most of my main characters were young men, violent and in violent pain. They had biblical names like Cain and Peter. One of them was black with yellow hair and green eyes whose fate was to rape sheep. For weeks after that one was read out in class, I was greeted in the college shop by a chorus of "The Whiffen-poof Song." "Ba, ba, ba," followed me everywhere. Another had an invisible band of steel around his head. The few realistic stories I wrote were about troubled relationships between fathers and sons.

So much of my own experience didn't seem to me experience at all, a mixture of daydreams and righteousness, out of which I could make nothing. My brother's suffering was dramatic, full of grand gestures and observable defeats.

His presence on campus changed my social status. The twin-set, rolled-sock clutch were suddenly very friendly, and everyone was candidly envious of me for having such a handsome and attentive brother. Unlike most young men who found having dinner at the hall an ordeal, Arthur enjoyed himself. An audience of a dozen young women sharpened his wit and warmed his charm.

Mother Packer sent us tickets to the opera. I'd come down to the living room and find him standing in front of the great round mirror in his evening clothes entertaining a group of girls. He'd take the coat over my arm from me and hold it, then offer his arm, enjoying the role of courtly brother. He was usually no more than slightly drunk, but his driving terrified me, as reckless and aggressive as the stories he'd tell on our way across the Bay Bridge and into the city. I don't think it was any longer his conscious desire to frighten me. He simply lived on the edge of hysteria and could at any moment have killed us both. It never occurred to me that I could say no to him, but it amazed me that everyone else would go out with him more than once.

But Edy did, and it did not surprise me that Arthur chose the person I found the most attractive of my friends. Edy had a taste for people more adventuresome than she was, and she liked being needed. What did she make of his transparent lying, his sudden flickering cruelties, the absolute isolation of his self-centredness? Perhaps they weren't so obvious to other people. Perhaps I unfairly exaggerated his faults. Edy once accused me of being in love with him myself and jealous of anyone else he was interested in. I was amazed, but of course Edy didn't see that his courtliness to me was a charade. If I ever asked him to do anything like drive down to see Mother Packer, remember our parents' birthdays or help out a friend, he simply didn't hear me.

Or he agreed and then "forgot." Edy then didn't have many such things to ask him and perhaps didn't notice how often he didn't hear what he didn't want to. And I'm sure she loved his future, as I still tried to.

Sometimes I wondered if Arthur wasn't like everyone else after all, and I was peculiar. Certainly most of the relationships I observed between the young women and men I knew had the same flavour of inauthentic romance I so mistrusted in Arthur. The men wanted sex as cheaply as it could be had. The women wanted sex for as much as they could charge in attention, entertainment and engagement rings. The women didn't want to be known as cheap lays. The men didn't want to be easy meal tickets. The ones who were, were called Hall Johnnys. One of them was known to have proposed to ten of the women on senior corridor. The impersonality of it all shocked me. When anyone claimed to have fallen in love, the frenzied exaggeration of feeling seemed to me even less genuine than the more calculated wrangling of dinners, dances, theatre tickets, weekends in the mountains.

My love for Ann, its eroticism so curtailed by guilt and fear, was something that had grown slowly out of my admiration for her singing voice, her painting, her willingness to treat me as a friend, the range of her experience and understanding. My love for Dr. Pope was chaste and passionate. It would not have occurred to me to charm or lure or make use of either one of them. Was it because we had nothing to offer each other but ourselves that our relationship seemed to me to exist in a world entirely apart from the courting games going on all around me? Those loves, so precious to me, so joyfully requiring of me, meant nothing, did not exist, in the world of my friends. If I had confessed them, I would have been seen as sick and depraved.

Sally and Edy both liked using me as a victim for their course in psychological testing. They discovered in me all kinds of pathological evidence for schizophrenia, manic depression and sexual perversion. They loved to reconfirm the moronic level of intelligence. They even found that only two percent of the population had less mechanical aptitude than I had.

Then Sally got into an argument with her psych professor about my IQ. I was too clearly a good student not to be a challenge to the validity of the tests. Tested in the department, I was told that I lacked a natural competitive spirit, failed at solving any meaningless problem like remembering nonsense syllables, at being able to repeat nine digits backward.

"You say you can't, but you really just don't see the point."

I failed in verbal skills because mine were too highly developed for the text. I avoided cliché opposites, defined words too subjectively, rejected oversimplified general statements.

"So," Sally said, "we're going to teach you to take IQ tests."

Her own skill was legendary.

I did learn. I worked my way up from 86 to 127 in a month. But I was a disappointment when I was tested in the following year. I'd skipped back down to 95. Like playing the piano, like tennis, intelligence obviously took a kind of practice I hadn't the competitive spirit to maintain.

The experience did relieve me of a secret fear that my competence was somehow a hoax.

"Mine is the hoax," Sally said, grinning.

In the one literature course we took together, she got As in quizzes from the summaries I gave her of what we were supposed to read. I very often didn't do that well, but on the essays and exams my method of actually reading the assignments worked better.

Sally's attitude toward her work bewildered me as much as her attitude toward useful young men did. It was a game played against teachers to do as little work as possible for as much credit.

In the few courses I had to take which I didn't enjoy, I was ashamed of high grades for so little effort. I knew my A in biology, achieved by a couple of nights of memorizing my notes, wasn't worth the C of a student too caught up in the real love of lab work to be bothered with memorizing details which would be forgotten in a week.

Most of the work I did in college I loved. Other students like Sally were perfecting an ability to avoid all but absolutely necessary work and to tolerate boredom. They are survival skills for a life I couldn't have lived, though it has always gone on all around me.

Except for Ellen, whose love of learning was pure of any other motive, my friends considered the seriousness with which I took my work a tolerable quirk as long as I didn't burden them with my enthusiasms. There were other good scholars on campus, but they tended to be conservative in their behaviour and looked askance at my breaking of rules or extravagant silliness. One of them told Dr. Pope she didn't think I deserved an A in Shakespeare because I didn't really take my work seriously.

I was hurt by the accusation because she was a student I admired. Before the final exam, I had begun to tape impossible-to-identify quotations on the floor beside her door late at night, things like "Bum, sir?" or "I take my leave, my lord." After the first several, she began to retaliate. For me such play was a way of dealing with the tensions of the exam period. The morning of the exam, she was sitting at breakfast memorizing speeches of important secondary characters.

"Why?" I asked.

"There's sure to be a question on there. Haven't you noticed how interested Dr. Pope is in them?"

I spent so much time talking Shakespeare with Dr. Pope that I couldn't possibly isolate such a narrow interest, nor would it have had occurred to me.

Sure enough, there was the question. I was full of admiration for such a divining skill, but it would have been useless to me. I had to focus on what seemed most important and interesting to me.

I'VE ALWAYS BEEN GRATEFUL to Donald Weeks for conducting our writing classes so that we could focus on those forms and themes important to us. He could, like Dr. Pope, be sharply critical of what seemed to him inauthentic or insubstantial. I remember a well-deserved "So what?" on a short piece of moody description. What manuscripts he dealt with in class he chose for the strengths he could see in the work. He, not the student, read the work aloud. I learned so much more about effectiveness and failure in my own work from those readings than I did from any discussion or written comment that having my work read aloud by a good reader continues to be an essential part of my working method.

If Donald Weeks didn't read the tone, it wasn't there. If he missed a rhythm, it was faulty. I could hear what explanations went on too long, what images were too complicated. I could also hear a line of dialogue that worked, a shift of pace that was graceful.

Because I did not have to go on from stories to poems or plays or novels or essays, I could work long enough at technique to see my own improvement. I could also watch Ellen's work grow and change. She learned by imitation and, though Dr. Weeks wasn't always enthusiastic about the models she chose, he didn't object to her method. Nor did he protest when another student found most of her poems in notes left on doors or scraps of conversation. As a consequence, we did not begin to sound more like each other but each more like herself.

I have heard it argued that all writing students should be exposed to all forms.

"How do you know you're not a playwright if you've never tried?"

In the same way I know I'm not a mountain climber, I suppose.

We were exposed to other forms both by other students' work and in our academic courses. Waki Ballard, for instance, wrote poems, children's stories, short stories and plays, and she went on to write a novel which was published. Ellen devoted herself to poetry, until she was in graduate school, when she began to write plays and act. Her volume of poems, published when she was in her twenties, was the first of our ventures into print.

Donald Weeks had open houses for his students. I went only once. The conversation was flippant and clever, full of punning rudeness and literary references. Barbara Carson was a regular, and so was Harry Bacchus, a young instructor Dr. Weeks had hired to expand the writing program. Harry's workshop methods included imposing his own tastes and his own theories about the creative process. He was an intense and shallow young man whose exclamations of approval tended to be "Boy!" and "Wow!" He seemed to me an odd choice for Dr. Weeks to have made. Dr. Weeks was given neither to jargon of creative theories nor to disarming enthusiasms. But he gave Harry every opportunity to show off, laughed in tight, excited approval at observations which seemed to me both pompous and puerile.

"What does he see in Harry Bacchus?" I asked Dr. Pope.

"He's very fond of him. Perhaps with two daughters, he's looking for a son."

I went away for a weekend to visit Mother Packer and to call on Nancy Lockwood who had just had a miscarriage. She had been told she could have no more children. She lay in a darkened room, hardly able to speak, having invested too much hope in a second round of babies to replace the three daughters who were growing up. Being there in the house behind which Ann had lived for so long in happier times for them both, I wondered how long Ann had lain in a darkened room in similar near despair, her unborn child threatened, her hands paralyzed.

Mother Packer insisted on sending me back to college in a cab, a thirty-mile trip, and she specified that the driver was to be a woman. When a nice-looking young man turned up instead, she nearly forbade me to go.

"I'm going to Europe by myself this summer. I really am old enough to take care of myself."

"Are you?" she asked sarcastically.

She was not enthusiastic about my plans. Mother had made the grand tour with a group of girls and a chaperone. Only the fact that I would be studying rather than be travelling around persuaded Mother Packer to consent to my going. I have sometimes wondered since if my own parents would have been more conservative in their attitudes toward their children if there hadn't been disapproving parents for them to defy in our name.

My return to college was uneventful, but it was late when I got in, and I had reading to do for my lectures the next day. I read through breakfast as well, a habit I developed to avoid early-morning conversation, at which I'd never been good. So I hadn't really exchanged more than greetings with everyone until I joined Dr. Pope at the college shop at ten in the morning. She was sitting alone with a glass of milk, always a clear signal that something had upset her.

"Don't speak to me," she said.

"Why not?"

"Just don't ask me any questions because I can't answer them," she said, the sound of tears in her voice.

"I don't have anything to ask," I said. "I've been away all weekend."

"You haven't even heard about Barbara Carson?"

"No, what's happened to her?"

"She was found wandering in a field in her nightgown at eight on Sunday morning, very drunk."

"What else is new?" I said, sighing, for Barbara Carson's antics had lost their sinister charms for me some time before.

"She said she'd been at a party at Donald's with Harry."

"And the dean is hopping mad at Donald and Harry? She can hardly accuse them of leading Barbara to drink!"

"I don't want to talk about it," she said.

I changed the subject. Yet I couldn't see why she was that upset.

"I'm so very glad you're not mixed up in any of this," she said as we got up to go to our next classes.

"I picked a good weekend to be away," I agreed, knowing I would have been called in on it if I'd been around.

Then, as the day passed, the rumour began to spread. Some said Barbara was to be expelled. Others said both Dr. Weeks and Harry Bacchus had been fired. Then we heard that other members of the faculty were threatening to resign in protest.

One of the senior majors said to me at dinner, "It's only the tip of the iceberg, you know. I can't understand why the president or the dean didn't blow the whistle on them months ago."

"On what?"

"On those parties, for one thing. Once Mrs. Weeks and the children left, they really got out of hand. And, you know, Donald and Harry are crazy, one minute inseparable, the next minute threatening to kill each other."

Barbara was nowhere to be found.

I phoned the dean.

"She's all right. She'll be back in the dorm in a few days' time."

"She's not going to be expelled, is she?"

"Over my dead body!" the dean replied.

"What do you want me to do?"

"Stay out of it, Jinx. Stay as far out of it as you can. Thank heavens you're not involved."

Harry Bacchus was not allowed back on campus. Donald Weeks finished his year's teaching and left. Only one man in the music department resigned in protest.

Barbara, back at the college, said, "It's really the president I'd like to seduce. He's the only really intelligent man around here."

"You seduced Harry?"

"That pompous little prick," she said.

Had Barbara stirred up this whole melodrama as a diversion for herself and then hidden behind her student status to see two men's careers ruined?

"Don't you feel guilty?" I asked.

"Why should I?" she said, opening her eyes wide. "It hasn't anything to do with me."

Several days later, when I passed Dr. Weeks on the creek bridge, he stopped and said, "You, after all, understand these things, don't you? I just couldn't do anything else."

I understood less and less.

Ellen said, "I've heard a really different story. Donald was in love with Harry, and that's why he hired him. When Harry had mono last fall, he moved in and Donald's wife nursed him. Then Harry fell in love with her, and she left with the children."

"Where does Barbara fit into all this?"

"I don't know. Maybe Harry was using her to protect himself from Donald."

I heard again Dr. Weeks's saying, "You, after all, understand these things, don't you?"

The students' loyalty to Donald Weeks didn't waver. He had been a good teacher, and he now appeared like a Macbeth or Othello, a man brought down by his own tragic flaw who had lost wife, children, his lover and his career. But we thought no more of interfering with his fate than we would have thought of interrupting the progress of a tragedy on the stage.

I continued to feel that, though Barbara's part in it was insignificant, she had been despicable.

For Dr. Pope and Ellen, the loss was more personal than it was for me. Each was also in a way disillusioned. There I was, closer to each of them than anyone else, carrying the flaw in my own nature which could also be exposed. I did not defend him to either of them. I couldn't have. I thought he was wrong.

My own moral state can on the surface of it confuse me as I look back on it. I'm sure I was confused at the time. I seemed to hold two mutually exclusive views, that my love represented what was best in me and that it was a sin. Or more ambiguously and truly put, what was specifically good and generally bad. Ann called my love "misdirected," and, as a general proposition I agreed that, if I could be as devoted to a man as to either of the women I loved, I should probably choose to. As long as I entertained the possibility that my emotional makeup would change, I did not really see that my devotion to either woman could effect the collapse of our worlds as Donald Weeks's passions had toppled his. My fears were of staircases, sidewalks, doorways, the image always of a way I must walk that I could not.

The imaginary man, Sandy, still figured in my defences occasionally. Sally and Edy were so skeptical of his existence that I once asked Grandfather Rule to wire flowers in his name. The excuse I offered was wanting such a demonstration of affection to discourage another young man who didn't interest me. I was embarrassed by such deceits. Still they were less painful in my conscience than the deceit of dating that I occasionally indulged in at Sally's and Edy's urging once or twice, even having my appetite roused by a technically competent young man about whom I didn't know, about whom I therefore couldn't care. Such experiences did teach me not to confuse desire with love. They may also have kept me open to the hope that I might, one day, love a man and welcome my ability to desire him.

Living with another woman, because it was a daydream fixed on either Ann or Dr. Pope, didn't occur to me as a real possibility. Ann was married with two children, and I was too much involved in her happiness to wish away anyone else in her life. For Dr. Pope, given her religious views and her position, it was unthinkable. If I had suggested by gesture or word that I was in love with her, I would immediately have been banished.

I was really not unhappy with the relationship as it was. Erotically constrained, I still had the abundance of her loving attention, the richness of her mind, the generosity of her imagination for my future. If she had not kept in mind that I would be spending six weeks among graduate students in England, I would have done nothing to prepare myself for it. Even as she did prepare me, I was hardly conscious of it. The summer meant crossing the continent to see Ann, then recrossing an ocean to get back to her.

She and Henry, with the two children, had moved to an apartment in a large house on the other side of the Hudson, whose grounds extended to the edge of the cliff above the river. It was a beautiful place with its view of the great river, the George Washington Bridge and the city skyline beyond, no fence or hedge of any sort to obstruct it. That drop, though not as dramatic as the fireball at Yosemite, was far enough to be mortal to the imagination. Carol was only two-and-a-half.

"I've taught her to be careful," Ann said, practical fatalist that she was.

I took picture after picture of that little girl in a dress I'd bought for her. In them, she looks as lively and serene as her mother, who laughs up at the camera with her.

The first night I was there, Henry and Ann and I sat up late, talking. I could read on their faces some of the strain of the last months, but Ann seemed entirely recovered, and Susan at four months was a contented, quiet baby, already displaying her father's curly grin.

When Henry finally decided to go to bed, he asked, "Shall I go to her tonight?"

"No, I will," Ann said definitively.

Then she said to me, "Carol has trouble sleeping. I think it was being with Mother all that time and then having to adjust to a baby sister."

She reached out to me, held me and held me away, beginning again all the sexual questioning I found so difficult to cope with. If I told her I'd made love with half a dozen men and thoroughly enjoyed myself, chances were she would come to my bed. Though I wanted her very much, I didn't want to lie to her, an ironic deficiency given all the lying about myself I was willing to do among my friends. I was constrained, too, by Henry's presence in the apartment, by children who might any moment wake and need her.

Carol did not call. We went in and found her playing in the dark in her crib. Ann picked her up, held her and sang to her, then put her back to bed.

We went back to the living room where I was to sleep, chain-smoked and talked quietly for another hour. When we checked again, Carol was still awake.

"I'll leave you with her now," I said and went to bed.

After that night, there was no suggestion that Ann and I might make love. As Carol became accustomed to me, I took my turn with her in the night. During the day, the two children kept us occupied, and Henry brought us news of the outside world in the evening.

"Oh, it's a tonic for Ann to have you here," he'd say. "And for me, too."

The erotic tension I created sweetened their nights together, and I didn't resent it. Though I wanted Ann, I felt no claim to her.

Ann sometimes said, "Henry would enjoy making love with you."

"I love Henry," I said. "I want you."

"We can't always have what we want," she said, the platitude of motherhood in her voice.

"No, but there's more than one alternative," I said.

"Meaning?" she asked, studying me.

"There's going without."

Ann mistrusted my chastity nearly as much as my desire for her. She talked always as if we were dealing with my feelings. Her own were outside the range of discussion. She could transmit them only if they weren't named.

"She doesn't look sick, does she?" Ann asked, looking at Carol.

"No, but I think she is. It isn't that she has trouble sleeping, she simply doesn't sleep."

Ann took her to the doctor who diagnosed infant insomnia and gave Ann sleeping medicine for her to be used just long enough to break the pattern. We put it in her milk that evening. She sat in her high chair drinking it, and then she put the bottle down and her small head dropped to her chest. Neither of us moved nor spoke for a moment. Then Ann picked her unconscious child up and took her to bed. When she came back to the kitchen, she was crying. I held her, stroking her hair, saying into its fragrance, "It's all right. It's all right," as I did to Carol in the night.

I spent some of my last few days with my grandparents, trying not to grudge the time to them. Grandfather was delighted with the trip ahead of me. He wanted me to model the clothes I was taking and had no more sense than Mother Packer did of how inappropriately lavish my wardrobe was. It took up four suitcases, and I also had with me a small portable typewriter, the only item of my own choosing. Mother Packer had asked the advice of her friends still travelling, as she had done in the years before she was an invalid, on the cost of the trip as well as what I needed to take with me.

Though I had pointed out that students travelling third class would not really be expected to dress every night for dinner on board ship, I had to take one evening gown against the three listed. I had a wide-brimmed, navy, straw picture hat, an argument I'd lost against the likelihood of my being invited to a garden party at the palace. I had two other hats for church services, to which I did not expect to go. No one suggested the mix and match travelling became for everyone only after plane travel overtook ocean liners as a way to cross the ocean. I had to have navy, brown, black and white shoes, heels and flats. I had to have theatre clothes and school clothes, city clothes and country clothes. There were handbags and gloves to match, three different coats.

There was no one my own age to ask advice. European travel, stopped during the war, was still in 1950 a doubtful enterprise, rationing still on in England, reservations uncertain, much of what people had gone to see in ruins. I was the only one I knew going to Europe that summer.

"If you meet the old queen," Granny said, "be sure to say you're Hugh Rodman's great-niece. He was a favourite of hers."

Grandfather gave me Uncle Hugh's silver flask filled with whiskey as an antidote to seasickness.

Ann and the children were on the dock to see me off on the *Queen Mary*. There was a band playing. I boarded the ship, found my way out on deck and could just make out Ann's face in the crowd. It was only at that moment that the folly of the summer overtook me. I had no desire to go to Europe at all. But the ship's whistle sounded. The tugs bullied that cumbrously large ship out on the river, and I was on my way.

Down in the cabin, I discovered three unhappy cabin mates, climbing around my mountain of luggage, on top of which was an enormous basket of fruit. The card was signed, "Sandy." So my darling, romantic grandfather had made his contribution to my embarrassment.

Jane Rule aboard the *Queen Mary* (en route to London, England)
Jane Rule Fonds, University Archives, University of British Columbia

I had to ask my cabin mates' patience while I sorted out my clothes as quickly as I could in order to get the steward to check three of my four bags. Sharing the fruit with them did improve their tempers, but I was tagged the first-class traveller in steerage.

Whenever I hear stories about brash American travellers, I can match them with errors of my own that summer, those suitcases more often than not playing some part in the drama. I would have been better advised to dump them overboard that first day.

After I recovered from the drowsiness of my first unnecessary pill against seasickness, I began like any normally adventuresome nineteen-year-old to enjoy myself. I was younger than most of my travelling companions. My cabin mates were teachers in their late twenties and early thirties, either desperately or resignedly single. The cabin across the hall was crammed with students from Notre Dame, lecherous but Catholic. One of them, tall enough to be as crippled as I was by the restricting short bunks, limped to breakfast with us every morning, challenged me to martini-drinking contests every evening and fortunately passed out before I was seriously threatened.

Barbara Carson was the only woman I knew who drank to get drunk habitually, but nearly every male I met drank himself unconscious at every opportunity. I was a show-off drinker who also welcomed the silly indifference which could come over me, muting fear or active boredom.

The novelty of ocean travel soon became regimentation. I was very grateful to disembark at Southampton, escaping the small quarters of the cabin, the repeating faces of my shipboard companions.

England from the train window was a miniature country, small houses, small gardens, small cars and lawns. Then suddenly, as we crossed the Thames, the London skyline was more impressive to me than New York's had ever been, the flat image the Houses of Parliament had been, there in three-dimensional stone. The station itself was huge, and I did not feel a Gulliver among the crowds of people.

Before I reached the English-Speaking Union, central and sedate, where I was to spend ten days, I passed a theatre advertising a play by Christopher Fry, starring Laurence Olivier. I went to it that evening for the price of an American movie, the ground still swelling under me from my six days at sea.

The following morning, I had a letter from my mother, telling me that Grandfather Rule had died suddenly of a heart attack the day I sailed. I was shocked to be so far away from everyone in my family, but I particularly wished I could be with my father. I knew for him my relationship with Grandfather Rule eased the half guilt he felt at his own impatient judgments of his father. I wanted to be with him on the trip down to Kentucky where Grandfather would be buried. But there was no question of my going back now. It was too late. I spent the morning writing to my father and to Granny.

In the afternoon, I went to Madame Tussaud's. It was an unfortunate choice. Wandering among those wax effigies, I had an overwhelming sense of the futility of all that vanity, kings and queens in their paste crowns and tacky robes, statesmen and actresses in melodramatic poses. I passed Sleeping Beauty, a sign stuck to her glass box reading "Out of Order." Her breathing apparatus was broken. Down in the Chamber of Horrors, one famous murderer wore a sign which read, "Dressed in his own clothes." Often that phrase has come back to me when I've been unhappily involved in some public event. "Dressed in her own clothes," I think. The murderers were arranged together in groups like juries, and dangling nearby were men hanging by their heads from ropes, by their eye sockets from hooks. All the people on the bus I took back to the English-Speaking Union looked like wax figures. I kept finding reasons to move, to keep from letting myself turn to wax.

That sense of the unreality of people stayed with me all the time I was in London. In the theatre, only the actors were real. I felt like a character in one of Charles Addams's cartoons of audiences, the one living person in a crowd of wax dummies. When I walked through the great parks, passing people sitting on benches, in deck chairs, lying on the grass, I willed them to move, to prove they were real and alive.

I would have been lonely anyway, I'm sure, but Grandfather's death made me more vulnerable to all that was surreal: a bombed building with only one remaining room, curtains at the window, a jar with flowers on the sill; a bomb crater lush with blooming bushes; the apparition of the palace guards galloping in formation down a city street.

At the Tower of London where the real crown jewels were kept, I was almost arrested for trying to take pictures of them and then I was ushered from dungeon to dungeon, all history, gore and death. At St. Paul's, I tried to imagine John Donne alive, reciting those incredibly long and cadenced sentences with tears streaming down his face, but his St. Paul's had burned down and been replaced. What was vivid was the crypt with its load of famous bones.

I needed to get away from so much death. I took a day tour to Canterbury, stopping along the way at castles in various states of decay. When we arrived at Canterbury, a service was just beginning, attended by hundreds of men—Rotarians? I stood outside the cathedral as they sang the first hymn and saw stone come alive with sound, deep and abiding.

My last day in London, a Sunday, I decided to attend a service at Westminster Abbey, understanding now that the only way to avoid a sense of these great cathedrals as nothing more than giant mausoleums was to participate in the living ritual. I dressed in a navy-blue suit and wore my navy picture hat. I arrived only a few minutes before the service was to begin and was dismayed at the size of the crowd, seats available only in the back rows of the outer chamber where nothing but the processions could be seen.

An usher hurried over to me and said, "Come this way." I followed him up the aisle right into the choir stalls originally used by monks, now the choicest seats for the congregation. One area was closed off by a red-velvet rope. He opened it and gestured me in. I couldn't think why he was giving me such a grand place to sit, but I was delighted. Then from the other side of the church came Eleanor Roosevelt and other members of her family. They were directed to my section. I could see people opposite us, naming each of the Roosevelts until they came to me. Had a granddaughter been expected and I mistaken for her? I did feel oddly at home, for the Roosevelts are tall, and we sang with American accents together.

When I told my mother, a staunch Republican, that I had
been mistaken for a Roosevelt, she said, "Nonsense! You don't
look anything like the Roosevelts."

Though moving again with all my luggage was a daunting
thought, I was glad to be leaving the solitude of London for a
place where I could surely make friends. I studied the faces of
other passengers on the small train which took us from Leamington Spa to Stratford. One in particular attracted me, a woman
in her early thirties, my height, with a face given to laughter, the
warmth of it in her eyes, in the dimples in her cheeks, in the tilt
of her nose; yet it was a strong face, too, the brows dark and
heavy, rather dwarfing her small, pretty companion. I wondered
if they were lovers.

I was the only one to wait for a porter when we arrived. All
the other passengers could carry their luggage. When the porter
and I arrived at the road, they were all standing, as if in line.
Fresh from having learned to get myself a cab in New York, I
told the porter to take my bags a hundred yards or so down the
road, and I signalled the next cab with a ten-shilling note. It
made a U-turn and picked me up.

I had been at Bishopton Lodge a full half hour before others
from the same train arrived, among them the two women I had
noticed. Their room was right across the hall from the one I
would be sharing with another American student. They nodded
rather coolly, and I made a note to teach them how to catch a cab
before the summer was over.

Again my luggage was an embarrassment. Even when I'd
packed away over half the clothes I had brought, there wasn't
room in the curtained corner of the room which served as the only
closet, nor in the bureau drawers. Mine was the only typewriter,
but, since I was willing to lend it, it wasn't held against me.

There were nineteen of us at the lodge, which was a large
family house converted into a lodge when the children had
grown up and gone. Mrs. Lucas, with the help of one maid, ran
it remarkably well. Very soon it was clear to all of us that, though
we were a mile out of town, our circumstance was far superior
to the accommodations in hotels and boarding houses in the
centre of Stratford.

Nearly half of the 150 students were American. The rest came from all over the world. At the lodge, we had a couple from Israel, an Egyptian, a man from China, a Canadian, the two Englishwomen across the hall and the rest of us were American. I was the youngest, but most of the Americans were only two or three years older than I was. The other students were older, in their thirties and forties, resuming studies after the interruption of war.

For the first few days, we were all busy attending general lectures, signing up for seminars and tutorials, finding our way around the library and picking up our theatre tickets. At meals, we exchanged practical information, and the Americans, having made easy acquaintance with each other, began the more difficult business of getting to know "the foreigners," who included the two Englishwomen.

To aid sociability in the evening, Mrs. Lucas sold us quart bottles of cider, and I suggested we set up a cider kitty rather than try to keep separate bottles. The Americans agreed readily enough, but it was a week before the others were persuaded it was a good idea. None of the Americans realized that the cider was alcoholic. That we sang our way to bed every night seemed only one more evidence of our good fortune to be among warm friends in a welcoming place.

As we settled to our academic schedule, the conversation at meals shifted into discussions of lectures, plans for papers and, most interesting of all, analyses of the productions of the plays we were seeing. John Gielgud and Peggy Ashcroft were the leads that summer, playing in *Lear*, *Measure for Measure*, *Much Ado about Nothing*.

I had never before been with a group of people as interested in their work as I was. I was adequately prepared as some of the other Americans, but most of my fellow students also became my teachers, and I challenged them as happily as I had Dr. Pope, arguing about interpretations of character, accuracy of texts, meanings of images.

When we went to the theatre, we not only saw brilliant performances of those great plays but afterward raced to the pub (it was named the White Swan but called the Dirty Duck) where we hurriedly bought all the beer we could and lined mugs up on the wooden tables on the terrace overlooking the river. There we could sit, joined by the actors, and drink and argue for hours after the pub had closed, helping ourselves to beer and tossing our money on the table to be retrieved by those who'd originally bought it.

For all the bright worlds I had come to know did not exist, no one had ever told me about this one. Not having anticipated it, not having imagined it in any way, I felt for the first time in my life at home, sure of work and welcome.

After we had been at Bishopton Lodge for several days, I found myself alone one afternoon in the lounge with Roussel, the Englishwoman I had admired on the train. She had been cool enough for me to feel a little shy of her, but I made some effort to be friendly.

"How old are you?" she asked me suddenly.

"Nineteen," I said.

She burst out laughing.

"What's funny about that?" I demanded.

"You're not an officious, arrogant American. You're just a baby."

So it was Roussel who taught me how to catch a cab in England, patiently waiting my turn in queue, Roussel who explained that we were mildly drunk every night on cider. Roussel also taught me that the toast was supposed to be cold in the morning, that cigarettes were too expensive to offer round without incurring debt, that lecturers were not to be casually asked for a drink, only formally invited to dinner. As she and her friend Sheena got fond of us in spite of themselves, they tried to educate us in civilized behaviour, complaining that they were so outnumbered they were beginning to be corrupted by American slang and indecent friendliness.

I caught a heavy cold shortly after I arrived, ignored it until I finally had to give in and spend a day in bed. When I didn't turn up for breakfast, Roussel presented herself with a cup of tea, which I was too touched by to refuse, though a Coke would have been much more welcome.

"Dewey thinks you've been a brick about being sick," she said. "He's very fond of you, you know."

Dewey was a tall, thin, pale American, brotherly I might have called him if I'd had a different sort of brother. There was really no pressure to pair off. Everything we did involved large groups of us. But on bus tours, which we took nearly every weekend, the Israeli couple always sat together as did Roussel and Sheena, and gradually I found I was sitting with Dewey. If he queued for extra tickets to the theatre, he got me one. If I was late to the pub, he saved me a beer. And one day he suggested we go to Oxford for the day.

We both had dreams of going to Oxford, mine only half serious because I really wanted to be a writer rather than a scholar, but the summer had intoxicated me with the joy scholarship could be. We spent the day wandering from college to college, buying dozens of books, and we argued most of the way home, about what I can't remember. We were both probably exhausted, and we had theatre tickets that night. One of us slept through half the performance. It's odd after years to think that what separated us at the time seems now an interchangeable experience.

Perhaps I had discovered that Roussel and Sheena were staying only three of the six weeks. Once I knew how little time I had, I wanted to spend it all with Roussel. I sat next to her at lectures, at meals, at the theatre. I sat behind her on buses. I waited for her to bike into town in the morning, to go home in the afternoon. Sheena made no objection, but quite often she either declined to join us on an evening walk or had other friends to see.

"You mustn't hurt Dewey's feelings," Roussel said.

"Oh, Dewey, I can see Dewey when you aren't here."

"He may have other ideas by then."

Would all women I found attractive insist on giving me up to men?

We were walking along a country road in the late, still-light evening. A black kitten had begun to follow us. Roussel knew we should discourage it, but its company amused her.

"Let's stop for a cigarette, and then we can walk it back," I suggested.

"Your idea of a walk is to go to the nearest tree and smoke."

We sat down under a tree, and the kitten climbed into Roussel's lap. I watched her play with it while we smoked, listening to the breakings in her voice, the laughter there in it. I reached over, took the kitten and set it down behind me. Then I kissed Roussel and said, "I love you."

"No, you don't," she said, startled.

"Yes, I do."

"You only think you do."

I kissed her again and felt her respond.

"We have to go back," she said. "Now."

The kitten followed us to its own gate, and we shooed it in.

At the lodge, Dewey was in the hall. Roussel said good night and went to her room. As I started after her, Dewey took my arm.

"Are you trying to avoid me?"

"No," I said.

"I thought we were making friends."

"We are," I said, feeling guilty as well as irritated.

"Then come have a drink."

There was no one else in the lounge. Most of the lights had been turned out for the night. We sat talking, then kissing. If Dewey had wanted to make love to me that night, I would have let him, and he knew it, but he didn't know why. He stopped abruptly and said, "Nice girls don't go any further than this." I laughed. He got up angrily and went to bed. I sat up, smoking.

Roussel had only one more day before she and Sheena left Stratford.

"Do you have any weekends free before you leave?" she asked. "Would you like to come to Horsham and meet my parents?"

The following weekend, I had agreed to go to Paris with Ann and Bobbie, two other American students. Easier to cancel was a tour the school had sponsored two weekends away.

"Maybe we could have breakfast in London on your way back from Paris," Roussel suggested.

But we finally arranged for a cab in Stratford to take us to the airport and meet us when we got back so that we would miss no lectures. I dropped Roussel a note, asking for a rain check for breakfast.

When I got back from that silly and exhausting trip, there was a note from Roussel which began, "Horrid, horrid child! What is a 'rain check' for breakfast? For all I know it's an American brand of cornflakes."

My more-immediate problem was finishing a paper on the imagery in *Macbeth* so that I could, in relatively good conscience, meet Roussel the following Friday in London and go down to Horsham with her.

Hurrying with a suitcase overloaded with Paris purchases of champagne and perfume, I climbed the high bridge over the railroad tracks at the Stratford station, caught a heel on the first step down and fell all the way to the platform. My suitcase broke open, scattering its contents. A young railroad worker, so handsome as to seem not quite real, came up off the tracks to help me. When he decided that I had broken no bones, he shyly gathered up my belongings, the bottles miraculously unbroken, and helped me into the waiting train. The conductor, having seen the accident, helped me change trains and got me a strong cup of tea, that English universal remedy. It didn't mend my stockings or heal my bruised knees, but it did quiet my alarm at so brazenly symbolic a fall.

I was as frightened as I was excited by the meeting I was going to, I was afraid of my inexperience. I was even more afraid that Roussel might have moral scruples which would leave me inexperienced. Yet even more important than those fears was the thought of simply being with Roussel again.

She was there on the platform to meet me, immediately concerned with the state of my knees, telling me I shouldn't have tried to make the journey after such a fall. I felt silly, heroic, lightheaded.

"But I'm fine. I've had a cup of tea."

How I loved to bring amusement into that voice, into that face made for laughter. It seemed incredible to me to be crossing London, city of my mourning solitude so few weeks before, with a woman I loved who lived there.

Her bed-sitter, five flights up, was quite near Victoria Station, and we stopped there briefly, time enough for her to collect her things, for me to see where and how she lived, before we caught the train to Horsham. Everything in the room interested me, from the books to the teacups, from the narrow bed to the view out the window. For I would be leaving her here in my imagination.

"Have you got a book?" she asked as we passed the bookstall in the station.

"Book?"

"For the train."

"I don't need a book," I said.

I had a lifetime of things to say to Roussel with no idea that she had a shorter-than-eternal attention span. When I was with her, the countryside was a background blur for her face. Nothing distracted me. My attention touched, amused and tired her by turns, neither as naturally sociable as I was nor as intense.

"Hush," she would sometimes say. "Hush."

I was surprised by her parents' house, a bungalow with French doors opening from the living room out into a large garden. It was the kind of house I might expect to find in California.

Both her parents were tall. Though Roussel looked more like her mother than her father, the strength of her brows and the vigour of her hair came from him. Mrs. Sargeant was a pretty woman, a face either wistful or merry. Roussel's had more authority and variety, as did her voice.

I was shown into the guest room right off the dining room, a wall away from her parents' room. Roussel's room had been added on to the house beyond the living room, one wall all windows looking out onto an apple tree, the long wall entirely books.

We sat there for a while after her parents had gone to bed until Roussel suggested I'd talked one ear off her and might save the other for another day.

"I'll say good night when you're ready for bed," she said.

When she did, she came into my arms, and we made love very quietly, very gently until nearly morning when she left me to sleep.

Roussel had made plans for the two days I was there. I met relatives. We took a bus to another town to have tea with Sheena. I by then knew Sheena had not been Roussel's lover. The only lover she had was a Canadian during the war, to whom she'd been engaged for a while. I sleepwalked through it all except in any moment we had alone together. I was used to managing on very little sleep but not from nights given to such astonishing pleasure.

Was it a bank holiday? Is that why we couldn't find a cab at Victoria Station, then split up and caught separate cabs, only to discover I'd missed my train anyway? We had a final night in Roussel's London room. I woke to find her dressed and preparing breakfast.

"Do you know you even talk in your sleep?" she asked.

Why did I have to go back to Stratford? Why was I booked for a week in Edinburgh for the festival before I sailed from Liverpool? I didn't know how to make a radical change in plans, and Roussel didn't encourage it. I took a train back to Stratford on Monday morning and was greeted so warmly by everyone in the household that I felt guilty at how little I any longer wanted to be there.

Certainly, if I had to be anywhere separated from Roussel, it was the right place to be. Dewey had resigned himself to friendliness. Frank, a brash young scholar from Brooklyn, was proposing to each woman in turn, saying, if he couldn't live with all of us for the rest of his life, at least he should be allowed one. Everyone was exchanging addresses, making plans to meet again somehow.

SEVERAL OTHER OF THE BISHOPTON BEAGLES, which we had been christened, were also going to Edinburgh, fortunately among them a strong and amiable young man, for I had added to my five suitcases and typewriter a small oak table made from the beam of an old mill which looked very like tables already in my parents' living room.

Roussel and Sheena came to Stratford for a last day to say goodbye to everyone. I tried not to resent the presence of eighteen other people I'd come to like well. Roussel and I had no more than five minutes alone in the clutter of my half-packed belongings and presents for my family. I had spent the crowded day memorizing the expressions on her face, the gestures of her hands with their long, elegant fingers, the tones of her voice, its breakings. For five minutes, I simply held her in my arms, unable to believe I could cross an ocean and a continent without her.

By the time I left for Edinburgh, I had another heavy cold, and the trip made it worse. When the train finally drew into the station late at night, I looked out the window with feverish eyes and saw what I thought was a giant billboard. It was Edinburgh Castle, illuminated.

I signed in at a small guest house, where a number of other Rules had registered in the past few months. In a city that felt much more foreign to me than London, I was near the lowland source of my family name. As I unpacked what clothes I intended for use, I discovered that I'd left all my tickets in my bureau drawer at Bishopton Lodge. I was advised to phone in the morning to get Mrs. Lucas to find them and read me the row and seat numbers from the tickets for the first few performances before she sent them on to me. I was allowed, with that information, to attend concerts and plays without a ticket.

Nearly every day a letter arrived from Roussel, and I scribbled notes to her late at night against a rising fever. I could have been seriously ill if I hadn't met Ginny Gilbert, a class and hall mate from college, wandering along a city street. She had been given penicillin and other useful drugs by her doctor against the chance of illness. She had planned to be in Edinburgh another week, but she had just had news that her mother was seriously ill with polio and was going back home at once. She gave me enough pills to take care of the secondary infections.

Her early return made me think not simply of my grandfather's death but of my grandmother who would meet the ship in New York. She'd probably find me a chore rather than a help; yet I'd always felt closer to her, more really known, though not so flatteringly, than by my fantasy-inventing grandfather. I was really too ill to take in much of what I was seeing. I was heartsick for Roussel and homesick for my family.

I left Edinburgh in the rain that had fallen for the ten days I'd been there on a night train to Liverpool, lay on a narrow bunk and coughed all night.

There was a letter from Roussel waiting for me on board the ship. I was in a cabin for ten days on the *Georgia*, a one-class ship which was grossly overcrowded because her sister ship had run aground, and we had to take a share of her passengers. Among our ten was one nun. In the cabin next door were nine nuns and one college student. We effected a swap for everyone's greater comfort.

The next day, off Ireland, more passengers were boarded from launches, and flowers came aboard, roses for me from Roussel. I no longer needed a grandfather to make romantic gestures, but, when a cabin mate asked who they were from, I hesitated before I said simply, "Someone I met in England."

It was an uncomfortable crossing without seats enough in the dining room, lounges or on deck. I was in no mood to meet new people, but it was hard to find a quiet corner for reading or writing. We were wakened every morning with the PA system blaring "Beyond the Blue Horizon," and similarly were ordered from meal to activity to meal like will-less robots. Then there was a storm, and I discovered I was among the few good sailors aboard. We were not allowed on deck, but I had a fine view from the forward lounge. The rhythmic power of enormous grey waves breaking over the bow of the ship, the pressure of the wind released me from my stupor of grieving into a sense of wonder at the power of my own feelings, to be young and alive and in love on that wild sea.

The storm delayed us nearly two days, and, by the time that voyage was over, even I had joined the bridge players and camp-song singers and game players to pass the last dull and crowded hours. As a result of that incarcerating experience, I was better able to entertain my sisters' friends and other children for years afterward.

It was 100 degrees on the deck in New York, the humidity nearly visible. I was nearly four hours in customs, and I was among the lucky first few. Ann was there instead of my grand-mother, who had elected to wait at a hotel with the car to drive me back to Westfield.

I was shocked to see Granny Rule arrayed in black. Mother Packer had not observed such mourning for the Colonel.

"It's a great comfort to me to have you here," she said as we drove out of the city. "You were your grandfather's favourite. I sometimes had to remind him that he had thirteen other grand-children."

The words were familiar enough, but the tone was completely different. What had created a tension between us while he was alive became a bond between us now that he was dead.

Through the few days I intended to stay, she spoke at length about her husband. She was aware that everyone in the family was all too familiar with his shortcomings, with the difficulties of their relationship. She believed that I, because I had been close to him, would understand her own love for him. It wasn't so much that she had restricted his dreams as that he had counted on her practicality to distinguish between the good and bad ones. If he was generous to a fault with his brothers, it was a good quality in a man to be loyal to his own.

She had taken over the running of his real estate business and was in the middle of a dispute about sewers and town lines. After one long phone call, she looked at me and grinned.

"I let them treat me like a poor widow as long as it serves my purposes, but I've always dealt with these problems. Your grandfather neither knew nor cared about sewers or town lines."

When I suggested I might come back for an extra week after a brief visit with Ann and Henry, she was delighted. My parents were disappointed that I'd have only a few days at home before going back to college, but under the circumstances they thought it was the right choice.

Ann brought the children to pick me up. Granny reached out for baby Susan. It was very rare that a baby wasn't at home on her ample lap, entertained by that strong string of beads she wore round her neck. The children, by now both my goddaughters, seemed so nearly my own flesh that Granny's welcome of them and delight in them was a gift to me.

I told Ann at length about Dewey, briefly about Roussel. Her eyebrows arched. Then she said, "I have no right to be jealous, I suppose."

"You haven't any reason to be," I said, and I meant it. My love for Ann was absolute. No one would ever be a challenge to it.

"Does she know about me?"

"Of course," I said.

It hadn't been difficult for me to talk with Roussel about Ann. It had reassured her that she was not my first lover. It was not difficult for me to talk to Roussel about anything because, though she teased me about how young I was, she didn't feel the same responsibility that Ann did, nor did she have ambitions for me, which Ann did.

I was newly restless with Ann's questioning. I knew she would think I should have chosen to spend time with Dewey, to get on with my heterosexual initiation. She had a Freudian rather than religious interpretation for my fall, for she was far more interested in my conditioning than in my morality. Yet she influenced my moral view without ever convincing me that heterosexuality was my only choice. From Ann I had learned how to love without being possessive, how to accept and rejoice in her love for husband and children. From Ann I had also learned that sexual fidelity did not necessarily mean what it did to my parents. It was possible for her to love me without threatening Henry. It was possible for me, therefore, to love Ann and Roussel without threatening either of them.

I had given up making any sexual demands of Ann, though my own desire was stronger, less inhibited by inexperience. It was, for the same reason, easier to live in its tension. The summer had given me a new sense of my own attractiveness, and I had discovered a world in which I felt at home.

I went back for a final week with Granny, newly related to her. I was no longer a troublesome adolescent but a young adult with whom she could really talk.

As I handed out lavish presents to my parents and sister (not including the oak table which I had shipped ahead from New York), I debated about whether or not to confess that, try as I could, with these purchases, with a weekend in Paris, ten days in Edinburgh, half a ton of books mailed directly to college, I had been able to spend no more than half the money Mother Packer had given me.

I decided instead to wait until I saw her. I had found her a beautifully woven shawl in Stratford which I gave to her when Dad took me to see her on my way back to college. I didn't have the opportunity then to speak to her alone. So, when I got back to college, I wrote her a long letter, telling her how much the summer had meant to me, how much I had learned, how many beloved friends I had made. I told her I wanted to go back the following summer, either to Oxford or the University of London. Then I confessed I'd spent only half the money and offered to return it. I didn't put much hope in her reply.

Did something of what I told her stir her own memories of Europe? Was she amused at my frugality? Did she like the fact that I had asked directly without first consulting my parents? For whatever reasons, she phoned and said, "Yes, you may."

The letters between Roussel and me, retelling each moment of our weeks together, changed from those elegiac tones at once to impatient planning. Though I really did this time want to go to Oxford or the University of London, love of not one but two women had turned me into a traveller.

Meanwhile Dr. Pope wanted to relive every lecture, play, concert, side trip with me. She quizzed me on details of performances I didn't know I had remembered until I needed to for her. As she had prepared me, she now taught me to fix that experience in my memory for future use.

I was sharing a sleeping porch with Sally Millett, who had elected to stay behind on junior corridor with me. Marty and Edy and the others moved on to senior corridor.

Though I had made up the credits I'd lost to illness the first semester the year before, I had decided, with the encouragement of the college doctor as well as Dr. Pope, not to try to graduate with the class of 1951 but to give myself the time I needed to work in more depth on fewer courses.

The world of Mills seemed smaller than it had the year before. I suppose I was also feeling spoiled and lucky. I saw a request for volunteer swimming instructors at the Y for handicapped children. One afternoon a week, for a couple of hours, I helped students from the handicapped wing of a local public school. For most of them, it wasn't a question of actually learning to swim. They were too badly spastic or too much paralyzed to be entirely independent in the water, but some of them gained a physical independence there that was greater than any they had sandbagged into their wheelchairs. It was physically tiring work, lifting sometimes quite heavy teenagers in and out of the warm pool water. I slept better on those nights than I had in a long time. I was as glad to find that I was not squeamish before their sometimes-grotesque deformities as I was to find I didn't get seasick. I suppose the suffering I went through from nameless anxieties had made me fearful of my competence before any test, markedly grateful to pass any of them. Once, while we were dressing the students after their swim, two daring twelve-year-old normal girls braved the dressing rooms to be first into the pool. I had to take them out in hysterics. Though I hated what their screaming did to my handicapped students, my instinct was to comfort rather than scold them. Fear is so often the source of cruelty.

I signed up for the speakers' bureau as well and was sent out to high schools, church groups, garden clubs to talk about the college, give book reviews. I always came back refreshed from contact with people not my own age.

I realized that it was not only our shared interested in Shakespeare that had made the group at Bishopton Lodge so congenial but our mixture of ages and nationalities. Only Dewey and I had temporarily snagged on conventional expectations. At college I was increasingly aware of them.

The seniors became a more cohesive group with the pressure of comprehensive exams ahead of them and beyond those the matter of what to do with the rest of their lives. Again I was involved in engagement parties, wedding plans, but I was not as detached as I had been my first term on senior corridor.

Sally who always refused group pressure nevertheless rebelled in angrier, less interesting, more predictable ways. She had enough units to declare herself either a history or psychology major and refused to make up her mind. Instead of focussing on one discipline, she neglected two and enjoyed gathering faculties' predictions that she would flunk either exam she took. She kept several young men busy courting her, claiming no one of them could afford her thirst. She was drinking heavily, and drunk she was surly.

Because of her taunts at my lack of social life, I did go to one or two of the hall's open houses and met Neils, a medical student, who phoned again suggesting not the usual frat party but dinner and the theatre in San Francisco. I accepted.

His intelligence and the wide range of his interests and talents attracted me. He played the violin, rode horseback, hunted. He was well read in several languages. His hard, disciplined body attracted me not at all, but, since he didn't press his sexual interest, I agreed to go out again, this time to the symphony and then a late supper.

I had been out with him half a dozen times before I realized I really didn't like him. He was entirely without humour. Everything he did was for his improvement. He never simply had fun. And he didn't know how to converse. He lectured on subjects that interested him, at least one of which was my improvement. A woman should be intelligent, healthy, tall in order to breed sons who would be princes. Neils lived at International House in Berkeley and made friends with exiled royalty from around the world.

I refused the next date. He waited two weeks and then called again, making so open an offer that I had no excuse to refuse but to say I didn't want to see him. He had, after all, been generous and thoughtful, and it seemed somehow too unkind to be that blunt: so I reluctantly accepted. This time, for the first time at the end of the evening, we parked. Instead of simply proceeding, Neils first laid out his plans for me: to be his mistress until he could afford to marry me. His intentions were honourable, his needs immediate, and I would be healthier, less neurotic with a good sex life. When I declined, he opened the glove compartment of his car and took out a pistol. I was overcome by an anger that left no room for fear. When I spoke to him, my voice was rich with stinging scorn. He put the gun away and drove me home.

Though later I was surprised by my lack of fear, it probably saved me from rape at gunpoint. Unfortunately, my anger excited his admiration. He wrote me long letters in green ink (I've never been able to stand the sight of green ink since), explaining that it had been a test which I had passed admirably. I had courage in the face of danger, etc., etc. Nothing induced me to see him again. Then came the postcards with theatre stubs stapled to them and messages like, "These are for your scrapbook, foul friend." He started dating another English major and pumped her for information about me. He went out drinking with my brother and developed a theory that we were incestuously involved. Neils could save me from an unnatural closeness with my family.

I felt unduly punished for my brief involvement with him; yet I felt guilty, too, thinking that, if I had been a normal woman, perhaps I would have found his forcefulness, his obsessiveness attractive. But surely the choice between being neurotic and spending the rest of my life with such a maniac was no choice at all.

I retreated into work, which has never been a safe haven for me in times of stress. The overcharge of excitement gave me insomnia, and the symptoms of anxiety began to return.

This time the doctor had a new solution. There was now a pill for the "fight or flight" syndrome. Then it was called Benzedrine, mixed with one or another of the sedatives. It was years before it was popularly named "speed." It worked. Oh, it left a nasty taste in my mouth, took away my appetite and my hands shook, but I could keep going during the day and sleep at night. I didn't take it routinely, but it was there when I needed it.

I was aware intermittently of my father's difficulties. The family who owned his business now that it was really thriving managed to oust him and return the profits to themselves. While Mother, with Libby, stayed on in Reno trying to sell the house they had built, he found work in Sacramento and gave Arthur a job there, too, all attempts at his schooling having failed. What Dad really wanted was to own a business. Mother Packer, too ill to go anywhere, was persuaded to sell South Fork to raise the necessary capital without interfering with her own income.

I, who had been away in England all summer and planned to be there the next, could make no counterclaim, and anyway my father's need was more important than my childhood love of the place. I didn't go to shut it up. I wanted it whole in my memory, as if it were still there, but the falling of thousand-year-old trees invaded my dreams and my prose for some years.

Now that Donald Weeks was gone, writers were invited to teach. Jessamyn West came that year, a woman of great energy and warmth, who gave us some insight into the practical business of being a writer, showing us editor's comments on her *New Yorker* galleys, talking about contracts and agents. Though each of us did dream of publishing work some day, we were more concerned with writing great works than in the rather soiling aspects of the marketplace. Surrounded with the attitudes academics had for writers who published in popular magazines, we were suspicious of Jessamyn's ability to instruct us in our rather higher calling. But we were polite, even friendly. I enjoyed celebrating with her when she sold her first poems to the *Ladies' Home Journal*. She went to the college shop and bought a magnificently silly sun hat and a new bathing suit.

Jessamyn was furious with me when I dropped her course second term. The swimming lessons had ended, but my interest in the students had drawn me to their school. I had volunteered to work in the classroom two afternoons a week, one of which conflicted with my writing class.

"You can't be a writer and a do-gooder, you know," she said. "You have to dedicate yourself to it; without that, no matter how great your talent, you're finished."

"I just don't seem to have much to say," I said and meant it.

I had plenty to say about Milton, the Old Testament, nineteenth-century novels, but about myself, outside of love letters, I had nothing to say, and I increasingly mistrusted my sense of what experience meant to other people.

I spent less time in the dorm. I sat with English majors or philosophy majors at the shop, talked ideas, systems of values, or I spent evenings with Dr. Pope and sometimes other members of the faculty. Ellen and I often worked together on papers, and I talked with her, too, about how much the summer had meant to me.

"I'd love to go," she said.

"Well, why don't you?"

"I don't suppose Mother would let me."

But Ellen's mother, hearing that I was going, too, was unexpectedly enthusiastic.

I tried to be unreservedly pleased. When I wrote to Roussel, I presented Ellen's being there, too, as an added delight. We'd by then agreed on the University of London, partly out of an appetite for more exposure to contemporary literature, partly for the availability of London, but also it meant I could see Roussel more often. She responded cheerfully enough but added that she intended to be demanding.

Roussel sent me more and more information about the Festival of Britain. We must plan weekends not only at Stratford but at Oxford, Cambridge, Canterbury. Everywhere there were to be remarkable plays, exhibits, lectures.

"They're going to perform *Samson Agonistes* at Oxford," I said to Dr. Pope. "It can't have been performed more than half a dozen times."

"It wasn't really written to be performed," she said, rather flatly, but her interest lifted again when I told her Lord David Cecil was going to lecture at Oxford, Dorothy Sayers at Canterbury.

I walked down the hill that late evening, hearing again the brief flatness in her voice. Surely being a Milton scholar, she should be interested, even if it was something of an oddity. Then it occurred to me, breaking through the egotism of my nineteen years, that she had simply had to stifle a moment of envy. So often the summer before I had thought and written to her that she and not I should be having the opportunity to see what I was seeing, would bring so much more to it, share it so well in her teaching.

Why shouldn't she go? If I went with her to deal with the physical difficulties of travel there was no reason why she shouldn't. I knew her well enough to understand her physical limitations, and I knew England well enough to manage it. I couldn't take a course, but that didn't matter. I'd get much more simply travelling around with her.

I turned and went back up the hill. She was sitting with a book in her lap, smoking a cigarette.

"Look," I said. "Come, too."

"I couldn't, Jinx," she began.

"Why not?"

The plan that had begun to form in my head grew as I talked.

"It's a much more expensive trip for you, travelling around, staying in hotels."

"I can find cheap ones."

"We'd have to take cabs sometimes instead of buses or the tube."

"No big problem. Cabs aren't that expensive," I suggested.

"Let me sleep on it."

I ran down the hill, nearly late for curfew, elated with the sense that finally I could do something for Dr. Pope, give her a world as rich as the world she'd given me.

Only when I finally got back to the dorm did I suddenly remember Roussel, and, for a stricken moment, I prayed that Dr. Pope would wake to know it was an impossible pipe dream. Why had I been so impulsive? Then I remembered the delight in Dr. Pope's face, the real hope in it. Well, damn it, I thought, we can all work it out somehow.

In the morning, Dr. Pope told me she had phoned her father, a retired banker in Washington, D.C., and he was delighted with the plan. He had set up a trust fund for her which gave her extra money. He suggested that she should pay the difference between what the trip would otherwise cost me, including a first-class flight across the ocean since ship travel would be very difficult for her.

"Well?" she asked.

"Well, wonderful!" I said.

Ellen had to be resigned to going on the course by herself, joining us some weekends, but I promised her we'd have time together later in the summer, perhaps on into the fall to go to the Continent. Ellen had racked up extra credits and could afford to take a semester off. I had only one semester left, which I could complete in the spring. She was generous enough to see how important the trip would be for Dr. Pope.

Writing to Roussel was more difficult. Her reply was downhearted. "Must I share you with all the world, my young Pied Piper?"

Yes, I answered, but it will finally be richer that way for both of us. Love mustn't cut us off but open us. I did believe it, or at least I thought I could will it.

I WROTE TO VARIOUS SMALL HOTELS, explaining that we needed a room up no more than one flight of stairs and near the bathroom. At Stratford, we could stay at Bishopton Lodge because Mrs. Lucas had decided not to take students again.

Evaline Wright, in the drama department, was on a year's leave of absence in Greece. She wrote to Dr. Pope to ask if she could join us for at least some part of our trip. After a year abroad, she'd particularly like some friendly company. I sent her our itinerary, delighted with her suggestion, for it might mean I was somewhat freer to take a day or evening away. Roussel wasn't as optimistic. For her, the summer was turning into a circus.

Mother finally sold the house in Reno and moved to Berkeley because Dad was now working in that area. I was glad to have my family nearby so that I could go home for an occasional meal, sometimes taking friends home with me. Edy was there often. Her own father had died before Edy was born. Her brother and sister were much older; so she grew up alone with her very reclusive mother. She loved the sense of family we had. My parents welcomed her in, and my sister adopted her as a much better older sister than I was. I know that part of Edy's interest in Arthur was the place he gave her among us.

Mother was interested in the work I was doing with the handicapped students, and one day I took her with me. I assisted the teacher who had the older students, fourteen of them from the ages of twelve to twenty-one. Only two were able to walk. They were our runners for baseball games. Most of the students had either cerebral palsy or polio. One was paralyzed from the waist down from a car accident. Because their IQs varied greatly, they couldn't be taught in groups larger than three or four. I taught everything from spelling to typing. Though their progress was very slow, there were moments of achievement that could never have been witnessed in another kind of classroom.

"Don't you sometimes get discouraged for them?" Mother asked me later.

"I suppose so," I said. "But when John first came, because he couldn't talk, we didn't know whether he could read or write. When I strapped his wrists onto the table in front of the typewriter and he typed, 'I can read,' I cried. He cried. We'd found a way to break the sound barrier."

Yes, it was true that I didn't want to be mistaken for a volunteer mother. On my way back to college, when I saw a boy running across the field, the tears that welled were for all those who could never do so simple and beautiful a thing.

Usually I enjoyed spending Easter vacation at college. I could work uninterrupted for hours, but this year, I needed to get away. I suggested to my mother that she join me for a week in Carmel, where we could celebrate our birthdays together. Other Mills students were in the same hotel, and we had drinks with them one evening before dinner, but mostly we kept to ourselves, walked on the beach, went shopping, rested, read and talked. Both of us were good letter writers, and we talked often on the phone; so we weren't out of touch, but we hadn't had such time together since the war.

She talked more frankly about our father than she had before, saying he was too good a man for the business world, both too honest and too trusting, but maybe it would be better when he had his own business. She didn't think Arthur should be working for Dad. Arthur should be learning what a real employer would not put up with. But without any qualifications or experience, he wasn't likely to get a job that interested him. She hoped Libby could stay as healthy as she had become in the high, dry desert air of Nevada. She hoped she could stay detached from Mother Packer once they lived nearer to each other again. My mother was very glad to be back in the Bay Area. She had never liked Reno.

I suppose she worried about me, too, though I'd never been in the habit of confiding in her, offering my good news when I had it and only the brighter colours of my experience. The only negative emotion she handled easily was anger; so I did occasionally report irritations and injustices. My fears and griefs I kept to myself. Yet I felt very close to my mother, sure of the loving bond between us. We were deeply companionable. It is not so necessary to be understood by one's parents as not to be misunderstood.

Occasionally my mother's zeal for our good health did embarrass me. Just before one of my trips to Europe, she read an article about blood transfusions for people who were tired and run down. She suggested to the college doctor that maybe a pint of new blood would set me up for the summer. The doctor explained that we had different blood types and that, in any case, I didn't need it.

I told that among a series of outrageous stories about my mother to entertain people, but I don't think any of my listeners were in doubt that I was as touched as I was embarrassed and amused.

I returned to college rested and reassured. Sally came back from her own adventures very sick. She had pneumonia. While she was in the infirmary, Edy remembered that Sally had for months been making a set penance at the Catholic church and would miss the last one because she was too ill to go. Edy phoned the priest, and he went to the infirmary for that purpose. Sally, seeing him, thought she was about to die and was furious with Edy for frightening her so.

Sally had only about a month to prepare for her exams. Her first week out of the infirmary, she spent with my parents. She was a little less thin and pale when she came back, but she had very little natural energy. She had decided for psychology simply because there was a smaller body of work to get through. She had the texts of all the psychology courses, and she read by the clock, hour after hour on a schedule which would see her done the evening before exams began. Since I was working hard toward my own exams, we were more companionable than we'd been all year.

The night before her exams began, Sally went out with some of the graduate students in the psychology department. She came home late, drunker than I'd ever seen her and was sick the rest of the night. In the morning, I phoned the doctor to say that Sally was too hung over to get out of bed.

"And you call yourself a friend of hers?"

"Look, I didn't do it. I was home studying."

I half-carried Sally to the infirmary, where the doctor gave her a shot. Then the doctor told me to go to the college shop and buy the full pitcher of fresh orange juice and take it into the exam room for Sally.

Sally did get to her exam on time, but, when I looked at her colour, I thought writing it was an exercise in gallant futility. I wondered what it was that drove her so angrily against her own intelligence.

When the exams were graded, Sally's marks were the highest ever achieved by an undergraduate. We were triumphant for her, and she was delighted to have dumbfounded her professors. She matched my doubt at the real purpose of it all with her cynicism. She saw no more purpose in the way I worked, and it took more time.

"But I care about it," I said.

She shrugged.

Sometimes, I complained to Dr. Pope, I'd like to refuse to take exams, which seemed to make so much competitive nonsense out of our learning.

"That's no way to get into graduate school."

My own exams by then were safely over, and the summer was too much upon us for me to worry the bone of principle for long. Soon we would be back among people who cared about learning the way we did.

Dr. Pope went to Washington, D.C., to stay with her father. I went home for a few days. Then, to save money, I took an unscheduled airline across the country. I was stranded in Chicago for twelve hours before I got a plane to Washington, D.C., where Granny was visiting Aunt Pat and Uncle Keg. I was wearing a new navy-blue and red linen dress. The seams of the panelled skirt did not last the trip, and I arrived with it in streamers. While I slept off my exhaustion, Aunt Pat sewed my outfit back together again so that it could withstand the strain of travel.

I had arrived the day the parks were desegregated in Washington, D.C. Granny, busy with handwork, looked over her glasses at me and said, "I suppose you think you've won."

"It's not my side, Granny," I said. "It's the right side."

She turned her attention back to the work in her lap, old matriarch who took responsibility for her black servants, cared for them when they were sick, sent their brightest children on to college, but knew that, in general, they were children, somewhat below par.

Granny and I met Dr. Pope and her father for dinner, and the two old ones got on very well. I was scheduled then to fly to New York to have lunch with Ellen's mother before Ellen and I went to Maine to visit Dr. Diller and his family. Ellen had taken a course in philosophy with him that year, and he had suggested we both stop at their summer place on our way to Europe. Lunch with Ellen's mother didn't bridge the generation gap. She was worried about our lack of definite plans after summer school and Dr. Pope's departure. She wanted us to promise we wouldn't go to Egypt. Ellen and I had enjoyed telling people we thought of bicycling down the Nile.

"Jinx's parents trust her judgment," Ellen said accusingly.

They didn't so much trust it as know I was old enough to have to depend on it. I often didn't trust it myself.

Both of us were relieved to board the plane for Portland, Maine. Just as we were landing, Ellen said, "I guess I should tell you about Dr. Diller ... Van and me."

I waited.

"Well, he seems to be, sort of, in love with me."

"Oh my God, E.K.," I said. "And we're going to spend a week on an island of only an acre with his wife and children?"

"I guess I should have told you earlier, but there never seemed to be time."

"Are you in love with him?"

"Not exactly."

"What are we doing here?"

The passengers were getting up to leave the plane. And there on the tarmac were Dr. and Mrs. Diller and the children.

Years later, I wrote a story about that week, called "In the Bosom of the Family." It is a tribute to our friendship that Ellen and I were still speaking at the end of it.

WE HAD DECIDED, as a forerunner to our experiments in cheap travel in Europe, to hitchhike to New Canaan, where I was planning to visit Ann and Henry. A farm couple gave us our first ride and were not amused when we said we were going to England. They wouldn't go there themselves.

"One of our girls wasn't good enough for one of their boys."

It took me a moment to realize they were referring not to a member of their family but to the Duchess of Windsor.

Out on the big road, we were picked up by a couple who wanted us to stop the night with them in Boston at their daughter's and drive with them to New York the next day. But their parental concern for our safety couldn't overcome our sense of adventure.

Our third ride was a lone man who asked us to get into the back seat. He was a pilot unable to drive less than ninety miles an hour, and he took us to the turnoff to New Canaan. A local resident delivered us to Ann and Henry's door.

Henry was alone. Ann and the children had not come back from visiting her mother in Chicago.

Once Ellen had been put on a train into New York, I asked Henry what was wrong. He said he didn't know. Maybe I should phone her. I did, and she said she didn't think her coming home right then was a good idea. Because of me, I wanted to know. No, she just didn't feel ready. I wouldn't ask whether she'd had a fight with Henry. Certainly he seemed as eager as I did to have her back. Between us, we did persuade her to come, but it was two precious days before she got there.

On the night before she was due home, Henry said, nearly peevishly, "Aren't you interested in me at all?"

The idea hadn't crossed my mind. Henry had been for so long a protective and considerate friend that staying with him while we waited for Ann had seemed uncomplicatedly natural. Only at that moment did Ann's saying Henry would like to make love with me seem anything more than Ann's perverse sexual pressure.

I had no way to refuse him. It seemed to me odd that he would be the first man, but my emotional life had left convention so long ago that I had no measure for anything outside my own perception of things. Since Ann had encouraged just this, I assumed for her it would mean no more than my making a meal for Henry. She would even be pleased at my willingness.

I couldn't tell Henry I had not made love with a man before because I didn't want Ann to know. Short of that, any reason for refusing seemed to me hurtful. So we made love through the night before Ann arrived, an experience curious and not unpleasant but for me without any of the intensity of feeling I had had briefly with Ann, briefly with Roussel.

When we met her and the children the next day, she was very much closed into herself. In the two days left, she stayed aloof and sad. She wouldn't answer my questions, nor had she any for me. I wondered if her being pregnant again might explain her mood, but I felt bewildered and afraid for her.

Only last spring Susan said to me, "Mother said you had an affair with Dad. I thought, how sad for her, how absolutely alone she must have felt."

"I was in love with your mother," I said.

Ann had had too many long and bitter years to reshape the past into cruelties to her. Yet perhaps at the time it did hurt her. I was too young to know that, particularly in sexual matters, people can say a lot that they don't mean, often without knowing it. I still thought Ann was wiser than other people out of her own complex experience and her quick intuitions.

Ann with the children took me to the airline terminal where we met Dr. Pope, her sister and her children. I felt like a patient horse in a pony ring, children climbing all over me, urging me into exploring the terminal. I was glad to have farewells done with.

We were flying first class. It was like a long leisurely dinner party for just the two of us, and we had more to say than the long flight could accommodate. It was a great relief to me to be with only one person I cared about, on whom I could concentrate with simple pleasure. Once we arrived, I would have to juggle time for Ellen, even more importantly for Roussel, but at the moment Dr. Pope and I were in balanced excitement.

When Roussel joined us for that first evening of dinner and the theatre, I realized how terribly difficult the summer was going to be. She and Dr. Pope got on easily enough as I expected they would with so many interests in common, and Roussel treated me with the natural affection of a friend. But we were in love. We'd had only one weekend together and had been waiting months to see each other again.

I had already talked with Dr. Pope about our not living in each other's pockets. It was easy enough for me to get away for a couple of hours every other morning, if only for a walk in the park, and Roussel's room was only a three-ha'penny bus ride away. But our time was too hurried and clandestine. Roussel tried to be patient, but she complained that we had time to make love but never to talk.

She was worried about the exams she had written, sure she hadn't achieved a first, which was her only hope of going on to graduate school. She had applied for a fellowship in Iowa for a year and wondered if that was an academic detour that would give us only a crowded Christmas holiday together with my family. She wouldn't know the exam results until August.

There were too many uncertainties, too many decisions to make in the half dark. Roussel was trying to get some work done and give some time to her parents while she also tried to accommodate my schedule, being in London when I was. She was going to be at Stratford with us where Evaline Wright was also joining us.

"But that will help," I reassured her.

Roussel gave me an amused, skeptical look.

Dr. Pope's delight in everything we did made the tension I was under a light burden in those first days in London. I was distracted enough by Roussel to be not at first very conscious of a new dependence Dr. Pope felt and felt fearfully. Once other friends of hers proposed to take her on a day's outing. Unthinkingly they arranged to take the tube. Escalators were one thing Dr. Pope couldn't manage. She was back at the hotel in an hour just as I was getting ready to meet Roussel.

"I'm a fool and a coward," she said.

"They're fools!" I shouted, murderous of people so stupid.

"You keep shielding me from things," she said.

"I'm not shielding you from anything. I just make plans that work."

"I'm going out shopping," she announced, "alone."

I couldn't go on with my own day, stayed at the hotel and waited until she got home.

"I even took a bus!" she announced triumphantly.

But we both knew it was a risk she shouldn't have taken. She was so small, so uncertain of her balance, so slow that even the crowds on the sidewalk were dangerous for her.

Being physically imaginative for her was no difficulty for me. It was simply an extension of what I had done at college. I ordered taxis to come back for us at the end of a theatre evening in Oxford or Cambridge so that we wouldn't have to walk to find one. When we had a fast train connection, which often meant climbing over a high footbridge of the sort I'd fallen on in Stratford, I arranged for the porter to take Dr. Pope across the tracks on the luggage van. In all such circumstances, she was gallant and amused, but, as they accumulated, she felt the loss of her independence.

She wanted to do things for me, wash out underwear, adjust my reading light, give me the aisle seat at the theatre. Such attentions, particularly in public, embarrassed me, and I often tried to joke her out of them.

"Everyone's saying 'Look at that great lout of a girl taking the best seat!'"

"They think my leg brace doesn't hinge, and I should stick it out in the aisle. Why shouldn't you have the legroom you need?"

Dr. Pope seemed to me essentially so strong and independent a spirit that I didn't really understand her frustration at my doing things for her. I was impatient with her concern that she was too much a burden. I, of course, enjoyed making each adventure possible for her. She gave me so much each day of her knowledge and her pleasure that I felt as much nourished as I always had in her presence.

She was also uncertain of the propriety of some things I suggested, like having drinks in our room.

"Surely it's as proper as two women having drinks in a public bar, and it's a lot cheaper."

"Are you sure it isn't a little sordid?"

I joked and teased, but in such matters she didn't trust my judgment and was uncertain of her own.

When Evaline Wright joined us at Stratford, she was a real grown-up and world traveller whose advice Dr. Pope could trust. We were given her permission to go on drinking in our room, where she joined us. Miss Wright proposed a day trip Roussel and I had done the summer before.

"I don't want to go if you don't," Dr. Pope said.

I realized she was speaking out of loyalty to me, having no reason to think I longed for time alone with Roussel. Reassured that I'd like a day to catch up on letters, she went off happily enough.

Roussel couldn't throw off a sense of inhibition as quickly as I could and she never trusted the privacy of the out of doors, quite reasonably since tourists turned up everywhere. We didn't fight, but we had to deal with my recklessness and her caution. In Stratford particularly, where the landscape seemed to me to belong to us, I hated to waste an hour, for again Roussel would be leaving while Dr. Pope, Miss Wright and I went on to Oxford and Cambridge.

MY CHOICE OF ACCOMMODATION in Oxford was a mistake. We were over a mile from the town, and the guest house was mainly a permanent home for old people with several rooms to rent to transients. Miss Wright was given a room she claimed was a not-quite-converted broom closet, and ours, though large enough, was threadbare and dusty.

"Don't go around in this room barefooted," Miss Wright admonished me as she joined us for a before-dinner drink.

The dining room was of the sort in which no one speaks, afraid of interrupting the conversation among the knives and forks. Only the loud, cheerful Irish maid broke the silence with her shouts down the voice tube to the kitchen. "Three soups, one of which is for Miss Garrett" and "Five dinners, one of which is for Miss Garrett."

In the lounge for coffee, Miss Garrett introduced herself to us. She was an ancient Canadian scholar who went home for wars. An honorary fellow of Magdalen College, she asked if she could show us around. We agreed readily enough, and she gave us an informative tour of her college. When she offered to take us punting, Dr. Pope declined. Even Miss Garrett's assurance that she was accomplished not only in a punt, but in a canoe, a skill learned from her girlhood in the Canadian north woods, would not persuade Dr. Pope to change her mind.

The next evening at coffee, Miss Garrett again introduced herself and offered to show us Magdalen. We made our uneasy excuses. Miss Garrett's memory for the present was quite gone. Each day she went to the library and was given the same book to read and take notes on.

"What is it about her meals?" Evaline finally asked the maid.

"She doesn't like white sauces or custard."

I hadn't the nerve to say, "Make it 'two of what is for Miss Garrett from now on.' "

The food was negatively memorable.

After our first night at the theatre, we came back to a house without lights. On the table by the stairs was a lighted candle, sitting in a dish of water, with a sign, "Light your candle from me, but don't blow me out." Surrounding it were candles in holders for us to take to bed.

"Where did you find this place?" Miss Wright hissed, as we slowly climbed the stairs in the flickering light.

I took Dr. Pope to call on Professor Dyson, whom I had met the summer before at Stratford. We went to his fifteenth-century rooms at eleven in the morning where he uncorked Spanish sherry and broke the cork.

"Which means," he said cheerfully, "we must finish the bottle."

Professor Dyson collected first editions, and he showed us a number of his rarest specimens. Then he took Dr. Pope's own book on *Paradise Regained* from his shelves and asked her if she'd honour him by signing it.

As we went back down the shallow, worn steps of that ancient building, Dr. Pope seemed to float.

"I am in Oxford," she said. "I am a scholar among scholars."

Her wonder touched me, but it also separated her from me, for I knew then very clearly how claustrophobic I was becoming in such beautiful rooms into which only the scholarly present were allowed. No novel or book of poems less than a hundred years old was worthy of a place there unless, of course, it had been written by a friend, Auden or Charles Williams, or C.S. Lewis. I was physically as well as intellectually restless, longed to hike, to go out on the river, to play like the young animal I was.

I did occasionally take an afternoon to myself even when Roussel was too far away to join me.

"Why don't you tell Libby where you're going?" Miss Wright asked one day.

"I often don't know myself," I answered, which was true enough in Oxford.

"She thinks you're meeting someone," Miss Wright said.

"If I were, it's no business of hers. She isn't on this trip as my chaperone."

"She's very dependent on you, and she worries," Miss Wright said.

"Oh, I do know that," I said.

"You've been very good to her and very patient. It can't always be easy."

It was a kind-enough invitation for me to unburden myself of my own problems, and I didn't mistrust Miss Wright, nor did I mind that Dr. Pope talked with her. But I really didn't need to talk. It would exaggerate difficulties which seemed to me manageable.

Miss Wright didn't go with us to *Samson Agonistes*, performed out of doors in the quadrangle of one of the colleges. Though too static for real theatre, the play was directed with lively imagination. When the sound of the crumbling temple was played over the PA system, it was hard not to believe the towers of the surrounding buildings were not falling on us.

The cab I had asked to return for us didn't materialize. We were directed to a cab rank several blocks away on the main road. Dr. Pope set out, uncomplaining, for she was absolutely self-disciplined about any physical challenge. Drunken soldiers from the nearby American base tried to pick us up. I was furious with the cab driver who had deserted us, furious that Dr. Pope had to walk such a distance, and those young drunks, offering to seduce rather than help us, got the full brunt of my anger.

"You know, you're kind of cute," one of them said to her, "but I don't like your big, mean friend."

We did finally get a cab, and it was Dr. Pope who comforted me while she put Band-Aids on her saddle sores.

In London, Roussel often joined us for dinner just moments after we'd parted at her room. She was reserved enough never to slip in making references to our time alone together. For me, it was so much an effort that I grew more and more on guard.

At the theatre, Dr. Pope more often watched my face than the stage, wanting to be sure I was enjoying myself. I was aware that the habit irritated me more because I would have enjoyed such concentration from Roussel, who went to the theatre to see the play. When Ellen was with us, I was conscious of how little she existed for either Dr. Pope or Roussel.

Ellen joined us for a weekend when we were in Bath. Though our hotel was satisfactory, the food was very good—I ate duck every night we were there—the time there had been disappointing. I did not share Dr. Pope's admiration for the eighteenth century.

"A row house is a row house, whether it's built in a curve or in a straight line," I said.

Nor was I her eager companion exploring the Roman baths and other sites familiar to Jane Austen enthusiasts.

"Are you trying to ruin this for me?" she demanded.

No, no, I really wasn't. We were both relieved when Wells Cathedral delighted me.

But I was so angry with Dr. Pope for addressing not a single remark to Ellen the whole weekend she was with us that I confronted her with her rudeness.

"Well, I suppose I'm simply so much more interested in what you have to say," was her defence.

I was not flattered by it. I felt like a cat in a gunnysack.

By the time we arrived in Cambridge, the tension was unrelieved. Miss Wright, who had joined us again, though she was staying in another hotel, suggested I walk her home one evening and then invited me in for a drink.

"You're discouraged, aren't you?" she asked.

"I'm ashamed of how impatient I get," I confessed. "I really did want it to be a perfect summer for her."

"It is," Miss Wright said, "as much as it can be."

Just before we were about to leave, Dr. Pope's leg brace broke. We had to get to the orthopaedic hospital in London to have it fixed. She would not let me go with her, made her own way out to a cab on the frail, unguarded leg, carrying the brace. She was determined not to allow her handicap to be my responsibility, yet how much easier it was to deal with that than to cope with her emotional dependence.

Be patient, I counselled myself. Be patient, Roussel encouraged. It's not much longer, Ellen reminded me, and we'll be free. I realized she was positively looking forward to the trip on the

Continent. I looked ahead only to the week Roussel and I would have alone together before she left for the States.

I was forward-looking enough, however, to know I must buy a bicycle. I had used up all my own purchasing coupons. Miss Wright volunteered her own. She would impersonate my mother. Her hair newly done for the occasion, she set out with me to a department store. In the cycle department, she was my disapproving, only half-resigned parent, since I didn't know enough about the world for the trip I was proposing, speaking no foreign language adequately, being an indifferent map reader, clueless about the maintenance of a bicycle. She insisted that I change a tire, replace a chain, remove and restore a wheel right there in the shop. She required me to buy extra safety lights, a canteen for water and a horn. By the time she finished with me, it would have been less expensive for me to pay the taxi, but I wouldn't have missed that performance for the price of "excessories."

"You never did as well in class," she remarked when we left.

"I passed out for you once," I reminded her.

One of our last excursions before Dr. Pope flew home was to Canterbury to hear Dorothy Sayers lecture. Both Dr. Pope and I were eager to hear her and persuaded Miss Wright to come along for the bonus of watching her. Roussel's cousin was Dean of the Arches at Canterbury and had offered to introduce us. I was nervous about introducing people to him, never having met him myself, unsure of the proper address. An English friend advised me to address him as "Venerable Sir" and to curtsy. When I got a postcard from him, telling me to look for a tall man in orange garters and signed "Cousin Alec," I relaxed a little.

We had to change trains and make a close connection on the way down. I never wanted Dr. Pope to feel hurried, so I kept my nervousness to myself. Miss Wright took care of her own suitcase. I helped Dr. Pope out with her suitcase, then went back into the carriage to get mine off the overhead luggage rack. In my haste, I lost control of it and it fell on the head of a woman sitting underneath it.

"I'm so sorry," I said frantically as she began to tilt sideways. "Are you all right?"

"Perfectly," she said, as I propped her upright.

Jane Rule, Dr. Pope and Roussel Sargeant in England
Jane Rule Fonds, University Archives, University of British Columbia

"Are you sure?"

"Perfectly sure," she answered politely, beginning to sag in the other direction.

The train was about to leave. I had to get off. I had to get us to the next train. I grabbed my suitcase and fled. We did make our connection, but for the rest of the trip, I had the image of that poor woman before me.

Once we'd got to the cathedral, we waited in a crowd of people for the doors of the lecture room to open.

"Get a look at that," Miss Wright said to me, nodding at a dumpy little woman in a shiny grey suit with a man's shirt and tie.

At that moment, Cousin Alec appeared, and, as soon as he had greeted us, he turned to the little woman and said, "May I present Dorothy Sayers?"

Had she heard Miss Wright's remark? At the moment before giving a lecture, Dorothy Sayers had nothing to say to us, and we were too tongue-tied with embarrassment to say anything ourselves. That experience put me off ever wanting to meet the famous if I could avoid it.

The lecture, given to help raise money to repair the cathedral's bell tower, was to be about bell ringing. Miss Wright gave me a skeptical look, Dr. Pope a nervous one. She didn't want me to be disappointed, particularly in an enthusiasm we shared. Dorothy Sayers explained she'd written *The Nine Tailors* some years before and didn't really remember much of her research about bell ringing, but perhaps we'd enjoy singing some of the chimes. She divided us up into sections, each given one tone to produce by singing "bong."

A week later, after both Dr. Pope and Miss Wright were gone, Roussel and I heard Dorothy Sayers give a perfectly intelligent lecture in London on medieval drama.

I took Dr. Pope to the airport and got permission to get onto the plane with her to see her comfortably settled.

"You'd get into Buckingham Palace to sit on the throne if you put your mind to it," she said, picking up my own bantering tone whenever I did anything to help her physically.

"Do me the favour at least to look as if you need help," I said as she started to walk off on her own.

Leaving her on the plane, I knew the summer had gone relatively well. Dr. Pope would teach with a richer head, enjoy remembering plays, lectures, the landscape and architecture. I wondered if I, too, would finally remember the festival rather than the tension between us, without guilt at my own emotional withdrawal. In those days, I wanted to forget failure because I had no use for it.

Roussel, when I reached her, was in a state of glum nerves about the results of her examinations. I had bought tickets for *Antony and Cleopatra*, played by Olivier and Vivien Leigh, to celebrate the day the results were posted on the Senate House wall, but Roussel had made me so apprehensive for her that I wondered if I'd made a mistake. I went with her and watched her find her number on the long list. She paused, looked, looked again.

"Either there's a mistake or the standards are much lower than I thought," she said.

She had a first. Only one English student in the whole of the University of London had a mark higher than hers. It meant she could, after her year in Iowa, come back to do graduate work on a fellowship. I was silly with relief, but I watched the play that night through the snarl of a migraine headache, so often with me at the end of long strain.

I took my luggage and bicycle down to Horsham to stay with Roussel and her parents. I was going to leave what I couldn't carry on my bicycle there. I was pleased with my first trial packing. All the clothes I needed, a change of shoes, notebooks and several books fit into my sidesaddles and my little eight-and-a-half-pound Skywriter typewriter strapped neatly on the flat back luggage carrier. But, when I got on it to test the balance, the bike rose up on its hind wheel like a rearing horse and stayed there. A pair of Roussel's elderly clerical cousins having tea in the garden laughed until they wept.

I took out the books and tried again. It was very little better. The typewriter was the next to go. The bicycle settled down on its front wheel, but, when I rode it out onto the street, it reared at the first bump of a pebble and stayed there. With the extra shoes gone, it rode docilely. I tried to lash the typewriter to the handlebars, a happy fantasy of myself riding along on the French countryside typing as I went. But finally I had to face the reality of being typewriter-less for the next months. Since I had written nothing but postcards in longhand for years, the sacrifice was a hard one.

Roussel, who knew from experience my modest skill and stamina on a bicycle, was dubious about the whole plan. Her mockery made me the more cheerfully confident, but I still gave no real imagination to the time beyond her departure, which seemed stranger and more ironic the nearer it approached. I felt as I had on my first trip to England when I left Ann behind on the deck, that my real reason for taking the trip had been left behind me.

"You will promise to make the whole world happy," Roussel said.

I was, without realizing it, emotionally exhausted by the time I met Ellen, just back from a week in Scotland, where she'd bought a first edition of *Paradise Lost*. She wanted to take it along, as well as some deer antlers she'd found in Oxford and enough Kotex to last the trip. In the luggage room of the Cumberland Hotel we argued until we were too pressed for time to do anything but load up and take off. We'd agreed to take a boat train from Victoria Station and begin bicycling once we arrived in France.

Just into Hyde Park, the coat fell off Ellen's bicycle. A young man on a motorcycle stopped, picked it up, lashed it back on with rope from his own pack and departed without even saying a word.

At the other side of the park, we were caught on a traffic island, double-decker buses and London cabs encircling us. An amused bobby finally came to our rescue just after Ellen had tearfully confessed she hadn't ridden a bicycle since she was seven years old.

"Why didn't you say so?" I asked.

"I didn't think it was something you forgot."

We did get to Victoria in time to catch the train. Neither of us was in much of a mood for the adventure by then, but Ellen got out a French phrase book and tried to coax me with learning a few before we landed in that country late that afternoon.

"Where we can afford to stay, nobody's going to ask if we want a room on the street or on the court," I said scornfully.

Disembarked at Dieppe, we both watched the train depart for Paris. We had no city map and so found our way to the main road by asking, "*Oo eh Paris?*" at every corner. When we reached the road, it rose, mile after mile before us, at a steep incline. We were about halfway up it, pushing our bicycles, when a truck on its way down stopped and the driver offered us a lift. We refused, pointing up the hill. He nodded vigorously, picked up Ellen's bicycle and put it in the back of the truck with several toilets. He took mine from me and then ushered us into the cab.

We drove with him back down the long hill, arrived at a house where he stopped, gesturing to us that he'd only be few minutes. When he'd delivered a toilet, he got back in and drove us back out of the city. We stopped at a farmhouse to deliver another toilet before we headed toward Rouen, the city where we had planned to spend the night. We reached it around ten o'clock that night. Miss Wright had suspected correctly; neither of us knew how to read a map. We could never have reached it on bicycles that night, even if the road had been entirely downhill.

The youth hostel where our driver left us was filthy, the only plumbing having failed some years ago, but we were too tired to complain, slept badly and woke to the problem of finding our way out of Rouen on cobbled streets Ellen hadn't the skill to ride on.

"We'll take the train to Paris," I decided, "and get rid of the bikes."

Ellen was guiltily apologetic and relieved.

I, who had decided to stop smoking for the time we rode our bicycles to give me more wind and to save money, bought a pack of cigarettes. The first cigarette, though I choked on it, improved my disposition. I was ready to laugh at myself when we were asked at the cheap hotel we had chosen in Paris whether we wanted a room on the street or the court.

Jane Rule, during her college years
Jane Rule Fonds, University Archives, University of British Columbia

In the time we spent in Paris, we never did figure out how to ride the subway or the buses. We walked everywhere, miles and miles a day. I loved exploring the city that way, finding new routes home, feeling my body restored by the exercise I'd lacked all summer, but Ellen got tired and discouraged at our inability to deal with the language. After a week, we admitted to ourselves that we were sick of cities, could not look at one more cathedral, one more painting. So we left our bikes at the hotel and caught a train for Barcelona, planning to go from there to Majorca, Georges Sand and Chopin country.

The two young men we met on that train and the time we spent with them on Majorca are described in some detail in *This Is Not for You*, but the motives of the two main characters are entirely fictional. Perhaps one of the thousand seeds for that novel was sown when one of the young men did ask me if Ellen and I were lovers. No one had ever confronted me directly before. Though I'd never had any erotic interest in Ellen, telling the truth, that we were "just friends," seemed also a lie about myself. It made me ask myself directly what I was doing there, again with a person I cared about who was far too dependent on me for reassurance, for decision making without a crippling disease for an excuse.

I was trying to write for a part of each day. Without a typewriter, I was missing the central prop of my ritual. I began stories I couldn't stay interested in. I wrote myself meaningless notes.

Ellen seemed far more content, building elaborate sandcastles on the beach, sketching, going on hikes with our companions, learning to spear fish. She began to talk of travelling on with them through southern Spain, assuming that I would go, too.

Finally, I asked her, "Could you go with them alone?"

"Without you?"

I nodded.

"Yes," she said simply.

I wanted to explain, but I didn't know myself why I had to leave.

"If you have to, that's all that matters," Ellen said. "There don't have to be explanations between friends."

She saw nothing in my desertion that she had to forgive. The guilt I felt was not strong enough to hold me there, though the flavour of it is with me still.

I left because I was too tired to carry responsibility for anyone but myself. I left because I was under sexual pressure I didn't want from a young man, in a growing complexity of a foursome I didn't feel a real part of. I left because I really did want to write and couldn't in those circumstances. I left because our money would not anyway have lasted very long now that we had given up our bicycles. I left because I was sick and frightened.

It was September. There was no way off the island for another three weeks, every boat and plane fully booked. I couldn't bear the sense of being trapped. I bribed my way onto the night boat and spent the night in the bar, being comforted by Spaniards because my king had just died.

"Not my king," I tried to explain, but they would not accept that and kept buying me drinks, not to cheer me up but to help me mourn.

I slept for an hour or so before the boat docked. Then I caught the train for Paris, travelling third class, both the compartments and corridors jammed with people and with animals. By the time I got to Paris, I had been on my feet for thirty-six hours. If I could just lie down on the pavement for a few minutes, I thought, no one would mind, but I forced myself to keep going on my grotesquely swollen feet and ankles until I got to the hotel. I nearly drowned in the huge, hot bath drawn for me, but I revived enough to go for steak and salad before I slept.

Before I caught the boat train the next day, I wired Roussel's parents to expect me that night. I had decided against going all the way into London and back to Horsham. I would take local trains instead. I had an hour to kill at the station, and a worker on the tracks offered me a cup of tea. I followed him not into the station but down the line to a shack where half a dozen workers were having tea. They rummaged round until they found a thin china cup for me, and I had to try some of each of their homemade cakes. Fortunately, I had a pack of cigarettes to offer round. All of them put me on the train, choosing a "ladies only" compartment for me and stowing my bicycle in the guard van.

As I pushed my bike up the front walk of the Sargeants' house at dusk, I could see the dining-room table set for three.

I stayed with the Sargeants for the five days it took to find space on a plane. They suggested, since I didn't have to be back in college until February, I could stay along with them in Roussel's room where I could write. I was touched by such welcome, and I had been there often enough to know how to be a daughter of the household, neither as thoughtful nor helpful as Roussel but forgiven my lapses by my age and nationality. I might have been more a distraction from their missing Roussel than a nuisance. But it was the place where I would miss her most, among her books and clothes, in the bed where we had made love.

At nineteen, not really knowing where I wanted to be, going home was the only uncommitting option. I'd had a letter from Mother saying that Dad hadn't been well. So I booked myself out of New York immediately when I arrived, not even stopping to check in with Ann and Henry.

I missed my connection for San Francisco in New York by only five minutes. I phoned Ann from the airport and met a welcome which cancelled the remote unease of our last meeting.

Ann's third child was expected at any time, and she and Henry wondered if I could stay for three weeks until Ann's sister would be free to come look after the children.

Only a week after I'd left Majorca, I phoned home to say I was staying in Connecticut for three weeks and would then come home.

"Why weren't you planning to be here?" Ann asked. "Was I that hard on you last time? I didn't mean to be. It didn't have anything to do with you."

I knew that. Being excluded and ignored for no reason had no comfort or reassurance in it. Also, I had not known what Henry might expect of me. But he also behaved as if our brief love-making had not taken place. I wanted to but couldn't quite erase the experience of that long-ago spring. It seemed to me the first in a long string of failures in friendship and love for which I felt variously responsible. Yet I also felt misused.

"You're so beautiful, someone must have loved you well. Who was he?" Ann asked.

I no longer had any appetite for such games. Ann's heterosexual demands of my life had finally made it impossible for me to talk with her, as I so much would like to have talked about what had happened between me and Dr. Pope, why intense dependency without erotic content was so claustrophobic, about my relationship with Roussel which had become important enough to me to make me apprehensive. Ann would have encouraged that apprehension, while I wanted it dispelled, for why should I be afraid of someone in whose presence I was so entirely happy? I could be candid with Roussel both as a friend and as a lover as I couldn't be with Ann, who was passionate lover one moment, remote judge the next.

"I want to do your portrait," Ann said.

While I sat and she reached across her large belly to the easel, both children were allowed to scribble on paper of their own, also propped on the easel.

"I remember the first time I drew your mouth," Ann said.

When she came to me that night and made love to me, I felt her hands asking questions of my body, which was more knowledgeable. I could also feel her fear of being inadequate now, even as she hoped she would be compared to the men she wanted me involved with. My desire for her, so long held in check, was more intense than ever. It amazed me that I could have contemplated not seeing her who had been the centre of my longing for so many years.

Yet she stayed afraid of and for me.

Ann finished the portrait before I left and sent it with me as a present to my parents. Of the three portraits she did of me, it is the most successful, in colour while the others were charcoal, my jacket bright with autumn colours, a clear autumn sky behind me. My face is brown from the Mediterranean sun, thin, the mouth full and bright, the eyes dark, watchful.

At five o'clock in the morning of the day my plane left, Henry woke me and asked, "Would you like a ride to New York?"

We left Ann's sister and the children still asleep, and I timed the labour pains while Ann read boys' names out of a dictionary.

I stayed at the hospital with Henry, but I finally had to leave for the airport before the baby was born.

At the airport in San Francisco, Mother called across the fence, "It's a girl, and they've named it after us!"

I went home to discover my room in the house they had bought in Berkeley. I liked the room, my furniture making it familiar, and opening off it was a flat roof over the enclosed sun porch where I could work outdoors on warm days. Libby was enrolled at Anna Head's, and her grey uniform took me back to the year I had spent there. My brother was working somewhere out of town and home only on weekends which he mostly spent with Edy, who was sharing an apartment with Sally Millett, not far from Mills. Dad, indeed, wasn't well. He had a skin disorder, probably from an allergy to the sun. Great, inverted blisters covered his arms and shoulders, and it had spread to the inside of his mouth. But cortisone was beginning to control it.

Mother was determinedly pressing Mother Packer to sell South Fork so that Dad could finally go into business for himself, for she was convinced that unhappiness in his work was as much to blame as anything.

There I finally did begin to write short stories to pass the time until Roussel came out for Christmas. I wrote her long letters, promising her relief from the Midwest winter, sunshine all day, flowers. I was promising her, too, that I could get back to England with her, where we would share an apartment in London while she worked on an MA and I wrote a novel. And, no, I wouldn't invite the entire world to share it with us. We would have time alone and make a life together. I had not yet broached those plans to my family.

My cousin Patsy came home from Japan where her father was on a tour of duty. We went to meet her, but there were already young officers assigned to see her through customs and deal with all the details of her arrival. I envied her the ease of that caretaking, but all my own unassisted border crossings did give me a sense of independence she never achieved, a world traveller who had no idea how it was done except in the care of the military. She stayed with us a while without much idea of what she would do next. She'd been teaching in a nursery school for military children while she was in Japan. She hadn't the grades or the interest to go on to college. Next to her life, mine seemed more ordered and purposeful. And perhaps her lack of direction made my parents look more favourably on my own resolutions when I offered them, impractical as they might have seemed. At least I knew what I wanted to do.

Mother did say to me, when I spoke about wanting a year in England to write, that it would soon be time for me to stop being selfish and start thinking about leading a life that involved people other than myself. The idea startled me, for I didn't think of the future in those terms at all. For the first time, it occurred to me that I would be expected either to marry or earn my own living before much more time had passed. But I couldn't imagine either course very clearly.

Roussel's visit was a natural disaster. It rained the entire ten days she was with us. When we crossed the Bay Bridge, we couldn't even see the bridge, and it was snowing on the higher hills in San Francisco. It was some years before she'd let me forget my false picture of sunny California.

Mother and Dad were very welcoming and hospitable, but I could sense a reserve in my mother which she didn't have with my other friends. It couldn't be Roussel's age because Mother was perfectly aware of how much time I'd spent with Dr. Pope. Was it her English manner? Or did my mother feel the intensity of my involvement with Roussel and mistrust it?

Once Roussel had gone back to Iowa, I was restless. I wasn't really looking forward to going back to college. I had more independence at home. I did want to have done with it.

There wasn't a room for me in Orchard Meadow. Ann McKirsty, an English major who lived in Olney, had at Christmas lost her porch mate to marriage or breakdown, I can't remember, and offered the space to me. Since I'd known my own classmates at Orchard Meadow, my close friends all having graduated, the shift was not difficult. There was a strong group of English majors on senior corridor. Because we all faced comprehensive exams even on courses we hadn't taken, we co-operated more in our studying than we had before.

Soon after I got back, Ann and I organized a series of seminars for all senior majors, at which a student gave a paper designed to help others review the subject. We invited the faculty to attend as observers. Dr. Pope was nearly always there, as impressed with us as we were with ourselves, for each of us chose the field we felt most competent to deal with, and we were, on the whole, an intelligent and hard-working bunch.

I was also taking Dr. Pope's course in nineteenth-century poetry and an independent study with her, asking that I write no papers, have no meetings with her but simply turn in a reading list at the end of term.

"How will I grade you?"

"I'll grade myself."

The nineteenth century was not her field, and her organization of the course was gimmicky and rigid. I, who had loved combative discussion in class, sat saying not a word. My papers were dutiful but uninspired. Both of us were unhappy, but we couldn't do more than be polite to each other over the gulf of our disappointment in each other.

The writing instructor that term called me into his office and carefully shut the door before saying in a nervous half whisper, "You know, you could be onto something here, writing about inversion." He went on to say that he couldn't officially encourage me, of course, but off the record there just might be quite a market for it. I stopped writing.

Roussel wrote to say she'd involved herself with Willy, a young woman whose readiness Roussel could not resist. Now she worried that Willy would be hard to leave. We wrote to each other about dependence, about how finally negative it was, destructive of love. We would never be possessive of each other or jealous.

I wrote to Roussel about Marilyn, a music major, with whom I listened to music and read Gertrude Stein, who had transferred from Reed, whose distractions from required work I'd never allowed myself before. When we first made love in her room, I knew it was dangerous, but I was already so tempted to quit that I needed the defiance of it.

I wasn't, in my view, learning anything. I was working for a degree, and I felt scornful of that motive. One night, when I came back from being with Marilyn, there was a note left in my type-writer from Ann, who was already asleep. Dr. Pope had called to notify us both that we'd been elected to Phi Beta Kappa. Ann had been asked to persuade me not to refuse. It was exactly the kind of gesture I was looking for; yet faced with the opportunity, I couldn't do it. It would have been insulting not only to Dr. Pope but to Ann and other friends accepting the honour.

I looked through my large collection of snapshots and found pictures of all eight of us who had been elected. I cut them into the shape of keys and strung them by their necks to swing over Ann's desk.

The president in his luncheon speech confirmed my gallows humour by saying most Phi Beta Kappas were not really creative people but masters of convention, which the secret ceremony afterward confirmed. I did it, handshake and all, to be "welcomed into the company of scholars." Whose company had I been in until now?

The other blackly humorous ceremony I attended was my brother's wedding. Because Edy's mother was a reclusive widow, there was no reception. Art and Edy left after the ceremony at the college chapel. The rest of the wedding party, my father as best man, Sally Millett as maid of honour, along with members of the family, went to Dr. Pope's for a glass of champagne.

"Remember, kiddo," my brother had said to me just before the service. "You can run your heart out, but I can beat you standing still."

Did he feel victory in marrying Edy? Did he resent my academic honours? I didn't know. He never explained himself beyond very occasional cryptic slogans.

My mother was distressed by the marriage as well as the service. She thought Arthur far too young and unstable to marry, but, if there had to be a wedding, it should have been a proper one to which all her old San Francisco friends could be invited bringing suitable gifts. I had long since given up believing that such a society really existed for us. Libby was the only one ever to put store in Mother's nostalgia.

I had weekly phone calls from Mother Packer who focussed her attention on my twenty-first birthday, which I'd asked to celebrate with the family at her house for squab dinner. Each time she called, she asked me what I wanted, and each time I replied, "Money for a year in England."

"I'll give you a car."

"Fine, I'll sell it."

"Would you like a house?"

"I'd sell it."

"How about my opal ring?"

"It's bad luck. You said so yourself. I'll sell it."

"You can't go away for a whole year. It would break your father's heart."

Such a sentiment amazed me. My father's heart had nothing to do with my plans. Nobody told him that selling South Fork broke my heart, and no one should have. He needed his own business. I needed to go England.

So, apparently, did Ellen. She had decided to go to the Royal Academy of Dramatic Art. Her enthusiasm infected two other senior English majors in Mills Hall to make plans of their own. I did not know either Judy or Waki well enough to be as concerned about them, though all of us were drawn closer by the pressure of exams. I know I couldn't declare London my private property, but I did remind Ellen that I'd agreed to share a flat with Roussel.

The day before my birthday, I went to the beauty shop and asked for a short cut. I came out looking as if a field of wheat had been planted on my head. It even rippled in the breeze.

"What will I do? Mother Packer will kill me," I wailed to Sally Millett who had dropped by with a birthday present.

"Put on dangling earrings, and pretend it's the latest style."

"I don't own any."

"Open your present."

For once, Mother Packer was struck speechless, and the rest of the family was kind enough not to comment. Already nervous about my hair, I was uneasy, too, about the mood in the room. Everyone seemed overly casual. Then I realized that there were no presents.

Dinner was announced. When I got to the table, I saw, instead of the usual bright bouquet of sweet peas, the ugliest piggy bank imaginable on a pedestal. The table itself glittered with small change. On the place cards were pasted silver dollars. At my place there was a fan made of paper dollars, a camellia backed in dollar bills. At Mother Packer's place was a toy cash register which replaced the bell for calling the maid, and, every time she rang it, everyone took handfuls of small change to put into the piggy bank. Dad presented me with a framed hundred dollar bill. The cake was not only filled with dimes, it was decorated with "Money happy returns of the day."

Late that night, I lay on my back, prying the last of the change out of the piggy bank with a nail file. I counted it to the last penny. My year in England was paid for.

With such good fortune secured, it seemed graceless to be so negative about the weeks that remained. I joined other English majors each night at dinner. Ann, more intensely working than any of us, also was best at breaking the tension by starting sudden, impossible conversations, usually with me.

"Did you let the elephant out?" or "Was that the duke who phoned?" They mostly developed into intense quarrels of faked jealousy, invented failures of responsibility for the benefit of a suitably amused audience. The game we played when we were alone was quarrelling over our shared servants, Gertrude and Bertrum, who finally became too expensive and jealous of each other to keep. It then fell to singular Bertrude to deal with our clothes and cleaning.

When I could take an hour off, I went to find Marilyn. We'd walk out to the lake, climb trees, play games with the local children. Or I'd go to the music building to listen to her practise. It was Marilyn my parents most liked me to bring home because, when she was there, we all sang after she sang for us. Her father was a minister, and she knew a wonderful range of hymns. She also told stories about stealing her allowance from the collection plate.

With Ann and with Roussel, it was I who lightened the day with nonsense. In Marilyn, I had a real playmate who didn't worry at any future between us, who took the pleasure we had in each other simply.

I had, when I first arrived at Olney, made a speech in hall council about not attending hall meetings. I was willing to pay a reasonable fine, but I simply didn't have time to spend arguing about whether we'd wear heels or flats to a dance I didn't have time to attend. When it came time for the English majors to give a dinner party for their faculty, none of us asked each other that friendly question, "What are you going to wear?" We went to our closets, creatures capable of making independent choices. Five out of six of us met in the living room wearing navy-blue linen dresses with white piping. The sixth wore navy with red piping.

"They'll think we're the waitresses in the restaurant," Ann wailed. "Bertrude told me you were wearing green."

"Bertrude always lies to you," I answered.

Brainwashed we were, and we tramped out chanting, "Remember who you are and what you represent," one of the more tasteless of the college mottos to fulfill another of what seemed endless rituals.

I didn't make top marks in my examinations. I felt dogged rather than intent, restless with so much generality. Even the paper I was interested in because I could set my own question was overworked in my head before I wrote it. Dr. Pope was more disappointed than I was. She saw my performance as one more act of rebellion.

"I do understand, Jinx. Because I was a mother figure, you had to rebel, and it was time for you to have friends your own age."

That would be how the dean and Miss Wright had tried to comfort her. I didn't like how much I'd withdrawn from her, how little I'd minded punishing her with my silence in class. She had given me everything she could, loved me in all the ways she knew how, and I could only spend time trying to figure out how to forgive her for it. Finally, she taught me that, too.

She and Miss Wright, whom I would now begin to call Libby and Evaline, gave me a special "faculty purse" for graduation, filled with money for martinis aboard the *Queen Elizabeth*, on which Roussel and I were booked to sail.

Mother went with me to Hink's to buy things I'd need for my year in England, and she also helped me pick out a full tea service for the Sargeants since it was still impossible to buy anything but white china in England. It didn't occur to me then how odd it was to be so easily extravagant at the beginning of a year in which I would be poor enough to think of an extra apple as a treat. Europe for so many generations' materially spoiled young was a basic financial education. We stayed in cheap hotels which would have terrified us in New York or San Francisco. We lived in cold rooms on inadequate diets which would have offended our sense of what we expected at home. None of us supposed, as many of our counterparts in those countries did, that we would go on living like that forever. Our poverty in those exotic settings was part of the romance. And our parents didn't have to visit us to be concerned.

Over the years, Ann stopped writing except to confirm times when I might be with her. When I arrived to spend a week, I did not know that she'd spent much of the spring in a mental hospital, suffering, Henry said, from melancholia. She had threatened to kill herself and all three children. Even now, she could not be left alone with them. During the day, she tended them well enough, but she hadn't the mind to get the washing done, the house cleaned, and the food she offered was out of cans. She talked very little until she began to drink after the children were in bed, and then she talked endlessly, wildly about suicide and murder. She said being a woman was simply too degrading. Henry did not love her. He didn't want to introduce her to any of his New York friends. He only made love to her after looking at his dirty pictures. Why should the girls grow up to be treated like that? In India girl children were killed. She'd seen it for herself when she was a child. Sometimes I argued with her, asked her why she'd made me godmother to them all if she thought she had absolute power over their lives, told her I was a woman and loved my life. To that she replied that I didn't yet live in the real world. I told her I never intended to. Henry left very early in the morning and came home late at night, taking advantage of my presence for some time to himself, for, once I'd gone, he'd have to be back to relieve a sitter, there to guard the children from their mother.

One afternoon I took the children to a neighbour's to play and stayed with them chatting with the mother of their friends.

"Ann's such a wonderful person," she said, "so much calmer and wiser than the rest of us. If ever there's a crisis in the neighbourhood, she's the one who knows what to do."

So the serene mask she had always worn hadn't cracked for anyone else. Her neighbours didn't even know she'd been in the hospital. She lived inside her house, inside that madness, and nobody knew, except Henry and me and the woman who watched over her while Henry was not there. It seemed to me so appallingly lonely. Yet to contradict her neighbour would be a betrayal of Ann. In the adult world people simply didn't know each other at all. How could they really help each other?

I knew, for the sake of the children, I should have stayed on, but I had made other promises I had to keep. Neither Ann nor Henry asked it of me, both so locked in their anger and grief that I was hardly more than a temporary relief. I had never been really very real to either of them. But what about the children?

"I'll commit her if I have to," Henry said. "The doctors think she's going to come out of it. It just takes time."

My meeting with Roussel, which should have been so joyful, was blurred with my fear and guilt for the children. I took her to Granny Rule's house which was full of aunts and uncles, cousins. One of my young cousins, Roddy, was so fascinated by Roussel's accent that he practised, "I'm going down the path in an hour and a half to take a bath." My father's twin brother, whom I'd told Roussel was a cold, stiff man compared to my father, arrived and kissed all his female relatives down the line until he got to Roussel, smiled at this unknown woman and kissed her, too. The whole family delighted her, and I was distracted enough by them not to think too much about those threatened and vulnerable children I'd left behind.

We'd been invited by Libby Pope to spend the last few days before we sailed with her at her family's summer place in upstate New York. Once there, I had a severe migraine. Roussel went with Libby to see the sights while I was left in the care of the old family servant who made me her special iced tea.

We nearly missed the boat. Only the first-class gangplank was still down, and we ran for it. We did have the luxury of a cabin for two, but it was airless, claustrophobic. One night, in desperation, we slept all night on deck under blankets, as a result of which we arrived in England with heavy colds. But I did get my trunk full of gifts through customs without duty. Roussel was made to pay on two pairs of nylons. Fortunately, most of her new things were with my luggage, and she didn't know about them until we arrived in Horsham. The tea set for her parents was a great success. So were the things I'd brought for her.

There were several long letters from Willy waiting for Roussel. I heard nothing from Ann. I suppose all relationships begin with burdens of separate sorrows, regrets, guilts that can be known but not adequately shared.

In the cold winter flat in West Hampstead a cousin of Roussel's had found for us, I made my first real home, learned after a fashion to cook, to entertain friends, to live with a lover and to write my first, unpublishable novel. In that process, I also began to learn how to live with the baggage of my life, its rhythms of failure and rebirth.

AFTERWORD

Linda M. Morra

Books are neither conceived nor written in isolation. So it is with Jane Rule's autobiography, *Taking My Life*, in which she illuminates those social interactions that gave shape to who she was to become, as a person and a writer. These kinds of interactions might be seen to characterize the process of ushering Rule's autobiography into print, of getting *Taking My Life* into the form it currently assumes. That I stumbled upon it in the Irving K. Barber Learning Centre, where the University of British Columbia Archives are housed and where I was perusing Rule's papers, was the very result of one such exchange: I had had a stimulating conversation with David Anderson, a profoundly generous and intelligent friend. I regard that conversation as the catalyst for getting this work into print. We had been discussing the nature of my academic research, which focuses on Canadian women authors and the publishing industry in Canada, when he mentioned the *Little Sisters* trial in which Rule had played a significant part. He alerted me to the fact that the Rule papers were being stored in the archives at the University of British Columbia and that little critical and archival work on her had been done up to that point.

So it was that, in July 2008, I found myself in the archives of the University of British Columbia, where I was patiently sifting through boxes and voluminous files from the Jane Rule Fonds. In one of the boxes, I found the manuscript for *Taking My Life*, written in her hand on yellow foolscap paper. I was startled: it had not been cited in the catalogue of her papers. As a researcher, I frequently rifle through the contents of archival boxes, in spite of what a catalogue promises (or denies). That practice did not detract from my surprise. There was a catalogued version of it that had been typed, against which I later checked my transcription and which I have used to shape the autobiography published here; the typed version had subsequently added mostly small changes that amounted to about thirty to forty pages of extra material, but it was the handwritten original text that held my attention. If there were other drafts that had preceded the latter, she did not preserve them; since Rule saved most of her papers, including early drafts of both her literary work and letters, I was inclined to approach this manuscript as if it had been an early, if not the very first, attempt. Even if it was an early attempt, I marvelled: the scarcely marked-up yellow foolscap manuscript demonstrated the kind of confidence and precision with which she wrote. Very little editing had been done in her hand and very few insertions and deletions had been made. She wrote with a self-assurance that was reminiscent of the way she spoke.

The process of preparing the manuscript involved transcribing the handwritten version, then checking it against the typescript. What has been published here is the typescript of *Taking My Life*—the version that seems to be the last one that Rule wrote. For the sake of scholars whose research expertise encompasses autobiography theory, book history and other areas of literary and critical theory, I have included passages that were omitted from or added to the typescript in a section titled "Omitted Text." Discussions related to two other editorial matters also arose between Ann-Marie Metten, Talon's eagle-eyed editor, the executors and me: whether or not changes should be made to dated language and whether or not to include breaks in the text. Rule made references to other races (specifically, Asian) in a manner that would these days be considered politically incorrect; yet, as one executor noted, since Rule was reporting the usage of either language by children at the time or the dialogue of her relatives, and since such usage was a reflection of the period, it was best to allow such language to remain. Conversely, the executors gave us permission to excise some equally dated terminology related to the Indigenous. The conversation then turned to the consideration of some section breaks, which Rule had clearly flagged in her typescript, but inconsistently so; Ann-Marie rendered these breaks with greater regularity and consistency.

Approximately 260 pages in length after my transcription of it had been completed, the manuscript was captivating not only because it was written in Rule's hand, but also because of the characteristic and disarming frankness of her prose, her engaging and straightforward style. She had written other autobiographical texts,[1] some published and others still in the archives, some focusing on her later career and others on aspects of her childhood. Many of the essays in *Loving the Difficult* (2008), for example, delineate family members and her interaction with them, or childhood experiences of importance to Rule; however, *Taking My Life* is uncharacteristic in its extended focus upon the entirety of her childhood through to her maturity into adulthood. As she herself notes in the manuscript, "I have never been able to use the years of my adolescence. In the great range of characters in novels and short stories, it is as if people between the ages of thirteen and fifteen didn't exist. And I not only lived through those years but taught students that age for two years with comprehension and delight."

In general, Rule eschewed protracted autobiographical forms in her own writing practices, for reasons in part related to discretion; as she noted in a letter dated May 12, 1981, addressed to Robert Weaver, the memoir "isn't usually something I do." The text that she had characterized as a memoir and that she had sent to him at that time, she claimed, was merely "an exercise for me in preparation for teaching that form."[2] She regarded autobiography and fiction, moreover, as discrete genres; so she observed in another letter to Weaver, "the proper place for autobiography is in an autobiography, not in fiction."[3] That it is not "something she usually did" is perhaps revealed in the fact that *Taking My Life* seems to have been written in the late 1980s, as the scholar Marilyn Schuster also suggests,[4] just before Rule retired from writing. By that time, her arthritis had become a painful impediment to her professional work. Writing this manuscript might have been her way of considering the origins of her successful literary career as it moved to closure. In a letter to a friend, written in 1994 as she and her partner Helen

Sonthoff cleaned out their basement "half an hour at a time," Rule reported that "old age has its strategies":[5] that is, writing the autobiography may have been one of those very strategies of grappling with her aging because, as she notes in the introductory paragraph with an unmistakable sense of resignation, "there is nothing else to do."

Taking My Life may be properly defined as an autobiography, because its subject is Rule herself and her world, as she constructs it with her passionate intellect. In examining the years of her childhood and adolescence, she looks intensely at family dynamics, tracks the emergence of her sexual life and alludes to the beginnings of her writing career. The manuscript thus struck me as bearing literary importance and cultural significance, because it traces the first twenty-one years of Rule's life and her development as a writer. As such, it operates like a *Künstlerroman*: that is, the storyline follows its prescribed narrative arc, from childhood to adulthood, and sheds light on those figures who were key to her moral, intellectual, artistic and sexual development. If we accept it as a *Künstlerroman*, it becomes evident why Rule would conclude *Taking My Life* with her twenty-first birthday: she had come of age, and had grown into her calling as a professional writer and mature adult. On the one hand, then, her autobiography is revealing of the politics of the era, from the 1930s to the 1950s; on the other hand, it probes in emotional and intellectual terms the larger moral questions that were to preoccupy Rule for the rest of her literary career, and showcases the origins of, and the milieu that gave shape to, her rich and vibrant intellectual life.

The title itself is resonant, even haunting, especially when contextualized within an understanding of Rule's rigorous editorial practices and her lifelong struggle to protect her freedom of expression and literary integrity. In her relationships with agents, editors and publishers, she was unflinching about her expectations: no word, no comma, no seemingly trivial part of the text could be touched without her permission. This tendency accounted for my deep surprise at finding the original manuscript of *Taking My Life* in the archives—and later, my deep anxiety as I began transcribing it. I wanted to respect the manuscript as I had found it, yet I was compelled to ask: how is it that Rule would leave an *autobiography*—the kind of text that is arguably the most consummate expression of self-agency, of autonomy, of the assertion of one's personal moral vision—unpublished and vulnerable to the editorial clutches of others, including, in this case, my own? An act of discretion on her part reveals itself here: in allowing for the possibility for the manuscript to be published long after it was written, she was also considering the ethical question related to those whose lives might have been affected by being represented in her work. The title sheds light on another possible answer to the question of why the manuscript remained unpublished in her lifetime: in writing about her early formative years, she is indeed "taking" or capturing her life, measuring it, assessing its pleasurable and painful contours, and accounting for how and why her life evolved as it did. Rule must have appreciated the implications of the title she chose. She was "taking her life," with all its implications of suicide: she gave up a literary rendering of her life to critical scrutiny and, in so doing, she allowed herself to be vulnerable to the interpretative critiques of her readers, academic and otherwise. In the introductory paragraph to *Taking My Life*, she suggests that its writing "may be a positive way" of assessing her life and rendering it to critical scrutiny, but the "may" she includes also suggests some measure of doubt. Positive or negative, Rule ultimately decides to write the autobiography, because "I may be able to learn to value my life as something other than the hard and threateningly pointless journey it has often seemed." This remark seems rather uncharacteristic for Rule, in whose fiction deep sorrow is often flanked by or intermingled with deep joy and even celebration, and in whose essays her voice is rather more feisty than despondent. Perhaps a function of her debilitating arthritis in the last years of her life, her sense of resignation is countered by the act of will the writing of her autobiography itself represents. Indeed, in transcribing this autobiography, I am asserting my own belief that her life was far from pointless.

She opens *Taking My Life* with perhaps the most traditional of autobiographical beginnings—her birth. On March 28, 1931, Jane Vance Rule was born in Westfield, a neighbourhood of

Plainfield, New Jersey. She was the younger of two children, until her sister, Libby, was born. Rule recollects her early years with her older brother, Arthur, and her younger sister; her parents and extended family; and the homes and places of which she was fond. She tracks the litany of residences her family occupied, and their travels across the country for the sake of her father's employment. Her parents had initially lived with her father's parents in Westfield, a neighbourhood of Plainfield, in a house known as the "Shingle Chateau,"[6] from which they moved to their own house, referred to as the "Gatehouse." From there, they moved to California, where they rented an apartment on Harrison Street in Palo Alto; then they moved again to 727 Cowper Street, where Rule reminisced about how they "began real life as a family." In the summers, they went to her beloved South Fork, which was located on the south fork of the Eel River in Humboldt County, California.[7] The "official name" for South Fork was Paradise Ranch, so named by her great-grandfather, John Macgregor Vance, who bought it but renamed it because it "was their farthest summer outpost from Eureka, California, the town in which [her] great grandfather was president of a bank, a railroad, and owner of extensive property." The regular summer home was closer to Eureka at Carlotta, "a widening in the road with stone and lumber mill named for [her] grandmother," Carlotta Mae Vance.[8] From California, when Rule was nine years of age, her family moved again to Hinsdale, twenty miles west of Chicago; then again to "Circle Drive" in Kirkwood, Missouri, a suburb of St. Louis; and then temporarily to 1111 Hamilton Street in Palo Alto, California, with the Packers, her mother's mother and stepfather. At this point, Rule's father had rejoined the navy, just after the Second World War began, at the urging of his classmates from the class of 1926 at the U.S. Naval Academy. From Palo Alto, they moved nearby to Orinda, California, where her father had been assigned to head up the pre-flight school at St. Mary's College.[9] He was then assigned sea duty; when his commitment to the U.S. Navy was over, Rule's father returned from the Aleutians—the islands from which Japanese-American and Unangax civilians were removed and interned.

In the midst of a peripatetic upbringing, Rule recollects charming anecdotes of childhood pleasures—such as the trout fishing, swimming, hiking, huckleberry and fruit picking at South Fork—and stories of childhood mischief. The former manifested itself in her literary passion for nature and her sense of connection to the environment, both of which were powerfully formed during this period.[10] The latter displays Rule in early possession of a keen sense of justice, what she described as "moral communism": her unswerving sense of logic that manifested itself in the manner in which she already questioned societal rules or assignments in elementary and secondary school systems. Such questioning, she notes, lacked the instinctive tactfulness of her brother, who "never made the blundering comments that were to become my trademark; yet he couldn't distinguish between what had happened and what he made up…I suspect it was I, a moral primitive, who first called him a liar. I had a passion for getting things straight."

As Rule delineates her childhood experiences, she also alludes to the complex layers of the cultural, economic and racial politics in the United States at the time: the family's "black servant," Josephine, who later returned home to die of consumption; the Filipino boarding house beside which the Rule family lived; and the friends who drew away from her family during hard times but rematerialized when the swinging financial circumstances of the Rule family improved. Even by definition of his own conservative Southern background, Rule's father might not have "escaped a sense of horror at exposing his own children to the multiracial population of our own neighbourhood school"; yet, these kinds of racist practices and intolerance were not to be part of Rule's familial legacy.

By the emergence of the Second World War, racial tensions flared, and Rule was exposed to such tensions both at home and on the playground. Her father read to her from the evening newspaper about the Japanese involvement in the Second World War. Yet on the school playground, Rule befriended a Chinese-American student named Wally, and another, a Japanese-American student named Chiaki. They initially performed and diffused such racial tensions by dividing up into "opposing

mixed teams at recess, called the Japs and the Chinks": "We
knew that, in the grown-up world, the Japs were bad and the
Chinks were good, but those two boys, best friends, were equally
liked." The friendship between the two boys, Rule observes, later
regrettably crumbled under the increasing hostilities of the
Second World War: when she returned to Palo Alto High in
California, she encountered Wally there again and inquired after
Chiaki. He disturbingly responded with a grim sense of flippancy,
"He got sent to concentration camp with all the other Japs."

Given such tensions and her own growing awareness of how
her sexual interests were located outside the bounds of hetero-
normativity, it is perhaps not surprising to discover the litany of
phobias, sometimes paralyzing, that Rule had to overcome: fear
of the dark, what she called "night fears"; fear of heights; fear of
being displaced by another move; fear of socially awkward situ-
ations; and fear, or rather the "familiar terror," of yet another
new school. In one momentous passage, she describes how she
threw herself into a stormy night in order to overcome her fear
of the dark:

> Too old now to call out to my parents with fake requests
> for drinks of water and more blankets, ashamed of the
> childish fantasies that terrified me, one night I got up, put
> on my shoes and a coat over my pyjamas, and went out
> the French doors onto the patio ... It was a wild night,
> wind pushing broken clouds across the face of a bright
> moon, setting the trees to dancing. I was not victim to it
> now but part of the spirit of the storm. I began to run,
> intoxicated with the energy in me and all around me. I ran
> the full circle of the lake, came home and slept. I was never
> afraid of the dark again. I had taken it into my nature.

These courageous encounters with her own fears bred a kind of
fierceness and resilience that would later serve her writing career
well, as she unswervingly negotiated the terms of contracts and
refused to compromise the moral vision of her work.

That kind of fierceness also characterized her loyalties to family members, particularly to her mother, with whom she seemed
to be most close. She and her brother were named after their parents: Jane and Arthur. Whereas her parents were harmoniously

inclined, by Rule's account of things, the relationship between her and her brother was discordant. Only sixteen months apart, she and her brother were in early childhood "central to each other"; however, their differences became increasingly pronounced. They initially played, and later even took ballroom-dancing classes together, but they grew distant, to the point of being hostile with each other as they approached their teenage years. From such disconnection, Rule experienced a sense of deep loss: "I didn't know how to replace or find for myself all that had gone from me in the broken bond with my brother, who felt required to root out of himself the gentleness that had linked us." It was a link that seemingly was broken for all family members; eventually, neither her mother nor her father was able to connect with their son, whose behaviour rendered the family increasingly distraught. Sometimes, he did not appear at home for days at a time and no family member knew where he was to be found.

In particular, Arthur's relationship with his father was competitive, markedly different from the attitude Rule's father fostered toward her. Their father's protracted absence, the result of wartime commitments, did not alleviate the tensions with Arthur, although his return from the war intensified them. He believed that he could reason with his son, could enjoy "man-to-man talks"—but these, Rule notes, were "wishful thinking" on her father's part. One way of accounting for Arthur's behaviour is suggested by Rule's own sense that many of her father's "tests for [Arthur] seemed designed to humiliate." Yet Rule also recalls with some degree of pain that her father would compare their report cards and chide him "with half [of Jane's] effort you could do twice as well."

Scholastically, Arthur was indeed considered, on the one hand, "unusually gifted," but, on the other hand, frequently "in trouble at school," and then in trouble with the police. He became sullen, detached and irresponsible in his dealings with his family; at last, his parents sent him to a private school in southern California, but he left it before the term was out. He joined the army, but was discharged and, upon his return, made an attempt to work for his father. He married one of Rule's friends, Edy Mori, and directly before the ceremony made a comment to his sister that revealed the competitive nature with which he viewed their relationship: "You can run your heart out, but I can beat you standing still." At times, there were teachers who expected the same behaviour of Jane as they did of her brother; in one instance, she found a message from one of her teachers on her desk, "Arthur Rule's Pig Pen Taken Over by Jane Rule." She found herself negotiating relationships with teachers over and over again because of the precedent set by her brother. The birth of Libby, her youngest sibling, may not have altered Arthur's increasing distance, but it removed the pressure Rule experienced, until then, by being the youngest child.

Rule describes her mother as gracious and kind, supportive and protective, prone to laughter and storytelling. She enjoyed a reassuring closeness in their relationship, although it was not one always marked by deep confidences. Rule's perspective in *Taking My Life* may reflect the proximity between her and her mother, the "loving bond" that existed between them: "We were deeply companionable." Some existing letters in the archive confirm Rule's recollections:[11] when she moved to take up her university studies, she wrote to her mother with great frequency and discussed a wide range of personal interests. By Rule's account, it was a relationship that was open, not "requiring" in terms of social decorum, like that of her grandparents, but rather joyfully indulgent. Her mother allowed her children to "run barefoot" and "occasionally forgot to brush [their] teeth." Her father, too, in his own way, was involved with his children's development: he was a champion swimmer, who taught his children to swim extremely well and took them to see the New York World's Fair. In general, her parents fostered traditional representations of masculinity and femininity, and played out roles conventionally associated with men and women respectively. Her father did not "question his masculine idealism" when he enlisted with the U.S. Navy, nor did her mother question hers as she assumed charge of the domestic sphere and of her children. These roles were bolstered by an education system that demanded Rule participate in home economics classes in which she seemed to wash dishes perpetually and, where later, in cooking classes offered by Westinghouse at

Castilleja School, she was given lessons in "makeup, wardrobe and deportment."

Rule also traces the emotional entanglements of her parents with her grandparents—those of her mother with her grandmother, the strong-willed, spoiled and critical Carlotta Mae Vance Hink Packer and her patriotic, moody stepfather, Colonel Gouvenier Vroom Packer.[12] From Carlotta, it would seem, Jane learned how to refuse to submit to demands and expectations imposed on her, or, at the very least, the means of dealing with such demands with irony or humour. As she notes, when Carlotta's first husband "shouted that the gravy should be dark brown, the colour of his shoe, [Carlotta] put his shoe alongside the gravy the next time it was served." On her father's side, she characterizes her grandfather as indulgent, a man who "ate ladyfingers instead of toast every morning," and who recklessly made business propositions, of which his wife would subsequently and astutely determine the value—or lack thereof. At times seeming to appear as a "naïve crackpot" whose lack of business sense was counterbalanced by the perspicuity of his wife, he regarded Jane as his favourite, much to the chagrin and resentment of her grandmother. Her grandmother, therefore, only became closer to Jane after his death. The relationship that these grandparents maintained was, for Rule, a way of life that "was receding into the past, would not be there for yet another generation of children to play their timeless games in the shadow and warmth of friendly ghosts."

Nonetheless, her grandparents insisted on private school for Jane. During her father's stint with St. Mary's College, Rule was sent to two all-girls schools, the first being Anna Head's, a prestigious private school that was designed by architect Soule Edgar Fisher and completed in 1892, then was completely relocated to Oakland Hills in 1964. In 1971, a coordinating school for boys, the Royce School, was established. By 1979, the schools became one. At Anna Head's, Jane experienced some kind of transformation, although not quite the kind her grandmother, Carlotta Packer, had envisioned: that a private school, as Rule notes perhaps parroting her grandmother, "could take a six-foot-tall, twelve-year-old barbarian in hand" and create a "civilized young

woman." There, she gained greater confidence in her person, her
stature:

> The absence of boys from that whole city block the school
> occupied gave me a sense of giddy freedom and then grow-
> ing power. Being the tallest girl in the school was a mark
> of distinction rather than a bad joke ... I was welcomed
> by the older girls, and my classmates were pleased with my
> distinction because it reflected favourably on them.

That confidence was strengthened by the protective group of
women, who both counterbalanced the "troubled and troubling
bond I had with my brother" and "put off the question of how
I could ever be a woman loved by a man." Her growing self-assurance was also fostered by supportive environments and com-
passionate teachers, such as Mrs. Knapp, who offered positive
reinforcement and extra tutorials to allow Jane to cultivate—
even to develop her own methods for cultivating—her own intelligence. Mrs. Knapp also seems to be a crucial figure in the development of Rule's moral understanding and sense of justice.
Finding individuals rather than institutions as sources for inspiration, as moral and educative guides, Jane specifically seemed to
flourish under her tutelage. Aside from daily comments about
principles related to self-discipline and kindness, Mrs. Knapp
functioned as a model for the preservation of dignity and kindness, even in the face of injustices—the likes of which Rule was
to confront repeatedly. Rule remained in touch with her, even
after she left the school, until Mrs. Knapp died of cancer some
years later.

After Anna Head's, Jane was enrolled in Castilleja School,
which was founded in 1907 by Miss Mary Ishbel Lockey at the
encouragement of Dr. David Starr Jordan, the first president of
Stanford University. By reputation and proclamation, its mission
was to provide a "comprehensive, college preparatory education"; it espoused and promulgated those values associated with
courtesy and kindness.[13] The all-girls school once again allowed
Rule to "put off the question of how I could ever be a woman
loved by a man" and even to invent a fictitious paramour named
David, a "more desperate order of lying, a defence against future

humiliations." And yet these threatening humiliations were not to be Rule's, for her initiation into her own developing sexuality is tenderly rendered; these are initially formulated around erotically charged, although not physically consummated, relationships with some of her instructors.

As is typical to the *Künstlerroman*, the artist experiences conflict in relation to the socio-political values of the period, as she is simultaneously challenged or guided by various mentor figures. Ann Smith was one such teacher in a series, a complex mentor who helped to usher Rule into maturity and adulthood. An art instructor of some talent, she brusquely corrected Rule's adolescent refusal to believe that a woman might love another woman: "It isn't silly," she informed her sharply. "Women do sometimes fall very deeply in love with each other." She lent her copies of *Lady Chatterley's Lover* and *The Well of Loneliness*, books that were likely formative or instrumental to Rule's later writing of *Lesbian Images*. The situation, however, was far from simple: at the same time as she seemingly approved of same-sex relationships and later even had a brief liaison with Rule, Smith also married, had children and encouraged Rule to acquire heterosexual experiences first. By the time she left high school, Rule was becoming "increasingly frightened" by her circumstances. She could neither accommodate nor resign herself to the situation in which Smith found herself: in a heterosexual relationship with children, and increasingly frustrated at the condition of being a woman, which "was simply too degrading." In view of Smith's own churning and repressed desires, Rule might well note that she "mistrusted the conventions for loving." She learned, therefore, to defy Smith's claim that Rule "didn't yet live in the real world." To this remark, Rule replied, "I never intended to."

But, at age fourteen, "shaped like a telephone pole," Rule had not yet found a sense of confidence, intellectually or physically, and certainly not sexually. She describes how sex education was first communicated to her by her father; the relief of getting her first period; the confusion of discovering what it meant to love for the first time; and her first physical experience at fifteen with a blond veteran whose attempts were clumsy and gently humorous, rather than embarrassing. There is no one moment, she notes, when she "confronted [her] own sexuality." Whatever assumptions were made about her—and Rule later realized that clear assumptions had indeed been made about her—she was consumed and blinded by a sense of "outraged innocence." Indeed, by Rule's account, innocence seemed to characterize many of her interactions and contradicted the "suspicion ... so often entertained by so many people, that I was a sexual adventurer." Whatever later views she espoused related to human sexual relationships or her involvements as a full adult, at this stage, she characterized herself as an observer, the "wardrobe mistress backstage" who was preparing young women for "their parts in a public show which had nothing to do with me." The toll it took on Rule to live in "restrained intensity" and "increasing anxiety" might be seen to be reflected in the migraine headaches, the bouts of insomnia and the blackouts that increasingly afflicted her.

If her academic performance improved, as it did, Rule increasingly resisted and challenged systems that purportedly measured her intelligence or that tried to inculcate in her heteronormative conduct for women. One of her teachers described her as merely being "an attention seeker and trouble maker," but categorizing her behaviour as such did not give justice to the real frustrations Rule encountered, ranging from patently ridiculous IQ tests, to classes on makeup and wardrobe. Her future participation with *The Body Politic* is anticipated by Rule's response to this form of "education"; the signs of her writing career manifest themselves in an article she writes that appears in the Castilleja school paper in which she protests against "such blatant nonsense." Not surprisingly, she was sent home for a week to reconsider these remarks. Upon returning to school, she was horrified to discover she would be obliged to forfeit participation in all extracurricular activities—and report to the principal others who made similar objections. In response to such "intolerable and unjust" restrictions, Rule walked out and enrolled herself in Palo Alto High, where she completed her secondary education.

Just before her seventeenth birthday, and after a brief stint as a typist in the purchasing department at Stanford University, Rule enrolled at Mills College.[14] Initially founded in 1852 as the

Young Ladies' Seminary in Benicia, California, but renamed as Mills College thirteen years later, it was devoted to women's education until 1990.[15] Her attempts to apply to Stanford had already been thwarted, and it seems that her application to Mills College was again being complicated by a former teacher's letter insinuating that Rule's "moral character" was questionable. In addition, Rule had not scored well in language and reading skills; as a result, she was given "provisional status," pending her performance during her first term there.

It is at this point, during her studies at Mills College, that she approached her writing with great seriousness. She took a creative writing class for which she "wrote obscure, symbolic stories" and in which were featured young men who were "violent and in violent pain." She also wrote a few "realistic stories" that tended to focus on "troubled relationships between fathers and sons." She studied under an instructor named Donald Weeks, who was at turns "sharply critical" and supportive. From these classes in which Weeks would read the students' work out loud, Rule "learned so much more about effectiveness and failure in my own work ... than I did from any discussion or written comment." It is this same instructor, however, who became involved in a relationship with another male instructor with disastrous consequences: he was dismissed from the school. The incident heightened Rule's personal confusion and erotic constraint: "I seemed to hold two mutually exclusive views, that my love represented what was best in me and that it was a sin. Or more ambiguously and truly put, what was specifically good and generally bad."

Also at Mills College, in her first term, Rule was to meet yet another instructor who would be crucial to her formative years, especially to her intellectual and psychological development: Dr. Elizabeth (Libby) Pope, her English professor who specialized in the work of John Milton. It was a relationship that was defined by a mutual sense of esteem for their respective intellects. Pope was stringent with her, but also allowed her great academic freedom, the kind which allowed Rule to flourish intellectually. If her relationship with Smith was erotic, that with Dr. Pope "was chaste and passionate." Indeed, as Rule notes in her autobiography, Dr.

Pope wrote many years later to observe that, on Mother's Day, when others "bragged about their children, she reminded herself that she'd had about five hundred daughters, 'Among whom, you are the most beloved.' " The proximity between them is suggested by the manner in which Rule and two other students routinely invited themselves over for supper and had long evenings of literary debate and discussions between them about C.S. Lewis, Charles Williams and Dorothy Sayers.

The friendship that developed would eventually result in Rule inviting Pope to travel with her on a second trip to England. Her first trip had been made the previous year, in 1952, when she applied for and was accepted into the summer session at Bishopton Lodge, at the University of Birmingham. She persuaded her mother that "a change of scene, an adventure, would be the right tonic" for her high-strung nature; and, in turn, her mother convinced Jane's abundantly generous grandmother to fund the trip. That her compulsion to write was strong even then surfaced in her desire to take a small portable typewriter with her, the only item she chose for herself as her parents and grandmother suggested an array of other items. In London, Rule enjoyed elements of both high and popular culture: a theatre production with Laurence Olivier; the wax museum, Madame Tussaud's; the Tower of London; St. Paul's; and Westminster Abbey. For the first time, she enjoyed a community of scholars, "a group of people as interested in their work as I was."

It is on this first trip that Rule met one of the more important figures to enter her life—Roussel Sargeant. Rule registered her attraction to and fascination with her immediately—the first time she saw her on the train to Leamington Spa. She was to discover that Sargeant was studying in the same program as Rule for the summer. Considerably older by about ten years, Sargeant guided her in terms of social conduct in England: she "taught [her] how to catch a cab," suggested that "cigarettes were too expensive to offer round without incurring debt," and noted that "lecturers were not to be casually asked for a drink, only formally invited to dinner." It is also Sargeant who initiated her into a fully and consistently sexual, adult relationship. When Rule continued on her trip to Edinburgh without her, they corresponded almost daily. The ease and affection with which they communicated with each other and understood each other marks Rule's assessment of their association.

Upon her return to America from this trip, Rule came to view the world differently: Smith's questioning about her relationships abroad began to give rise to Rule's impatience and restlessness, although Rule credited Smith with teaching her "how to love without being possessive." In returning to Mills College, she came to realize that the group at Bishopton Lodge in London was much more congenial because it was much less likely to become "snagged on conventional expectations." She herself made a half-hearted effort to adhere to convention by dating a male student at Mills, which ended in a harrowing attempt on his part to threaten her into submission to his desires. Poignantly, she reflected upon what might have been if she "had been a normal woman"—and humorously concluded that "the choice between being neurotic and spending the rest of my life with such a maniac was no choice at all."

One positive aspect of her return to Mills College was her introduction to the creative writing instructor who had replaced Donald Weeks: Mary Jessamyn West, who educated the students in the more practical aspects of being a writer, including the use of "contracts and agents."[16] She enjoined the students to try to publish in popular venues, such as *The Ladies' Home Journal*, and not merely to be concerned with "writing great works." Rule and the other students were suspicious and reluctant about "soiling" themselves by participating in the marketplace, attitudes fostered by many of the other academics; nonetheless, West was regarded congenially by the students. Indeed, Rule's subsequent understanding of the various markets and the successful submission of her stories to popular venues may have found their roots here.

Rule made a second trip to England the following year. It was again funded by her grandmother. Upon her return from her first trip to England, Rule had continued to write to Sargeant, with whom she decided that the University of London was the most appropriate place for her studies abroad: "partly out of an appetite for more exposure to contemporary literature, partly for the availability of London, but also it meant I could see Sargeant more often." They planned on attending the Festival of Britain; spending weekends at Stratford, Oxford, Cambridge and Canterbury; and going to lectures, plays and exhibits. But these plans were initially complicated, first by the inclusion of the fellow student and Rule's friend Ellen Kay, who would join her on weekends, and then again by Dr. Elizabeth Pope, whom Rule had initially and impetuously invited. Rule's sensitivity meant that she understood not only how much Dr. Pope wanted, even needed, to go to England—but also recognized that the inclusion of others in her travels would be taxing for Sargeant and for their relationship. When Dr. Pope decided to join Rule, Sargeant was "downhearted": "Must I share you with all the world, my young Pied Piper?"

The trip had its challenges. Dr. Pope was not easily mobile because she had suffered from polio as a young woman: she was not certain of her balance and crowds were often too difficult to manage because she wore leg braces and used elbow canes. Perhaps Rule's own experience with "two grandmothers afflicted with severe arthritis and dependent on canes, walkers and wheelchairs,"[17] and her own self-consciousness about her height would have rendered her more sensitive to the physical and psychological challenges of Dr. Pope. In writing the autobiography retrospectively, perhaps her own arthritis also gave her even greater insight. Although Dr. Pope's "delight in everything [they] did" made her dependence on Rule easier and although she was "absolutely self-disciplined about any physical challenge," even Dr. Pope felt the frustration at the loss of her own and her companion's independence. When Rule did find time to be alone with Sargeant, the differences in their natures showed themselves: Sargeant was more publicly inhibited, whereas Rule was more reckless. Although Rule tried to be patient about the situation, she grew restless and "looked ahead only to the week Sargeant and [she] would have alone together." But the heightening tensions between them were not greatly alleviated after Dr. Pope returned to North America, and Rule departed to France on her cycling trip with Ellen.

The challenges of the language and the form of travel that Rule and Ellen had chosen proved to be too difficult. Upon arrival in Paris, they abandoned their bicycles and decided to walk, "miles and miles a day." Eventually, they caught a train for Barcelona, and went on to Majorca, "Georges Sand and Chopin country." Without her typewriter, which she could not strap to her bike and which was the "central prop of [her] ritual" of writing daily, her work was impeded. When they were joined by two young men, the strain of the summer finally took its toll. Rule decided she was obliged to leave on her own:

> I left because I was too tired to carry responsibility for any-
> one but myself. I left because I was under sexual pressure
> I didn't want from a young man, in a growing complexity
> of a foursome I didn't feel a real part of. I left because I
> really did want to write and couldn't in those circum-
> stances. I left because our money would not anyway have
> lasted very long now that we had given up our bicycles. I
> left because I was sick and frightened.

At this point, Rule was nineteen. She had no sense of what else to do at this point but to return home, "the only uncommitting option."

Upon her return, Rule refused to respond to Smith's demand that she adapt to heterosexuality, which closed the avenue of communication between them. Pregnant with her third child, Smith did several portraits of Rule, who stayed with her for a few days. Upon reflecting on this period, Rule came to appreci-ate fully the importance of her relationship with Sargeant, in whose presence she was "entirely happy" and with whom she could be unreserved and candid. Rule had grown into herself, both as a woman and artist. After leaving Smith, she returned to Mills and entered into a lively correspondence with Sargeant. They planned Rule's third trip to England together, during which Sargeant would start her Master of Arts and Rule would write her first novel: "And, no, I wouldn't invite the entire world to share it with us." The plan came to fruition: on Rule's twentieth birthday, her family gathered money to help pay for her coming year in England. Carlotta Packer paid for the rest. The following year, in "the cold winter flat in West Hampstead," which Sargeant's cousin had found for them, Rule "made [her] first real home, learned after a fashion to cook, to entertain friends, to live with a lover, and to write [her] first, unpublishable novel."[18] She learned, as she herself so evocatively observes in the concluding lines of *Taking My Life*, "to live with the baggage of my life, its rhythms of failure and rebirth."

Notes

1. See Boxes 13 and 14, Jane Rule Fonds, University of British Columbia Archives.

2. Jane Rule to Robert Weaver, May 12, 1981. Robert Weaver Fonds. MG31-D162, Container 4, File 27 (1957–1982). Library and Archives Canada, Ottawa.

3. Undated letter Jane Rule to Robert Weaver. MG31-D162, Container 4, File 27 (1957–1982). Library and Archives Canada, Ottawa. It is true that Rule frequently invoked aspects of her personal life or autobiographical experiences for the purposes of her fiction. For example, she notes in *Taking My Life* that she wrote a story called "In the Bosom of the Family," based on an incident that occurs when Ellen Kay invites Rule to share a weekend with a professor (with whom Ellen is having an affair) and his family. She also suggests that the two young men she meets on a train in England and the subsequent time they pass together on Majorca are "described in some detail in *This Is Not for You*, but the motives of the two main characters are entirely fictional." She observes that the family house in Eureka "where Aunt Etta spent the winter much less well ... became one of the settings in my novel, *Against the Season*."

4. See Marilyn Schuster's *Passionate Communities: Reading Lesbian Resistance in Jane Rule's Fiction*, page 21.

5. Jane Rule to "Tiff" (Timothy Findley), circa December 1994. MG31-D196, Container 144, File 38. Library and Archives Canada, Ottawa.

6. I am grateful to the executors of the Jane Rule Fonds for pointing out this fact to me in "From Notes on Linda Morra's Manuscript." They added that Jane Rule's mother "came home from the hospital to the Gatehouse after Arthur was born, and the family, eventually including Jane, lived in the Gatehouse."

7. The executors of the Jane Rule Fonds noted that "South Fork was on the south fork of the Eel River, 11 miles north of Garberville on HWY 101 ... The ranch was sold in 1952. HWY 101 was rerouted through the property several years later."

8. See also the article "Carlotta—A Pioneer Family Named It," *Humboldt Times*, March 20, 1949, page 11, in which the author, Chet Schwarzkopf, notes that John M. Vance "started the town and named it after his daughter Carlotta."

9. St. Mary's College was one of many colleges at which the U.S. Navy had established pre-flight training schools in response to the shortage of fighter pilots after the bombing of Pearl Harbor. Between 1942 and 1946, the campus accepted navy cadets and officers who were temporarily housed in barracks. John Grennan, "Pipe Dream Fulfilled," *St. Mary's Magazine* Spring (2008), accessed May 13, 2011, http://www.stmarys-ca.edu/news-and-events/saint-marys-magazine/archives/v28/spo8/features/o1.html. Also, I am using the notes provided by the executors of the Jane Rule Estate.

10. I am grateful to David Anderson for pointing out this fact to me (and some other ideas throughout the course of his reading of the afterword). He referred me to the work of Catriona A.H. Mortimer-Sandilands, whose book *This Is for You: Walks with Jane Rule*, is currently being considered by UBC Press and whose current research is titled *After the Fire, What? Jane Rule, Lesbian Politics, Environmental Ethics*. He also shared ideas from his unpublished paper, titled "Impossible Bargains: Queer Rule in *The Young in One Another's Arms*," presented at a conference at the University of Victoria (Literatures of the West Coast) in October 2009. His paper was written from an ecocritical perspective.

11. See Boxes 19, 32, 42 and 43, Jane Rule Fonds, University of British Columbia Archives.

12. See also essays such as "Loving the Difficult," "Refrain," "Choosing Home," "Much Obliged," "Against Those Who Would Forget" and "Peanut Butter Summer," which appear in *Loving the Difficult*; therein, Rule tracks her childhood experiences, her writing career and familial relationships.

13. "About Castilleja School," accessed May 13, 2011, http://www.castilleja.org/page.cfm?p=119.

14. See also essays from *Loving the Difficult*, such as "Money" and "Things."

15. The website for the college states that "missionaries Cyrus and Susan Mills bought the Seminary in 1865 for $5,000, renamed it

Mills College, and moved it in 1871 to its current 135-acre oasis. At the time, Oakland was a bustling metropolis of about 10,000." See "About Mills," accessed May 13, 2011, http://www.mills.edu/about/mission_and_history.php.

16. For letters from West to Rule, see Box 22, Jane Rule Fonds, University of British Columbia Archives.

17. From "Notes on Linda Morra's Manuscript," as submitted to me by the executors of the Jane Rule Estate.

18. Likely Rule is referring to the unpublished novel "Who Are the Penitent?" (typed manuscript, Box 11, File 1, Jane Rule Fonds, University of British Columbia Archives).

Works Cited

"About Castilleja School," accessed May 13, 2011, http://www.castilleja.org/page.cfm?p=119.

"About Mills." *Mills College*, accessed May 13, 2011, http://www.mills.edu/about/mission_and_history.php.

Anderson, David. "Impossible Bargains: Queer Rule in *The Young in One Another's Arms*." Unpublished conference paper. University of Victoria (Literatures of the West Coast), October 2009.

Grennan, John. "Pipe Dream Fulfilled." *St. Mary's Magazine*, Spring (2008), accessed May 13, 2011, http://www.stmarys-ca.edu/news-and-events/saint-marys-magazine/archives/v28/sp08/features/01.html.

Robert Weaver Fonds. Library and Archives Canada, Ottawa.

Rule, Jane. *Against the Season*. Kansas City, MO: Naiad, 1971.

———. *Loving the Difficult*. Sidney, BC: Hedgerow, 2008.

———. *This Is Not for You*. Kansas City, MO: Naiad, 1970.

Schuster, Marilyn. *Passionate Communities: Reading Lesbian Resistance in Jane Rule's Fiction*. New York: New York University Press, 1999.

Schwarzkopf, Chet. "Carlotta—A Pioneer Family Named It." *Humboldt Times*, March 20, 1949, page 11.

Timothy Findley Fonds. Library and Archives Canada, Ottawa.

COMMENTARY

For the sake of clarification, explanations of places, persons, events, literary texts or other matters to which Rule alludes in her autobiography are provided below.

Addams, Charles Born on January 7, 1912, Charles "Chas" Samuel Addams was an American cartoonist who is perhaps most renowned for creating the characters known as the Addams Family. His cartoons appeared in, among others, the *New Yorker, Collier's* and *TV Guide*. He drew more than 1,300 cartoons, some of these published in *Drawn and Quartered* (1942), *Monster Rally* (1950) and *Dear Dead Days* (1959), and others in calendars and other forms of popular merchandise. His work has been famously characterized by macabre and black humour. He died on September 29, 1988.

Child Ballads Rule relates how she had fainted spectacularly in class as she finished reciting, "And I will lie lay me down and bleed a while, / And then I will rise and fight again." Rule is quoting from one of the 305 Child Ballads that were assembled largely from England and Scotland by Francis James Child. They were then published by Houghton Mifflin as *The English and Scottish Popular Ballads* in the late nineteenth century. Rule specifically cited a passage from Child Ballad number 167, titled *Sir Andrew Barton* or *Andrew Bartin*. Born in 1466, Sir Andrew Barton served as High Admiral of the Kingdom of Scotland, even as he was at turns described as a "pirate" or "privateer." Although he had a letter of marque issued by the Scottish crown, which should have protected him from harm, he was beheaded in 1511 after a fierce battle with Sir Edward Howard and his brother.

English-Speaking Union The English-Speaking Union, an international educational charity, was founded in 1918 by the journalist Evelyn Wrench and received in 1957 a Royal Charter, with Queen Elizabeth II as its patron. Its international headquarters are at Dartmouth House, in London, England. With approximately forty branches in the United Kingdom and more than fifty branches worldwide, the ESU has several objectives, two of which are as follows: first, to connect and empower individuals across the globe by equipping these individuals with "communication skills, confidence, and networking opportunities" and, second, to draw attention to issues related to current affairs through activities such as conferences, exchange programs and public debates (esu.org).

Godey's Lady's Book In papers Rule finds after Mother Packer's death, her grandmother refers to childhood experiences that Rule discovers she has shared with her, despite the difference of years. Rule grew up reading old copies of her grandmother's *Godey's Lady's Book*. Alternatively known as *Godey's Magazine and Lady's Book*, *Godey's Lady's Book* was published by Louis A. Godey in Philadelphia between 1830 and 1878, although the magazine did not cease publication well until 1898. It was most known for its fashion plates for women's dress; by 1860, it had 150,000 subscribers.

Madame Tussaud's A wax museum established in London more than two hundred years ago, and named after Madame Tussaud, a Parisian woman who had learned to model wax likenesses under the tutelage of her mentor, Dr. Philippe Curtius.

Milhaud, Darius (September 4, 1892–June 22, 1974) was a prolific French composer and teacher and a member of *Les Six* (*Groupe des Six*). His most popular work includes *La Création du Monde*, *Scaramouche* and *Saudades do Brasil*. He taught at Mills College at alternate years between 1947 and 1971.

Oak Knoll Naval Hospital in Oakland, California Rule's younger sister, Libby, was prone to ear infections, and once had to be taken by military ambulance to Oak Knoll Naval Hospital, which was opened during the Second World War (in 1942) and closed in 1993.

Petri, Egon (March 23, 1881–May 27, 1962) was a German-born classical pianist who had recorded with several labels, including Columbia Records. He had moved to Poland in 1927, escaped the day before the Germans invaded in September 1939, and moved to the United States, where he taught at Cornell University and then at Mills College. He became a naturalized American citizen in 1955.

Powers model Mary Lily Rule, a much younger cousin of Jane's father, ran away from the family farm to New York, where Grandfather Rule got her a job as a Powers model. John Robert Powers had established the first modelling agency in 1923 in New York City.

Sarg, Tony Rule's grandfather told her about his friend, Tony Sarg, who is likely Anthony Frederick Sarg (April 21, 1880–February 17, 1942), a German American puppeteer and illustrator, described as "America's Puppet Master."

Steig, William Rule refers to her brother Arthur's favourite Steig cartoon, which was captioned, "Whenever I'm a good guy, people walk all over me." William Steig (1907–2003) was an American cartoonist who contributed regularly to the *New Yorker*. He first achieved fame by transforming the way cartoons were created at the magazine.

USO shows In 1941, President Franklin D. Roosevelt drew upon existing organizations—including the Salvation Army, Young Men's Christian Association, Young Women's Christian Association, National Catholic Community Services, National Travelers Aid Association and the National Jewish Welfare Board—to found the USO, the United Service Organizations. The focus of the USO was and continues to be the support of American troops and their families (uso.org).

Vivien, Renée Born Pauline Mary Tarn on June 11, 1877, Renée Vivien was a well-cultivated and well-travelled British poet who wrote in French and followed the Symbolists' writing practices. She was an ardent admirer of the Greek poet Sappho, and she thus translated her work into modern French and even tried to revive a women's artist colony on Lesbos. Her poetry, much of it apparently autobiographical, explores paganism, feminism, love and androgyny; in one volume, *Dans un coin de violettes* (1908; *In a Violet Garden*), she explores her passion for a childhood friend, Violet Shillito, who died in 1901. Vivien also became renowned for her bohemian and lavish lifestyle, in part supported by the fortune she inherited from her father at the age of twenty-one. She was openly lesbian, and had an extended public affair with writer Natalie Clifford Barney, but more private ones with Kérimé Turkhan Pasha, the wife of a Turkish diplomat, and the Baroness Hélène de Zuylen, one of the Paris Rothschilds. Vivien died on November 18, 1909, at the age of thirty-two, from what seems to have been pneumonia.

West, Mary Jessamyn After Donald Weeks left Mills College, other writers were invited to teach. One writer that came that year was Mary Jessamyn West (July 18, 1902–February 23, 1984), author of numerous stories and novels, including *The Friendly Persuasion* (1945). She helped to establish the Palmer Society in 1921.

"The Whiffenpoof Song" Jane Rule wrote obscure, symbolic stories for her writing class at Mills College. One was about a man who raped sheep, and, for some time after, Rule was taunted with snippets from "The Whiffenpoof Song." The Yale Whiffenpoofs were the oldest collegiate *a cappella* group, established in the United States in 1909. "The Whiffenpoof Song" was their most popular, based on a tune written by Tod Galloway.

Taking My Life

Writing an autobiography may be a positive way of taking my own life. Beginning in the dead of winter, mortal with abused lungs and liver, my arthritic bones an incentive for old age, I may be able to learn to value my life as something other than the hard and threateningly pointless journey it has often seemed. I have never been suicidal but often stalled, as I have been now for some months, not just directionless but unconvinced that there is one. No place for a story or ~~but~~ can ~~pause~~ my explanation, which resolutely stops, feeding on the fat of summer. And so I take my life, with moral and aesthetic misgivings, simply because there is nothing else to do.

I remember remembering when I was born. My practical young mother said nobody could. But ~~$~~ I did remember dreaming and dreaming and that first waking to the harsh light. By the time she read me Mary Poppins, I realized that I, like most people, had forgotten not just my birth but apparently the language of birds, the ability to fly, to walk into the landscape of pictures, and to be at home among the stars. Just that one sensation remained, the painful brightness. It was not enough to make me into Mary Poppins but memory because for me the earliest self discipline I had. I couldn't, after I learned to write, keep a diary, just as I couldn't later take notes in lectures. Writing anything down seemed a way of forgetting it. I wanted to memorize my life so that whatever experience taught I would not forget. The difficulty, of course, is that what we seem to be static reference ~~could~~ could be restored ~~maybe~~ the very pulse of life, the dismissed clutter the real furniture of the soul. For fear of such loss, even our ~~stab~~ starkest nightmares are consolation, for they store and restore to us things we have not chosen to ~~remember~~ recall.

I remember Josephine, our black servant, the more avidly for the nightmares she inspired. Perhaps because she was real, she spared me a random racial bigotry harder to sort out. I did not, at three, confuse her with "real black beasts" on the playground with whom my brother and I were not allowed to play. They were

opposite
Page 1 of original handwritten manuscript for *Taking My Life*, circa 1980s
Jane Rule Fonds, University Archives, University of British Columbia

this page
Page 1 of original typescript for *Taking My Life*, circa 1980s
Jane Rule Fonds, University Archives, University of British Columbia

I remember remembering when I was born. My practical young mother said
body could. But I did remember dreaming and dreaming and that first waking to
rd light. By the time she read me Mary Poppins, I realized that I, like most
ople, had forgotten not just my birth but apparently the language of birds,
e ability to fly, to walk into the landscape of pictures, and to be at home
ong the stars. Just that one sensation remixained, the painful brightness.
was not enough to make me into Mary Poppins, but memory became for me the
rlyst self discipline I had. I couldn't , after I had learned to write, keep
diary, just as I couldn't later take notes in lectures. Writing anything down
emed a way of forgetting it. I wanted to memorize my life so that whatever
perience taught I would not forget. The difficulty, of course, is that what
y seem to be static interference could be instead the very melody of life,
e dismissed clutter the real furniture of the mind. For fear of such loss,
en our starkest nightmares are consolation, for they store and restore to us
ings we have not chosen to recall.

I remember Josephine, our black maid, the more vividly for the nightmares
e inspired. Perhaps because she was real, she spared me a random bigotry
der to root out. I did not, at three, confuse her with "that black trash"
the playground with whom my brother and I were not allowed to play. They were
mply children like us, victims of adult whim and temper, as were the kitten
ephine kicked out of the kitchen back down the basement stairs. Nor did I

OMITTED TEXT

In transcribing Jane Rule's handwritten version of *Taking My Life* and then comparing it to her typescript, I realized that she had made several changes. I wished to reflect these changes—the text that Rule either omitted from or added to her typescript—for the purposes of academics or for those whose interests focus upon textual production. The passages to which changes were made follow below. Text that Rule was to omit from the typescript version of her autobiography is surrounded here by square brackets; text that she was to add to the typescript version is shown here in italics.

(PAGE 3) **I became such a problem to feed** that my mother turned to the nursery school ... I would have shamed her as well as myself if I'd let the school do what she hadn't *been able* to.

(PAGE 3) **Arthur had an odd combination of talents.** He was instinctively tactful, never made the blundering comments that were to become my trademark [I became famous for]; yet he couldn't distinguish between what had happened and what he made up. [Perhaps both were his defences against a dangerous world.]

(PAGE 4) **I don't think for the first five years of my life** I had a very distinct sense of myself as a separate human being. I was half of what made up Arthur and Jane ... But we were central to each other. [The loss of that closeness, which began when we moved to California just before my fifth birthday, is a greater grief to me than *any* of those mythical losses that occur before memory or any of the later failures of language with people I have loved. As an odd consolation, it coincided with the loss of Josephine.]

(PAGE 5) **Josephine moved with us when we left the Gatehouse** just before my fourth birthday ... What I remember of that house on Harrison Avenue are nightmares and sickness. All of us were sick: Dad with appendicitis, Mother and Arthur with mumps [measles], and I had the only real earache of my life.

(PAGE 8) **At 727 Cowper Street, we began our real life as a family** ... My parents, in their prosperous old age, have forgiven or forgotten those slights, attend the weddings of grandchildren, the fiftieth anniversaries of old San Francisco friends[, tolerant of their complacency and bigotry].

(PAGE 12) **Free of Sunday duty, I expected other kinds** of adventures with my brother ... Kids did jeer at us ... I, the pugilist, jeered back, called our tormentor "a nigger, black trash," using the weapons Josephine had given me. *One boy* retaliated by tying Arthur up.

(PAGE 13) **The first Christmas at 727 Cowper,** we were given a set of phones to be set up between our two rooms ... Mine stayed on my bedside table and for some time received the secrets and questions Arthur no longer wanted to hear[, symbol of the silence that had fallen between us, more grievous to me than any loss I have had since].

(PAGE 13) **The first-grade reader was as personally insulting** [to me as food had seemed threatening]. I would not read "Dick and Jane." I said "Arthur." Corrected again and again, I finally wouldn't read at all, for the story not only confirmed my separation from my brother, but [the fact that boys ran and played while girls watched or helped Mother] revealed the source of his growing prejudice against girls, who only watched boys play or helped Mother.

(PAGE 14) [We were all given tests.] **Given tests, Arthur was labelled** unusually gifted, one of the children to be studied by a Stanford research team.

(PAGE 31) **Mother sheltered us the more** with her loving attention ... Mother Packer was ready for a game of cards, a pastime her own mother wouldn't have allowed on Sunday, though she saw nothing wrong with playing mah-jong [came in for a game of cards. Mother Packer loved cards and she felt happily wicked playing on Sunday. Her brother had not allowed it, but she had seen nothing wrong with playing mah-jong. Dad slept on the living-room floor. The Colonel read the Sunday paper]. At home for Sunday supper, we always had something delicious, waffles with maple syrup or cottage pudding with chocolate sauce and large glasses of cold milk, just the four of us, like children together.

(PAGE 33) **The dancing lessons she insisted I take** are as bleak in my memory as those San Francisco trips are bright. I had taken ballet lessons ... I had begun to ride [I was developing a passion for horse-back riding].

(PAGE 34) **Because the Colonel had kept horses** in the army, Mother and he had always ridden ... But that, too, was a world irretrievably gone. [Having a horse of my own was only a daydream.]

(PAGE 39) **Arthur and I were both enrolled** in ballroom-dancing class ... I actually enjoyed myself. [I even remember the dress Mother Packer sent for the Valentine dance which I couldn't go to because Dad had been promoted to the position of district sales manager in St. Louis.]

(PAGE 39) **I could not, as I had in California,** simply mount a horse and ride off into a forest. There were a dozen other children to ride with, all with proper riding habits ... I went back occasionally [I don't remember even going back. Perhaps I did once or twice, but there wasn't the money for a proper riding habit. Often, we had no car to get there], but, since the riding was far more a trial than a pleasure, I gradually gave up any interest in horses.

(PAGE 40) **An unplanned and, for Mother,** alarming family reconciliation took place soon after we got back to Hinsdale. [The other family experience of that year was a trauma for Mother.] Mother's father phoned her from Chicago, on a honeymoon with his third wife ...

(PAGE 41) **Granddad was not as big a man** as we were used to for a relative ... Gretchen was a slight, dark woman, too young to be a grandmother. [She was shyer than we were and I'd never ever seen her trying not to like somebody.]

(PAGE 43) **Granny Rule,** [perhaps as a gesture of forgiveness,] **perhaps aware** that Arthur's behaviour and moods puzzled and worried my parents and, confident in her ability to handle children, offered to take Arthur and two other cousins on a trip to Washington, D.C.

(PAGE 44) **For me [us] the peculiarities of the household** were a great comfort, for there was always someone awake to dispel night fears, and there was never a family meal to test either my table manners or my appetite.

(PAGE 45) **Those were Mary Lily's last few months on the farm.** That fall she ran away to New York where Grandfather Rule got her a job as a Powers model, making his own daughters and Granny Rule the more jealous and critical of her. [He adored her.] Mary Lily was for me a revelation. Even at my stubborn worst, I had never stood at the top of the stairs and screamed at anyone, Mary Lily's tactic when she was crossed by any of them. The old men and her mother were worried about her and frightened of her, the very image of Eve, the temptress, for [she was so beautiful] she attracted every man in the country.

(PAGE 47) **Again there were rumours at Dad's office** of promotion and transfer. The first snow had fallen, the day I lined up to get on the bus with the notebook finally completed. The girl next to me knocked it out of my hand, the papers scattering in the slush. I tried to turn away, to run home, [I did not want to get on the bus,] but the kindly driver— surely not the one who had reported us the winter before?—got out and collected my soggy leaves for me and coaxed me to school.

(PAGE 49) **It seemed** ["seemed"] **a happier place** for Mother, mainly because Dad was much more often at home.

(PAGE 52) **The new lawn was up at our new house,** measuring for me the century I'd been away. Mother did momentarily gloat at my being glad to be home. [My mother thanked my rescuers who told her I'd entertained them grandly all the way home. I knew they were amused by me, but they'd been very kind.]

(PAGE 54) **His sisters were on the move now** ... Patsy, taller than I was, ... had *a* tiny record she had cut which she played over and over again.

(PAGE 55) **My father went on working on the house** on weekends, finishing the upstairs where Arthur already had his room and where I would eventually move, but he was restless and distracted. [Once he nearly electrocuted himself while I was helping him.]

(PAGE 56) **I even began to feel a bit cocky,** brave enough to object when, week after week, [my friends and I were] I was always assigned to wash dishes in a home economics class.

(PAGE 57) **There I [we] sat in the cafeteria** with the principal, having an amiable lunch while my friends looked on, amazed. I [We] never did dishes again, but I [we] didn't learn to cook either. I [We] lived in stiff truce with that teacher all term.

(PAGE 57) **The day after my father told us** he decided to enlist, he left for Chapel Hill. [I don't remember what my father said when he told us he had decided to enlist. We were supposed to be proud of him and of ourselves for helping make the sacrifice. The day after he told us, he left for Chapel Hill.] When he came home months later, he was in a lieutenant commander's uniform.

(PAGE 58) **Mother, left to sell the house** and be ready to move either with him or back to California if he was ordered overseas ... Mother adored sales, "My merchant blood coming out in me." [Dad had his orders to St. Mary's pre-flight school in Orinda, California. We rented a house on a small lake, very near the college. Art was signed up at the local school, and Lib enrolled in kindergarten, but I was finally to be sent to private school in Berkeley, three-quarters of an hour's drive from where we lived. The father of another student would drive four of us in each morning, and mothers would take turns picking us up. I had to have a uniform, grey shirt, white blouse, grey sweater. Drab as it was, I was delighted not to have to think what to wear every morning. And I would be entering a world that had nothing to do with my brother.

He is the one who should have been given that opportunity, far more alienated than I was, in much greater need of the attention he would have had in small classes. Even though I had a serviceman's scholarship, Mother and Dad couldn't afford to send me on his navy pay. Mother Packer paid the bill because nothing but private school could take a six-foot tall, twelve-year-old barbarian in hand and make a civilized young woman out of her. She had no similar interest in Arthur, whose natural manners had always been better than mine, whose even greater height was a social asset rather than a disaster.]

(PAGE 58) "You should have asked for help," he said gruffly [but backing off].

(PAGE 64) The school physically was so different ... The school buildings, too, had nooks and crannies, having been built before people were concerned about waste *of* space, which has always made a place liveable.

(PAGE 64) About half of us were new girls, and those who had come up from the lower school, rather than banding together to exclude us, the only social strategy I expected, went out of their way to make us feel welcome. ["The students are nice to each other," I told my mother in amusement. "I like all of them."]

(PAGE 68) She had the virtues *of* cheerful respect and fairness, and, though she devoted herself to us, she stayed aloof.

(PAGE 69) I could not look at her or at anyone, feeling at once betrayed and ashamed and in terror of being shut out of the only school I had ever liked [world I had ever loved].

(PAGE 75) My brother was fair and blue eyed and full lipped ... In most crises, he vanished, but he could, like Granddad, suddenly take on a gallant role for himself. [There was a graduation dance at Anna Head's. I don't know how Mother talked Arthur into going with me, but he picked out a corsage himself.]

(PAGE 76) He stayed long enough to move us back to Palo Alto to the square house on Waverly Street where we would live until the war was over. [Mother Packer and the Colonel, who earlier might have been some help to Mother, however critical they were, were now so frail themselves they were an added burden. They needed the help they were used to and couldn't find any. The Mexican cleaning woman and gardener stayed on, but Mother Packer had to cook. Often she hadn't the strength to, suffering from a range of real ailments and nervous disorders. I used to bike over to run errands for them, but more often Mother had to go on emergency calls.]

(PAGE 79) **I could hardly remember now what Mother and I had found** to quarrel about when I was younger. [I listened to my friends' complaints about their parents (very few people my age had fathers overseas) without anything of my own to contribute.]

(PAGE 81) **The troubled and troubling bond** I had with my brother ... I loved all poems about the death of lovers, particularly Amy Lowell's "Patterns," ending with that fine, "Christ! What are patterns for?" which she may have written with motives similar to mine. [Sara Teasdale, Edna St. Vincent Millay both mourned death satisfactorily.]

(PAGE 91) **One night I woke vomiting** and had to wash out my sheets and blankets without letting Mother Packer know. To my great surprise, my brother offered to take my place for a night [two nights].

(PAGE 97) **These were not problems to discuss with Mother** ... She was willing to discuss all the sense I had of my family and tell me about her own, her unconventional childhood, trailing around the world with an artist [unfit] mother and alcoholic father, problematic older brother and sisters.

(PAGE 99) **My parents, my grandmother,** even Arthur liked Ann ... Mother Packer like*d* Ann's serenity.

(PAGE 110) **I was fifteen years old.** My sexual experience went no further than a single struggle in the back seat of a car with a tall, blond veteran [included a couple of struggles in the back seat of a car with a young veteran] who was really more interested in finding a wife than in deflowering a virgin.

(PAGE 110) **There was no one moment** when I confronted my own sexuality. Consciously, I didn't desire any of these young women. If they desired me, [as now it seems they must have,] they were too frightened to be anything but circumspect.

(PAGE 111) **In the spring, I discovered that I couldn't graduate** because I hadn't had four years of gym. I had to return in the fall and take two periods of gym and whatever else might pass the time, finish in February and then have some time off to look around. [The counsellor's advice was that I should return the next fall and take two periods of gym and whatever else interested me for the first term. I could finish in February and then have some time off to look around.] I was really too young to start college anyway.

(PAGE 112) **From the moment she moved in, I sensed something was very wrong** ... If any of my friends came over, she pleaded a migraine headache and retreated [went] to her room ... When she woke and threw up, I changed her bedclothes and her pyjamas, then sat wiping her face with a cool, damp cloth[, did what I could to make her more comfortable].

(PAGE 114) **Ann and Henry did not move east,** and I did not get into Stanford ... I reapplied for the winter quarter. [My energy came from my anger rather than my confidence.]

(PAGE 116) **Ann's guilt and fear** [and restraint] troubled me more for her than for myself.

(PAGE 117) **I made my application** ... I had what I knew were good references from teachers, from my German tutor who was angry [annoyed] that I'd been refused at Stanford.

(PAGE 118) **I not only didn't know what was expected** of me in assignments, I didn't know that anything in particular was expected ... I was simply suspicious of questions like "Does a Drowning Man Really Drown?" I didn't want *to be made a fool of* [my leg pulled] by a bunch of condescending, smart-aleck male professors.

(PAGE 120) **Our own self-obsessed and sheltered life** ... In a way I didn't much think about, Carol seemed somehow mine as well. [I was awed.]

(PAGE 122) **I discovered some days later** that he was Egon Petri ... Darius Milhaud taught composition every other year at Mills, the alternate years in Paris *at the Paris Conservatoire*, and some students commuted with him.

(PAGE 134) **In 1948, Dr. Pope was in her early thirties.** Her PhD thesis on *Paradise Regained* had been published, and she had been at Mills long enough to have established herself as a central power in the department, cherished and admired by Donald Weeks, the sensitive, cynical head of the department. [Though the majority of the faculty at Mills were unusually dedicated teachers, most of them also had lives apart from the campus. Elizabeth Pope did not.]

(PAGE 135) **Because Dr. Pope went to chapel, I began to attend** ... Discussions of morality tended toward various kinds of [political] responsibility rather than definitions of sin.

(PAGE 135) **Still, often when I bowed my head in prayer,** it troubled my conscience ... It was among the few important things we didn't discuss. [I had told her all about my battles in school, the bitterness I still felt at how I had been treated. She told me of her own lonely adolescence, the sadism of a particular nurse, the difficulties there were for her in college.]

(PAGE 136) **When the lovesick graduate student asked** me outright how I managed to win such favour, I was frightened as well as embarrassed, for I knew she recognized the nature of my own devotion as clearly as I recognized hers. [If I'd been older I might have been able to tell her that wanting to die for someone else was not a sentiment to be shared, even with the beloved.] I felt sorry for her, but I wanted nothing to do with her or her self-despising, painful devotion.

(PAGE 139) **Arthur had joined the army.** [*added and then deleted from page 115a of the typescript:* I don't remember my last summer at South Fork, probably we weren't there very long. My father, who had taken over a family-owned building supply company, had so much improved it that the family was having second thoughts about the percentage of profit they had offered him. He began to instruct the company lawyer, so he would not have wanted to be away for long. I do remember long, tedious days in Reno, the tension in the family and my pledge to myself that I would never again spend a summer at home, isolated with problems without solutions.

What I wanted to do was to go east again to see Ann. She was pregnant again, the baby due in March. Late that fall, Ann came down with polio and was temporarily partially paralyzed. It was some weeks before she could use her hands. Susan was born prematurely, and they both spent some time separately in the hospital.

I saw an ad for summer schools in England and phoned Mother to tell her it was exactly what I had to do the following summer. She, in turn, persuaded Mother Packer that I should go. So I applied to Stratford for the session on Shakespeare and was accepted. I gave very little thought to what I had contracted to do. What mattered to me was that I would see Ann, Henry, Carol and the new baby in June and again late in August.

It was Dr. Pope who was excited about the prospect of my going to England. She had never been.]

[*An alternative version, added to and then deleted from page 115b of the manuscript:* Part of the summer we spent at South Fork. Mother Packer, who did not walk alone at all now, uncertain of her balance and fearful of falling, did when we were at South Fork practise walking with the help of my arm and her cane. One day we'd walk from the house up to the fig trees, the next town along the honeysuckled fence to our gate. One day we disagreed about which way to turn and she struck out on her own. We were both very proud of that few minutes of her independence.

Libby, who didn't really like the place, made friends with some elderly neighbours, who tamed squirrels, chipmunks and birds. But she was often bored, missing her friends in Reno. Since she wasn't interested in fishing or hiking, disliked the moss in the river, the deer droppings in the orchard, she was a reluctant and complaining companion we were glad to leave behind. She and Mother Packer bickered.

My father, who had taken over a family-owned-building supply company in Reno, had so improved it that the family was having second thoughts about the percentage of profit they had offered him. He began to mistrust the family lawyer, so he did not want to be away for long.

Art was in the army.]

(PAGE 141) **One midweek evening, they persuaded me** to give up my books and go out for a *friendly* beer. In the ladies' room of a local bar, a very drunk and handsome woman tried to pick me up.

(PAGE 141) **At home, I was far sicker than I had been** at college. The altitude had always troubled me. Now I fainted if I went upstairs too quickly, I couldn't go anywhere by myself, not even into a store. I didn't know from moment to moment what negative trick my body would play on me, against which will seemed helpless. [I was frightened in the car. Not allowed to work, I was desperate.]

Mother was attentive, patient, reassuring. She was willing to have me home for the year to let my overtaxed nerves mend. The thought of not going back to college horrified me. After several weeks, I begged to go back. Once I agreed to drop at least one course, Mother agreed to let me try it. [I felt as weak as if I'd just had major surgery and anxious.]

Dr. Pope, worried and inclined to blame herself for the academic pressure I'd been under, [behaved less my tutor and more my affectionate friend,] offered to feed me herself if the dormitory dining room was too much for me.

(PAGE 151) **I remember the shock of recognition** when I read *On the Road* ... I accepted the literary judgment of the book as undisciplined, negative romance [that it was], but I couldn't dismiss it.

(PAGE 153) **Sally and Edy both liked using me** as a victim [guinea pig] for their course in psychological testing.

(PAGE 154) **Sally's attitude toward her work bewildered me** as much as her attitude toward useful young men did. [Most other students' attitude toward their work bewildered me as much as their attitude toward their love affair did.] It was a game played against teachers to do as little work as possible for as much credit.

(PAGE 158) **We were exposed to other forms** both by other students' work and in our academic courses ... Her volume of poems, published when she was in her twenties, was the first of our ventures into print [successes].

(PAGE 161) **My own moral state can on the surface** of it confuse me as I look back on it. I'm sure I was confused at the time. I seemed to hold two mutually exclusive views, that my love [for Ann and for Dr. Pope] represented what was best in me and that it was a sin ... As long as I entertained the possibility that my emotional makeup would change, I did not really see that my devotion to either woman could effect the collapse of our worlds as Donald Weeks's passions had toppled his. [That it was misdirected, as Ann so often claimed, I hold to be specifically loving, though generally right. If I could be as devoted to a man as I was to either of them, I should probably choose to be. But I could not imagine it, any more than I could imagine that my devotion to either of them destined to collapse our worlds as Donald Weeks's passions had toppled his.]

(PAGE 162) **The imaginary man, Sandy, still figured** in my defences occasionally ... I was embarrassed by such deceits. Still they were less painful in my conscience than the deceit of dating that I occasionally indulged in at Sally's and Edy's urging once or twice even having my appetite roused by a technically competent young man about whom I didn't know, about whom I therefore couldn't care [cared nothing].

(PAGE 164) **The erotic tension I created** sweetened their nights together, and I didn't resent it. Though I wanted Ann, I felt no claim to her [and honoured Henry's].

(PAGE 167) **After I recovered from the drowsiness** of my first unnecessary pill against seasickness, I began like any normally adventuresome nineteen-year-old to enjoy myself ... The cabin across the hall was crammed with students from Notre Dame, lecherous but Catholic. One of them, tall enough to be as crippled as I was by the restricting short bunks, limped to breakfast with us every morning, challenged me to martini-drinking contests every evening and fortunately passed out before I was seriously threatened. [I could explore the ship, make acquaintances with the passengers at all the mindless amusements provided and retreat into attention if I needed to.

The day before we sighted France, a young woman from first class, which she assured us was simply an elegant old people's house, asked us to come up as her guests for a swim. When we tried to cross into first class, our way was barred by a polite but adamant steward. Our friend, distressed to have put us through such an embarrassment, sent us a case of champagne when she got off at Cherbourg, and we spent the final night as we crossed the channel drinking champagne.

I had ten days by myself in London before I had to be at Stratford. I might meet some of my shipboard friends at the Embassy's Fourth of July party. Otherwise I had no plans but to discover what I could of London. I was staying at the sedate English-Speaking Union. The dining room there where nothing could be heard but the clinking of silver made a good preparation for public dining rooms all across England. It was like being in a silent movie. But before I had time to have my first meal there, I discovered a theatre in the neighbourhood offering a Christopher Fry play for the price of a movie.

"You should have been with me," I was to write to Dr. Pope again and again that summer, whether I'd been to the theatre or to Oxford, shopped for books or gone to a gallery. To Ann I wrote the love letters I always had, but resignedly.]

(PAGE 170) **Though moving again with all my luggage** was a daunting thought, I was glad to be leaving the solitude of London for a place where I could surely make friends. I studied the faces of other passengers on the small train which took us from Leamington Spa to Stratford. One in particular attracted me, a woman in her early thirties, my height, with a face given to laughter, the warmth of it in her eyes, in the dimples in her cheeks, in the tilt of her nose; yet it was a strong face, too, the brows dark and heavy, [she held herself proudly,] rather dwarfing her small, pretty companion. I wondered if they were lovers.

(PAGE 171) **As we settled to our academic schedule,** the conversation at meals shifted into discussions of lectures, plans for papers and, most interesting of all, analyses of the productions of the plays we were seeing. John Gielgud and Peggy Ashcroft were the leads that summer, playing in *Lear*, *Measure for Measure*, *Much Ado about Nothing* [and two others which have blurred in my memory now with other summers. I did not know it then, but I was to be at Stratford each of the next three summers as well].

(PAGE 172) **For all the bright worlds I had come to know** did not exist, no one had ever told me about this one. Not having anticipated it, not having imagined it in any way [my joy in it was absolute]. I felt for the first time in my life at home, sure of work and welcome.

(PAGE 172) **I caught a heavy cold shortly after I arrived,** ignored it until I finally had to give in and spend a day in bed. When I didn't turn up for breakfast, Roussel presented herself with a cup of tea which I was too touched by to refuse, though a Coke would have been much more welcome [however filthy I thought tea in the morning].

(PAGE 174) **There was no one else in the lounge** ... He got up angrily and went to bed. I sat up, smoking[, shaking with tiredness and need and confusion].

(PAGE 180) **Her early return made me think** not simply of my grandfather's death but of my grandmother who would meet the ship in New York. [A strong, independent woman, suspicious always of my relationship with my grandfather,] She'd probably find me a chore rather than a help; yet I'd always felt closer to her, more really known though not so flatteringly, than by my fantasy-inventing grandfather.

(PAGE 180) **There was a letter from Roussel** waiting for me on board the ship ... I was in a cabin for ten *days* on the *Georgia* ...

(PAGE 182) **Ann brought the children to pick me up.** Granny reached out for baby Susan[, were absolutely suited to each other]. It was very rare that a baby wasn't at home on her ample lap, entertained by that strong string of beads she wore round her neck.

(PAGE 182) **I was newly restless with Ann's questioning** ... From Ann I had learned how to love without being possessive, how to accept and rejoice in her love for husband and children. [And she influenced my moral view without ever seriously shifting my sexuality. From Ann I had learned how to love without being possessive, how to extend love to a husband and children.] From Ann I had also learned that sexual fidelity did not necessarily mean what it did to my parents.

(PAGE 183) **I had given up making any sexual demands** of Ann ... The summer had given me a new sense of my own attractiveness, and I had discovered a world in which I felt at home. [A world to live in which I had been welcomed, challenged and loved.]

(PAGE 185) **I had been out with him half a dozen times** before I realized I really didn't like him ... He lectured on subjects that interested him, at least one of which was my improvement[, at least one of which was the fulfillment of women]. A woman should be intelligent, healthy, tall in order to breed sons who would be princes.

(PAGE 186) **I refused the next date.** He waited two weeks and then called again ... it seemed somehow too unkind to be that blunt: so I reluctantly accepted [so I went]. This time, for the first time at the end of the evening, we parked.

(PAGE 187) **Now that Donald Weeks was gone,** writers were invited to teach ... Surrounded with the attitudes academics had for writers who published in popular magazines, [who made money,] we were suspicious of Jessamyn's ability to instruct us in our rather higher calling.

(PAGE 189) **"No big problem. Cabs aren't that expensive[**. You pay the cab fare]," I suggested.

(PAGE 192) **Usually I enjoyed spending Easter vacation** at college ... I suggested to my mother that she join me for a week in Carmel, where we could celebrate our birthdays together. [Libby must have had a sitter or gone to stay with a friend.]

(PAGE 192) **She talked more frankly about our father** than she had before ... She hoped Libby[, when they finally moved back to California,] could stay as healthy as she had become in the high, dry desert air of Nevada ... My mother was very glad to be back in the Bay Area[, looked forward to coming back]. She had never liked Reno.

(PAGE 195) **Granny and I met Dr. Pope and her father** for dinner ... Lunch with Ellen's mother didn't bridge the generation gap [wasn't such a success]. She was worried about our lack of definite plans after summer school and Dr. Pope's departure.

(PAGE 197) **It took me [us] a moment to realize** they were referring not to a member of their family but to the Duchess of Windsor.

(PAGE 205) **At the theatre, Dr. Pope more often watched** my face than the stage ... I would have enjoyed such concentration from Roussel, who went to the theatre to see the play [never gave any indication that I existed when we went to a play].

(PAGE 206) **"A row house is a row house,** whether it's built in a curve or in a straight line," I said. [She stamped down on her braced leg and said, "What have I done to see Bath with a barbarian?"]

(PAGE 207) **"I passed out for you once,"** I reminded her. [I went out to the airport with Dr. Pope and got permission to take her right onto the plane.

"You'd get into Buckingham Palace to sit on the throne if you put your mind to it," she said, picking up my own bantering tone whenever I did anything to help her physically.]

(PAGE 214) **I was trying to write for a part of each day.** [So was Ellen, but without a typewriter ...] Without a typewriter, I was missing the central prop of my ritual. I began stories I couldn't stay interested in. I wrote myself meaningless notes. [My stomach couldn't tolerate the food. I took nothing but tea and toast for days.]

(PAGE 216) **At nineteen, not really knowing** where I wanted to be, going home was the only uncommitting option. I'd had a letter from Mother saying that Dad hadn't been well. So I booked myself out of New York immediately *when* I arrived, not even stopping to check in with Ann and Henry.

(PAGE 216) **Ann's third child was expected at any time, and she and Henry wondered if I could stay for three weeks until Ann's sister would be free to come look after the children.** [If Ann had to go to the hospital, I'd be there to take care of Carol and Susan.]

(PAGE 220) **I wrote to Roussel about Marilyn, a music major,** with whom I listened to music and read Gertrude Stein, who had transferred from Reed, whose distractions [whose lonely voice and playful spirit was the first real distraction I'd ever had from work ...] from required work I'd never allowed myself before. When we first made love in her room, I knew it was dangerous, but I was already so tempted to quit that I needed the defiance of it. [I knew we were courting disaster, but I was already so tempted to quit that I didn't care.]

(PAGE 221) **Did he feel victory in marrying Edy?** Did he resent my academic honours? I didn't know. He never explained himself beyond very occasional cryptic slogans. [His resentment, always there just below the surface, only erupted in moments of great tension, in such cryptic slogans.]

(PAGE 222) **So, apparently, did Ellen ...** Her enthusiasm infected two other senior English majors in Mills Hall to make plans of their own. [I made it as clear as I could that I was not making friendly promises to any of them. Earnestly, Ellen agreed.]

(PAGE 222) **"Open your present.** ["I'll lend you mine."]
      For once, Mother Packer was struck speechless, and the rest of the family was kind enough not to comment ... Then I realized that there were no presents. [Was this the moment then when I was to be confronted with the fact of my selfishness, the impracticality of my dreams?]

(PAGE 223) **With such good fortune secured,** it seemed graceless to be so negative about the weeks that remained ... Ann, more intensely working than any of us, also was best at breaking the tension by starting sudden, impossible conversations, usually with me. [Ann McKirsty was helping me deal with Chaucer, a course I had managed to avoid, and I was lecturing to her on the seventeenth century. We sat with other English majors every night now and talked work. Ann, more intensely working than any of us, also was best at breaking the mood by starting sudden, impossible conversations, usually with me.]
      "Did you let the elephant out?" or "Was that the duke who phoned?" They mostly developed into intense quarrels of faked jealousy, invented failures of responsibility for the benefit of a suitably amused

audience. The game we played when we were alone was quarrelling over our shared servants, Gertrude and Bertrum, who finally became too expensive and jealous of each other to keep. It then fell to singular Bertrude to deal with our clothes and cleaning[, mending, washing, shoe polishing].

(PAGE 223) **With Ann and with Roussel,** it was I who lightened the day with nonsense. In Marilyn, I had a real playmate who didn't worry at any future between us, who took the pleasure we had in each other simply. [Roussel, meanwhile, had a suicidal Willy on her hands.]

(PAGE 224) **That would be how the dean** and Miss Wright had tried to comfort her. I didn't like how much I'd withdrawn from her, how little I'd minded punishing her with my silence in class. [Such an explanation seemed to me idiotic, but I did have enough sense to leave her with it if she could draw some comfort from it. I didn't like how much I'd withdrawn from her, how little I'd minded punishing her with my silence.]

ACKNOWLEDGMENTS

Linda M. Morra

It is to David Anderson, first and foremost, to whom I owe much gratitude for inspiring me with the idea to peruse the Jane Rule Fonds, where I later found her unpublished autobiography; yet, I could not simply walk into the University of British Columbia Archives and work on Rule's papers without permission to explore what she had deposited there in 1988. When I began this research, Rule was still alive and, as I was trying to determine how to get in touch with her, I spoke to both a colleague and a warm and caring friend, Janice Stewart. She suggested that it would also be wise to interview Rule and that, if I so desired it, she could arrange to put me into contact with her. I was struck by Janice's generosity. She offers a remarkable array of qualities that serve as a model for academics and for their exchanges: she is considerate, kind, willing to share what she knows. I am deeply thankful to her for getting me through a crucial stage of the project.

When I received Rule's contact information from Janice, I directly thereafter sent a letter to Rule, to which she kindly responded. I and my research assistant, Andrea Szilagyi, thus found ourselves travelling to Galiano Island, where Rule allowed us to interview her. In spite of her deteriorating health, she made *us* lunch and was at all moments gracious and accommodating with our questions. When Andrea and I returned from Galiano Island, we proceeded to bury ourselves in the boxes upon boxes of Rule's archival material at the University of British Columbia. I appreciated Andrea for her impeccable work habits, her passionate interest in the papers and her initiative in the process.

I was able to hire such an assistant because of the support of a Social Sciences and Humanities Research Council (SSHRC) Standard Research Grant: these grants are invaluable for the kind of research that would otherwise not get done. Archival work is both time consuming and costly, and so a grant becomes indispensable to being effective in such work. I was also awarded a Bishop's University Research Grant that paid for one of my research trips to the University of British Columbia, at which time I compared the typescript to the handwritten version of *Taking My Life*. Later, I received a grant from the *Fonds de recherche sur la société et la culture* (FQRSC) for the purposes of continuing this work. I am deeply grateful for having had consistent support, such that I was able to complete the work on this book.

I owe a debt of gratitude to Christopher Hives (the university archivist responsible for establishing the Jane Rule Fonds and safeguarding her papers), Candice Bjur and Leslie Field—all professional, generous and helpful archivists and library assistants at the Irving K. Barber Learning Centre. Indeed, at every stage of development on this manuscript, both Candice and Leslie were giving with their time—from providing me with a temporary copy of the handwritten manuscript, to retrieving box upon box for me to rummage through, to scanning those images that appear in the book, to offering suggestions that had not even occurred to me, to looking up queries in the copy-edited manuscript. I was initially permitted to work with a copy of the handwritten manuscript for a brief period, after which time I was obliged to return the copy to the archives. Thereafter, I called upon Candice, who was completely accommodating: she looked up all queries on my behalf. (Candice, I am herewith referring to you as the archival saint of the Irving K. Barber Learning Centre.) She was especially important to the whole process.

After having done all this work, Rule's autobiography would still not have seen the light of day if the executors of the Jane Rule Estate had not agreed to its production. They were flexible with deadlines and permissions, and, at all points of exchange, courteous with me. They read over Rule's manuscript and my afterword, and provided corrections to the spelling of names and to other details about which I had been inaccurate. They made other suggestions about the shaping of the manuscript and gave Talonbooks the permission to use the images included in the publication and on its cover. The selection of the images eventually included in the autobiography was no small feat: there are easily thousands of photos that have become part of the Jane Rule Fonds, but the persons represented therein are not clearly identified. It took some guesswork on my part to determine who these figures were; when I had narrowed down the images to about twenty, Candice and Leslie scanned them and sent them to the executors for their proper identification. The executors—and Candice and Leslie—generally made the process so uncomplicated that it was a delight to work with them.

There are those to whom I feel immensely grateful for a variety of reasons: Marilyn R. Schuster, the scholar who kindly had her own research assistant look up some details for me with respect to the dating of the manuscript and who provided thoughtful and provocative questions along the way; Gary Kuchar, for asking his assistant to copy some documents from the University of Victoria archives on my behalf; Tony Power, the head archivist at Simon Fraser Archives; Jean Matheson and Janet Murray of Library and Archives Canada, both of whom helped to provide a digital copy of the image on the cover of this book; Jessica Schagerl and David Anderson, friends and scholars who read over and provided feedback about the afterword and who assessed its accuracy and readability; Janice Braun, the associate library director at Mills College, for answering so expeditiously some inquiries about persons who worked at the college at the time Rule attended; Vicki Williams and Karl Siegler of Talonbooks, both of whom were responsive to my initial proposal to publish this manuscript; Karl Siegler, for his thorough editing of the afterword; Ann-Marie Metten, a goddess in the field of copy-editing who worked with me through the decision to render changes to the Omitted Text section and whose eagle eyes caught so many of my typographical errors; Greg Gibson, a fine proofreader and production editor; and my dear and loyal friends, and my supportive and loving family, who have dealt so patiently with me as I deferred visits with them to complete the transcription and preparation of this manuscript. Now that this book is ready for publication, I am making a promise in print to spend more leisurely time with you—at least for a little while, before I move on to my next research project.

ABOUT THE AUTHORS

Jane Rule was born in New Jersey in 1931 and came to Canada in 1956, where she later taught at the University of British Columbia. Her first novel, *Desert of the Heart* (1964), in which two women fall in love in 1950s Reno, Nevada, was successful as a 1985 feature film titled *Desert Hearts*.

Rule emerged as one of the most respected writers in Canada with her many novels, essays and collections of short stories, including *Theme for Diverse Instruments* (1975). She received the Canadian Authors Association best novel and best short story awards, the American Gay Academic Literature Award, the U.S. Fund for Human Dignity Award of Merit, the Canadian National Institute for the Blind's Talking Book of the Year Award and an honorary doctorate of letters from the University of British Columbia.

In 1996, Jane Rule received the George Woodcock Lifetime Achievement Award for an Outstanding Literary Career in British Columbia. She passed away in 2007.

Linda M. Morra holds a PhD in Canadian literature from the University of Ottawa. She teaches at Bishop's University and lives in Montreal. Morra is the editor of the critically acclaimed *Corresponding Influence: Selected Letters of Emily Carr and Ira Dilworth*. She is currently working on a monograph in which she explores Canadian women writers' self-agency and textual integrity in relation to the publishing industry in Canada.

Taking My Life is set in Sabon, a mid-twentieth-century typeface based on Claude Garamond's sixteenth-century punches. Sabon was designed and cut in metal by typographer and designer Jan Tschichold (1902–1974) in the period 1964–1967. Tschichold determined the face's weights and proportions with an eye to the practicalities of modern typesetting and layout. Sabon was first used in 1973 by American book designer Bradbury Thompson to set the Washburn College Bible. Sabon is also used as the official logo typeface of Stanford University, to which Jane Rule always planned to attend.

The cover of *Taking My Life* shows an original portrait of Jane Rule painted by her friend and lover Ann Smith during a stopover visit on Jane's return from England. The portrait is signed "Ann Hibbard Burnham Smith / October 6, 1951" and elicits the following comment from Rule: "Of the three portraits she did of me, it is the most successful, in colour while the others were charcoal, my jacket bright with autumn colours, a clear autumn sky behind me. My face is brown from the Mediterranean sun, thin, the mouth full and bright, the eyes dark, watchful." Majorca, "Georges Sand and Chopin country," had been good to the young Rule.

All photographs, with the exception of the frontispiece, are used with permission of the Jane Rule Estate, courtesy the Jane Rule Fonds, University Archives, University of British Columbia. The archival photographs were scanned and digitally restored to remove damage and the effects of aging.

Frontispiece photograph is used with the permission of Alex Waterhouse-Hayward.